'You, Madeleine Lafayette, are a captivating wee witch.'

'I am not a witch,' Madeleine said, flustered and indignant. She could feel the heat of his body, though they were hardly touching.

'No? Maybe a fairy, then,' Calumn said, wondering fancifully if she had indeed cast a spell on him. Mere foolishness—but he hadn't come across her like before, and he didn't seem to be able to make himself stop what he knew he shouldn't be doing. For he wanted suddenly, urgently, to kiss her. He leaned closer and caught a trace of her scent, remembered that too, from last night, like the wisps of a dream.

'What are you doing? Let me go.' Madeleine's lungs seemed to have stopped working. Her heart was pumping too hard. Calumn's eyes sparkled blue like the summer sea. *He looked as if he was going to kiss her*. Surely he would not dare? Surely she would not…?

Calumn kissed her. It was the softest of kisses, just a touch of his lips on hers. A warmth, a taste, a curl of pleasure inside her, and it was over. '*Oh!* You should not…'

AUTHOR NOTE

In the eighteenth century it was relatively common for young Scotsmen like Calumn, the hero of my story, to join the British army as part of their education—just as the sons of English noblemen were accustomed to do. Prior to the '45 Rebellion there was little conflict between the British Government and the Highland clan system, since both operated almost independently.

The Young Pretender changed all of this. Contrary to popular myth, the Jacobite uprising wasn't a case of Highlanders led by Bonnie Prince Charlie fighting an English army. It was a much more complex and far more harrowing scenario than that.

The forces of the Crown, led ultimately by the King's brother, the Duke of Cumberland, were made up from the regular army, supplemented by a number of clans loyal to the King (mostly but not exclusively Presbyterian, including my local clan, the Campbells of Argyll), who did not want to see the Catholic Stuarts on the throne. Though efforts were initially made to keep Highland regiments out of the fighting, by the time of Culloden there were four Scottish regiments involved. Ranged against them, the Jacobite army comprised a mixture of Highland clans (largely Catholic and Episcopalian), lowland recruits, plus French, Irish and even some English volunteers and mercenaries. Kin faced kin across the battlefield, just as Calumn finds himself doing.

Following the defeat of the Jacobites, the feudal power of the clans was systematically removed and the landscape of the Highlands changed for ever, regardless of whether the laird had supported the Government, as Calumn's father did, or Bonnie Prince Charlie.

Charles Edward Stuart fled to France from where, having become an embarrassment to the French court, he was packed off to Switzerland. He eventually died in Italy, reputedly of drink. He never returned to Scotland.

The retribution which followed Culloden—the disarming of the clans and the ban on Highland dress, the confiscation of lands, the burning of crofts and the decimation of the population (commonly known as the Clearances)—which is depicted in my story—is entirely factual. 'Butcher' Cumberland's nickname, and reputation, was well earned.

THE HIGHLANDER'S REDEMPTION

Marguerite Kaye

First published in Great Britain 2011
by Mills & Boon, an imprint of Harlequin (UK) Limited,
Eton House, 18-24 Paradise Road, Richmond, Surrey TW9 1SR

© Marguerite Kaye 2011

ISBN: 978 0 263 88801 0

Harlequin (UK) policy is to use papers that are natural, renewable and recyclable products and made from wood grown in sustainable forests. The logging and manufacturing process conform to the legal environmental regulations of the country of origin.

Printed and bound in Spain
by Blackprint CPI, Barcelona

Born and educated in Scotland, **Marguerite Kaye** originally qualified as a lawyer but chose not to practise—a decision which was a relief both to her and to the Scottish legal establishment. While carving out a successful career in IT, she occupied herself with her twin passions of studying history and reading, picking up first-class honours and a Masters degree along the way.

The course of her life changed dramatically when she found her soul mate. After an idyllic year out, spent travelling round the Mediterranean, Marguerite decided to take the plunge and pursue her life-long ambition to write for a living—a dream she had cherished ever since winning a national poetry competition at the age of nine.

Just like one of her fictional heroines, Marguerite's fantasy has become reality. She has published history and travel articles, as well as short stories, but romances are her passion. Marguerite describes Georgette Heyer and Doris Day as her biggest early influences, and her partner as her inspiration.

Marguerite would love to hear from you. You can contact her at: Marguerite_Kaye@hotmail.co.uk

Previous novels by the same author:

THE WICKED LORD RASENBY
THE RAKE AND THE HEIRESS
INNOCENT IN THE SHEIKH'S HAREM
  (part of *Summer Sheikhs* anthology)
THE GOVERNESS AND THE SHEIKH

and in Mills & Boon® Historical *Undone!* eBooks:

THE CAPTAIN'S WICKED WAGER
THE HIGHLANDER AND THE SEA SIREN
BITTEN BY DESIRE
TEMPTATION IS THE NIGHT

For Johanna, Catriona and Fiona,
who amazingly claimed to be flattered to have a lochan
named after them!

Prologue

The wind ripped mercilessly across the bleak, rolling moorland, driving the icy sleet straight into the grimly set faces of the Jacobite forces ranged opposite. Calumn peered through the haze of smoke at the ragged Highland line in a desperate attempt to make out the Macleod colours, but it was useless. There was no doubt Rory was among them somewhere. Best not to know exactly where.

The big three-inch guns pounded across the narrow gap which constituted no-man's land. The air was acrid with the stink of gunpowder. Calumn's ears rang with the noise—the tumultuous blast of artillery, the drums, the snorting and whinnying of the Dragoons' horses stationed on the left flank. And above it all the eerie banshee wail of the wind.

He readied his company of fusiliers for battle, rousing the men, straightening the line, barking last-minute orders. His heart was pounding so hard he could hear it even above the thud, thud, thud of the guns. He was afraid, but not of death. He cared not a jot for his own life, but he was terrified none the less. Terrified that he would look up in the heat of battle and come face to face with his brother.

A spine-tingling roar, starting low and rising to a crescendo, as if from the maw of a thousand lions, carried across the moor from the Jacobites. A fearsome, chaotic line of Highlanders, standards flying, began to charge. Calumn automatically checked the fixing on his bayonet. Saw Cumberland give the signal. Gave his own company the nod. And slowly, inexorably, moved forward into the hellish fray.

A shot whistled past his ear. *Traitor, traitor,* the voice in his head sang out, yet onwards he went, step after disciplined step, towards the heaving mass of wild-eyed clansmen in their plaids. His feet sank into the brackish water of a burn. The wounded screamed, crumpling beside and in front of him. The ferrous smell of fresh blood rent the air, mingling with the heart-wrenchingly familiar scent of sodden wool coming from the *filleadh begs* worn by the Highlanders. With leaden arms, he raised his musket, aimed and fired. High. Mutinously high. Far above the heads of the men who were his kin.

A riderless horse bolted, the high-pitched whinny like the scream of a frightened child. He saw the Macleod colours directly in front of him and paused, frantically searching, seeking Rory's distinctive mane of gold hair, the exact same colour as his own. A hissing noise, which he thought at first was the wind changing direction, made him look up just in time to see the murderous glint of metal arc through the air towards him. In time to turn away from its fatal path, but not in time to avoid it completely. The heavy, double-bladed claymore sliced into the flesh of his belly, the force of the impact sending him flying backwards into his own line. Finally, he saw Rory. As he cried out his brother's name, his legs gave way beneath him and he felt himself falling, falling, falling…

Calumn woke with a start as he always did, sweating profusely. The dryness of his mouth told him he had been shouting in his sleep. Trembling, like a man with the ague, he reached for the decanter of whisky he had taken to keeping on the nightstand by his bed, gulping down a generous dram of the fiery golden liquid. He touched the large scar, which weaved a jagged path across the taut muscles of his abdomen. The physical wound had long since healed, but on nights like this the scar felt burning hot, inflamed and aching, as though he had been branded by an iron.

Eventually the vivid memory of the nightmare faded. Calumn slumped back against the damp pillows, clutching his glass. The furious beating of his heart slowed. The sheen of sweat on his chest dried.

But other, less visible scars still burned, deep in his psyche. The all-pervading sense of desolation. And the heavy blanket of guilt which enveloped his soul.

Chapter One

Madeleine Lafayette huddled forlornly in the entranceway of a close, the narrow passageway leading to the tenements which Edinburgh's residents called home. Even in the dim glow cast by the flare of the nearby brazier which served as a street light, it would have been obvious to any passer-by that the young woman was no native Scot. Her slim figure was clad in garments of a decidedly foreign cut, the dark blue tippet she clutched around her shoulders woven in an intricate design that was neither plaid nor stripe. Her flaxen hair showed almost white in the ghostly light, but her skin had neither the pallor of the city dweller nor the swarthiness of the Gael. Rather it was translucent, like a pearl tinged with colour by the sun. With a generous mouth, the soft pink of coral, and slanting green eyes under fair brows, she had the appearance, against the grey of the city's sandstone and granite, of an exotic sea-creature out of her element.

Shivering, Madeleine hugged her tippet closer. At the top of Castlehill she could see the dark hulk of the castle looming, forbidding and—as she had discovered to her dismay—impregnable. Perhaps it had been a mistake, coming all this way alone with no contacts and no plan, nothing save the one objective in her mind. To find Guillaume.

The exhilaration of her impetuous flight and the trials of the rough sea voyage with the Breton fishermen had prevented her from thinking too much about the danger she was courting in coming here alone, the overwhelming odds which were stacked against her, or the terrifying possibility that despite all her certainty she was wrong. That Guillaume really was dead.

No! He was alive. He *must* be alive.

Above her, from the castle ramparts, someone barked out a staccato order. Footsteps rang out over the cobblestones as another rushed to obey, then silence descended again.

At home in Brittany her father would be asleep, for in the summer months they both rose with the sun. She loved those early morning rides around the estate, checking on the progress of the year's planting. The scent of dew-drenched grass beneath the hooves of their horses mingled with the tang of salt and the sweet smell of the crops in the fields. By the time they returned for breakfast, the mist from the sea which hung over the land like a cloak of the finest lace would have burned away to reveal the clear azure of the Breton sky. Here in Edinburgh the air smelled so different, of stone and people and dust and dirt. Though she knew the slate-grey North Sea was only a matter of miles away, she could detect no trace of it. A pang of homesickness clutched her.

Guillaume had been here, in Edinburgh. She knew that much from his early letters home. This morning, landing in the port of Leith just to the north of the city, the castle had been her first thought. She'd made straight for it, for she'd been told that Jacobite prisoners were held there still. The discovery that she could not gain entry had been a blow to her hopes. The sensible thing then would have been to look for lodgings, but she had been unable to tear herself away, tormented by the thought that Guillaume might be just yards away on the other side of those thick walls. An endless stream of people passed in and out of the garrison, but all were checked by the vigilant guards. By the time Madeleine had concluded that she must enlist the help of someone with legitimate business there, it was dusk and the city gates were locked. With no clue as to how to go about finding a bed for the night, she fought the urge to shed some tears of self-pity.

She wondered how Papa had reacted to her flight. Perhaps he was regretting the harsh words which had triggered it. He had been so changed since Maman died, throwing himself into the management of the estate as if he needed to fill the void in his life, leaving no room for dealing with his grief. At home, he had retreated into his shell, like one of those hermit crabs she and Guillaume used to race across the sands, teasing them with sticks to make them scuttle forwards—though mostly they went sideways. Without doubt Papa would be furious to find her gone, knowing full well whither she had come, though she had left no note. Recalling the extent of her wilfulness, Madeleine shuddered.

A burst of hearty laughter startled her out her reverie. A group of soldiers were staggering up the steep incline towards their barracks. Instinctively, she shrank back into the gloom of the passageway, but it was too late, they had spotted her. Three of them, clad in the distinctive red coats and white gaiters of the British army, loudly and raucously drunk.

'What have we here, lads?' the largest of the group said with a lascivious grin. Faced with a pair of large green eyes set in a strikingly lovely face framed by white-blonde hair, he whistled. 'A beauty, by God.' Grimy fingers grasped Madeleine's chin, forcing it up so that he could examine her face. 'What's your name, darling?'

'*Laissez-moi,* let me go,' Madeleine said haughtily. She was frightened, but not overly so. They had obviously taken her for a lady of the night, and would leave her be when they realised their mistake. She shook herself free.

The man laughed and tried to snake his arm

around her waist. 'Give us a kiss,' he said, manoeuvring Madeleine so that her back was against the
sandstone of the close wall. The other two joined
him, grinning and egging him on. She could smell
the ale on their breath, the dirt and sweat on their
bodies. Now she was afraid. There were hands on
her, touching her face, her hair, her breasts. She
struggled. 'Let me go,' she said again, her voice
betraying her fear, but the man merely tightened his
hold, so she kicked out, her foot in its sturdy boot
making contact with his shins.

He yelped. 'You little wild cat, you'll pay for that.'

On the other side of the street, Calumn Munro
was returning from an evening in his favourite
tavern down in the Cowgate where the whisky,
which came from the landlord's own illegal still,
was mellow, and the company convivial. As he made
his erratic way home, a woman's cry for help pierced
the balmy night air, causing him to halt abruptly.

Across the road, at the foot of Castlehill, a group
of men were bundling something—or someone—
into a close. Despite the potent effects of the whisky
swirling around his brain, Calumn's body was immediately on full alert. He strode purposefully towards
them, his long legs covering the short distance
effortlessly, his golden hair and the heavy skirts of
his coat flying out behind him. When he arrived his
fists were already clenched in readiness. There were
three of them, soldiers in uniform, he saw with disgust, surrounding their victim. He caught a glimpse
of pleading eyes and fair hair, noted that the woman

was young and extremely pretty. She was also struggling frantically.

Concern for her plight and loathing for its perpetrators filled his mind and fuelled his body. With a roar like a battle cry, Calumn launched himself at the soldiers, with nary a thought for his own safety. He took the largest of the three first, hauling him clear of his intended victim before landing his own mighty fist smack in the middle of the man's face. With immense satisfaction he heard the crunch of bone. A swift follow-through with a double punch to the abdomen, and with a whoosh of breath the man collapsed, moaning. Calumn turned his attention to the other two, fighting dirty, using his feet as well as his fists.

Heart pounding, legs shaking, a cold sweat breaking out on her brow, Madeleine leant back against the wall and took deep, gulping breaths of air while in front of her, in the narrow space, her rescuer set about the soldiers with a devilish fury. He was a tall man and, beneath his expensive evening clothes, a very well-built one, with broad shoulders and powerful thighs. His hair, the colour of ripe corn, unpowdered and untied despite his formal dress, flew out in a bright halo of colour behind him as he dealt efficiently with her assailants. Of his face she could make out little, gaining only a fleeting impression of cold menace.

A cruel blow to the jaw took his second opponent out. A vicious kick and an arm-twisting had the last one at his mercy. On the stairway which wound its way from the close up to the first of the tenements, a man appeared in a nightcap, brandishing what looked like a poker. Her rescuer glanced up, telling him curtly to go back to bed, at the same time frogmarching the third soldier out of the close and hurling him into the gutter. Madeleine forced herself to move. Quickly retrieving her small bundle of belongings from beneath the stairwell, she picked her way over the comatose bodies of her attackers out into the street where her rescuer waited.

'Are you all right?' he said anxiously, his voice a soft, attractive lilt, very different from the harsh tones of the soldiers.

Madeleine nodded. 'Yes, thank you,' she managed through lips made stiff with fear. Seeing he was not yet convinced, she tried to reassure him. 'Truly, I'm all right, I took no hurt.'

The tension in him eased, his mouth curling into a smile, the fierce lines on his face relaxing, so that she saw he was young, perhaps five or six and twenty, and almost unfairly handsome. His eyes were dark blue, his smile engaging. Despite her ordeal, she could not but return it.

'Calum Munro,' he said with a flourishing bow, 'I'm happy to have been of service.'

'I'm most happy to meet you, Monsieur Munro,' Madeleine said with a curtsy which was almost steady.

'You're French,' he exclaimed in surprise.

'Mais oui.'

She was enchantingly pretty, all big green eyes

and silken hair, with a mouth made for kissing. Alone, at such a late hour and in the vicinity of the castle, he had assumed she must be a courtesan, but, looking at her more closely, he wasn't so sure. Of a certainty, she was no common harlot. 'May I know your name, *mademoiselle?*'

'I am Madeleine Lafayette.'

'*Enchanté.*' His exertions, on top of the whisky, were beginning to take their toll on Calumn. He needed his bed, but he could not simply abandon the poor lass to the whim of the next group of soldiers who were even now making their raucous way up the hill. 'Let me escort you home, *mademoiselle,*' he said, proffering a gentlemanly arm. 'It's not safe for any woman to be out on her own here at this hour.'

His knuckles were bleeding. There was a bruise forming on his cheekbone. She saw now what she had not noticed before, that he was—albeit charmingly—in his cups. 'I am thinking that you too should be in your bed, *monsieur,*' Madeleine said, 'you look as if you have had too much wine.'

'Not too much wine, too much whisky,' Calumn corrected her gravely. 'Let's get you home. Come now, which direction?'

The words were very slightly slurred. She began to fear that he would collapse if they stayed here for much longer. 'Which direction are you taking?' she asked, and when he pointed vaguely down the hill, told him that she, too, was going that way. She would see him to his own door and then claim to have lodgings nearby. She tugged on his arm. 'Come along, *monsieur.*'

'Calumn, my name's Calumn,' he said, taking her bundle and throwing it casually over his shoulder before tucking her hand into his other arm. *'En avant!'* He seemed to rally, setting off down the brae with an easy grace, the loping stride of an animal built for speed, not the mincing step of a city man. Clinging to his arm, Madeleine had to run to keep up.

They crossed into the Lawnmarket, which during the day teemed with tradesmen selling butter and cheese as well as the wools and linens for which the place was famed. At this time of night it was eerily quiet, difficult to imagine that in just a few hours it would be nigh on impossible to get from one side of the street to the other without running the full gamut of maids, merchants and pickpockets.

At the far end, Calumn stopped at Riddell's Court where his family kept rooms. 'Where to now?'

Madeleine shrugged. 'Not far. I can make my own way from here,' she said, trying for a confidence she was far from feeling. The reality of having to spend the night outside and alone was only just starting to sink in.

She reached for her bundle of belongings, but Calumn held on to it, seeming to notice for the first time what it actually was. 'You've just arrived, haven't you?'

Madeleine nodded reluctantly.

'And you've nowhere to stay?'

'No, but there is no need to…'

'You'd best come up with me then.'

Madeleine shook her head.

'I don't blame you, after what you've been through, but you've nothing to worry about. Apart from anything else, I'm fit for nothing but sleep. I've a spare room with a lock on the door that you're welcome to, and I promise I won't try to take advantage. Word of a Munro.'

She had a fleeting sense of a shadow when he said his name, like a cloud crossing the sun, then it was gone. Weighing up a bed in a house and a door with a lock, against a draughty stairwell and a backdrop of late-night marauders, Madeleine was extremely tempted to accept his offer. Instinctively, she felt Calumn Munro was trustworthy. Had he not already proved himself a knight errant? She nodded her cautious acceptance. 'You're very kind, *monsieur.*'

Calumn led her through the wrought-iron gate which protected the close entrance into the courtyard and up the steep wooden stairs to the second of the building's four storeys. He had some difficulty in fitting the heavy key into the lock, but eventually threw the door open with a flourish. 'Here we are.' He pulled Madeleine into a narrow hallway and thrust the door shut behind them.

Inside, in the warmth, the after-effects of the whisky hit him abruptly. In the light of the lamp which burned on the table by the door, she watched the colour drain from his face. 'Make yourself comfortable,' Calumn said, waving vaguely at a door almost directly opposite. 'I'll just stop here for a wee minute.' He started to slip down the wall.

Though she was taken aback by the rapidity of his decline, Madeleine gamely tried to catch him before he fell unconscious on to the floorboards. 'You can't go to sleep here.' Placing Calumn's arm around her shoulders, she staggered as she heaved him upright. 'Which is your chamber?' she asked, and then all but dragged him towards the door he indicated.

'No, no, I'll be very well where I am,' he mumbled in protest, but she continued to propel him forwards, managing to reach the bed just before the weight of him pulled them both on to the floor. 'You're a fine lass,' he muttered appreciatively, collapsing backwards onto the bed without releasing his hold on her. Madeleine tumbled forwards, sprawling full length on top of her host. 'Perfect,' he murmured happily, pulling her closer, one arm around her waist, the other hand proprietarily on her bottom, before falling instantly asleep.

Pressed tight against his body, Madeleine could not decide whether to be shocked, annoyed or amused. She could not move. Her head was tucked into the crook of his shoulder, her face pressed into his neckcloth. He smelled of clean linen and warm man. Different, but not at all alien or repellent as her attackers had been. Reassuring almost. It must be his size. He was not just tall, but solid muscle and bone. The contours of his body seemed to complement hers, as if they were two halves of something designed to fit. Her curves melded into his hollows.

It was an unexpectedly pleasant feeling. Though she knew it was imprudent, she was not at all inclined to move just yet. Guillaume had never held her like this. That last day, before he had sailed to the aid of the Scottish Prince, he had not held her at all.

The buttons on Calumn Munro's jacket were digging into her chest, and something else was pressing insistently against her further down. His hand tightened on her robe. She could feel his heart beating slow and steady through his jacket. She could hear him breathing, feel his breath on her hair. His proximity was making her hot. A trickle of sweat ran down the valley between her breasts. She realised what the something else was which she could feel through the layers of her petticoats. A shiver arrowed through her.

Minutes crept by, and still Madeleine lay pliant on top of him, listening to his breathing in the dark of the room. She stopped thinking. Exhaustion rolled over her like a mighty breaker on to the beach. The temptation to close her eyes and give in to sleep was almost overpowering. Two days it had taken the fishing boat to sail from Roscoff to the port of Leith. She'd felt its rocking under her feet for hours after she had landed. The bustle and noise of the sailors and stevedores at the port had been intimidating. Edinburgh itself was smaller than she had expected, but much more foreign, too. Had it been a mistake, coming here?

Beneath her, the tone of Calumn's breathing changed and his grip on her loosened. Madeleine inched cautiously off the bed, back out to the hallway. Picking up the lamp, she opened the door at the far end and found herself in a large reception room with a huge fireplace. The boards were polished and scattered with rugs. Two enormous wooden chairs of carved black wood sat side by side at the hearth, with a settle opposite. Under the window was a chest of the same wood, the fittings brightly polished brass. A table and four chairs sat in another corner. Heavy rafters showed dark against the tempered walls, on which were two companion portraits. A fierce man in full Highland dress with Calumn's deep blue eyes, and a woman, golden-haired and very beautiful, equally stern. His parents, unmistakably. They were obviously a wealthy family.

A muffled groan drew Madeleine back to the bed chamber where Calumn lay sprawled on top of the covers. She ought to make him more comfortable. Placing the lamp carefully on the nightstand beside a decanter of amber liquor, she unlaced his shoes. He did not stir, so she unrolled his stockings. His calves were muscular and finely shaped. His legs, with their cover of dark golden hair, felt rough and warm. His feet were long and narrow. Bare, they made him look vulnerable.

The water in the china jug was cold, but she poured some into the bowl anyway, and found a clean linen towel which she used to carefully bathe his knuckles. She had nothing with which to bandage them, but judged they would heal more quickly exposed to the air in any case. The bruise on his cheek was purpling. At home she would have applied an arnica paste for the swelling.

Engrossed in her task now, Madeleine set about removing Calumn's jacket, a more difficult operation, for the dark-green velvet fitted tight across his broad shoulders. By the time she had finished she was out of breath. His silk waistcoat was easier. She unwound his neckcloth and placed it at the foot of the bed beside his jacket. His shirt fell open at the neck, giving her a glimpse of his chest she could not resist touching. His skin was cool. A dusting of hair. Not an ounce of spare flesh. She should not be doing this.

With an immense effort, she rolled Calumn to one side, tugged up the heavy counterpane and sheets and rolled him back. He sighed and snuggled his head deeper into the feather bolster. His profile was so perfect it could have been sculpted, save for the tiny cleft in his chin. A long strand of gleaming golden hair caught in his lashes. Madeleine smoothed it back. It was surprisingly soft.

'*Bon nuit,* Calumn Munro,' she said, pressing a tiny kiss to his brow. Treading softly, she retrieved her bundle and opened the second door leading off the hallway. It was a small windowless chamber obviously intended for a maidservant, simply furnished with an iron bedstead, a wooden chair and a wash stand. As Calumn had promised there was a lock in the door and a key in the lock. Madeleine hesitated, then turned it. Quickly disrobing, she placed her shawl, dress and stockings on the chair and sank gratefully on to the rather lumpy mattress, pulling the rough woollen blanket over her. Within minutes she was asleep.

The next morning Madeleine padded through to the scullery on bare feet with her tippet wrapped over her shift and poured herself a glass of water from a large stone jug. Returning to the main reception room, she walked straight into Calumn, who growled something low and vicious in an unfamiliar language. Startled, she jumped back, spilling some of the water down her shift. He towered over her, clad in a long woollen robe tied loosely at the waist. In the bright light of day his eyes were dark blue and heavy lidded. The stubble on his jaw was a tawny colour, darker than his tousled golden hair, giving him a raffish look.

'Who in the devil's name are you?' he barked.

Madeleine's heart sank. 'Madeleine Lafayette. You don't remember?'

'You're French?'

She smiled nervously. 'Yes, I'm still French.'

To her relief, Calumn's flash of ill temper faded. He raked his hand through his hair and grinned ruefully. 'French, and obviously not a housebreaker. I need coffee.' He opened the door leading out onto the stairwell. 'Jamie,' he roared, 'where are you?'

A patter of feet preceded the arrival of an urchin of some nine or ten years with a mop of dirty blond hair and a face which would benefit from the application of a washcloth. 'Nae need to ask how you are this morn, Mister Munro,' the lad said with a cheeky grin, handing over a tray on which was an enamel pot of coffee and a large jug of ale. 'You're like a bear wi' a sore head.'

Calumn took the tray wordlessly. Tossing the boy a coin, he caught Jamie's curious glance towards Madeleine. 'I'll not be the only one with a sore head if I catch you blathering, do I make myself clear?'

'Clear as day, Mister Munro. I didn't see nobody.' Whistling tunelessly and somehow managing to grin at the same time, a feat which impressed Madeleine immensely, Jamie banged the door shut behind him.

Calumn poured them both a cup of coffee before helping himself to a long reviving draught of ale. 'Jamie's family live on the ground floor,' he said by way of explanation. 'Andrew Macfarlane, his father, is dead. His mother takes in lodgers and looks after me, too.' He dropped gracefully into one of the seats opposite Madeleine. Under his robe he still had his shirt on, but not his breeches.

Embarrassingly aware of her own dishabille, Madeleine pulled her tippet closer and tried to redistribute her shift, a manoeuvre which simply succeeded in drawing Calumn's attention to her bare ankles. Shuffling her feet as far back under the settle as she could manage, she shook out her hair in an effort to disguise the flush creeping over her cheeks. 'Do you remember nothing of last night, *monsieur?*'

Calumn inspected his knuckles ruefully. 'Aye, it's coming back to me now.' His mouth thinned as an echo of the menacing look from last night traced a path across his handsome countenance. 'It's men like that who give soldiers a bad name. You took no harm?'

Madeleine shuddered as the image of the men's faces flickered into her mind like evil spirits. 'None, thanks to you. You were very brave to take on three of them alone. You could have been killed.'

He gave a twisted smile. 'Perhaps that was my intent. I sometimes think I'd be as well dead.' His eyes glittered, like the glint of granite on a Highland peak.

Madeleine shivered, frightened by the bleakness in this expression. 'You should not talk so.'

'Should I not now?' he growled at her. 'And what business, *mademoiselle,* would that be of yours?' he demanded, frowning fiercely and staring off into space, so that she dared not reply.

Fortunately he did not seem to expect her to. His frown eased, then as suddenly as it came on, his mood shifted and his attention refocused on his visitor. She looked mighty uncomfortable in her state of undress. Far too uncomfortable to be the type of woman he had taken her for. And she was younger than he had taken her for, too. What the devil had he got himself into?

'It was a sorry introduction to Scotland for you, but if you don't mind my saying so, you were asking for trouble, hanging around the castle like that. They no doubt mistook your calling. I did so myself, but I take it I was wrong?'

Madeleine stared at him in consternation. 'Indeed,

you are mistaken,' she said indignantly, clutching her tippet even more tightly.

'That's what I just said,' he responded, unmoved by her embarrassment. 'But as I've also just said, you can't blame me for thinking it, anyone would have made the same mistake.'

She could not deny this, so remained silent.

'What the hell did you think you were doing there? Had you no money for a lodging?'

In the cold light of day, after a night's refreshing sleep, Madeleine struggled to come up with an answer to this perfectly reasonable question. Her actions seemed stupid even to herself. 'I don't know,' she said, feeling singularly foolish. 'I mean—yes, I had money, but I don't know why I didn't find a place to sleep.'

'Do you know why you're here, at least? In Edinburgh, I mean?'

'Of course I do,' she responded, drawing herself up haughtily. 'I was trying to get into the castle, but they wouldn't let me pass.'

'Why on earth…?'

'I wanted to speak to the prisoners there. I'm looking for someone.'

'A man, I presume.'

Madeleine nodded.

'And what has this man done?'

'Nothing,' Madeleine said indignantly. 'He's not a criminal.'

'Then why—ah, your man is a Jacobite.' He waited on her nod. 'And what makes you think he's in there?' Despite his pleasing lilt, the worlds were sharply spoken.

'I don't. I don't know where he is.' Madeleine paused, swallowing hard as the many, many things she didn't know about Guillaume and his fate threatened her ability to think clearly. 'The castle is as good a place to start as any. I thought someone in there—one of the other Jacobites—might know him, or of him, might be able to help me trace him.'

'It's a bit of a shot in the dark if you ask me.' Calumn pressed a hand to his brow. His head had begun to thump. His tried to think, but his thoughts fled from his grasp like a hare from a hound. 'How do you come to speak such good English?'

'A woman in our village, Madame le Brun, who is married to the school teacher, is from a place called Dover.' Confused by the sudden change of subject, Madeleine eyed her host warily. 'She teaches me embroidery—or she tries to—as well as English. She would be pleased at the compliment,' she said with an attempt at humour, 'for she despairs of my stitchery.'

Calumn rubbed his eyes and shook his head in an effort to clear away the fog befuddling his brain. A shaft of sunlight slanted in through the leaded panes of the window, making him wince. Too much whisky, but at least it stopped him from dreaming. He focused his gaze on his unexpected houseguest. She was a slight thing, with long flaxen hair trailing down her back. Beautiful in a fey, ethereal way. 'You look like a mermaid,' he said.

His smile curled like smoke. His voice had a teasing quality, a lilting, sensual tone, which connected to her senses at a very basic level. Looking at him from under her lashes, the sunlight making his hair a burnished halo, Madeleine thought anew how strikingly attractive Calumn Munro was. Perhaps his ill temper was simply morning crotchets. 'My mother used to say that, too,' she said.

His eyes crinkled as his smile deepened. 'Did you put me to bed?'

'I just made you comfortable.' The vivid memory of being held hard against him made Madeleine's toes curl up into the soft pile of the rug at her feet.

'Did I behave myself?'

She wondered nervously if he knew that it was she, not he, who had taken liberties. 'You behaved perfectly. You promised you would. Word of a Munro, you said.'

Calumn's smile faded. His eyes darkened, as if a light had gone out. 'Word of a Munro,' he repeated, his tone bitter. 'I must have been drunk.'

He got up and stretched, rolling his shoulders, which were stiff from tension. He needed food and fresh air. 'I can't think on an empty stomach. We'll get some breakfast and you can tell me your story properly.'

'You've done too much for me already,' Madeleine protested, but it was half-hearted. She was ravenous. Calumn Munro looked like a man with influence, and last night had proven him also a man of action. What's more, he was her only friend in this foreign country; she would be foolish to turn down the opportunity to enlist his help.

Foolish, but also wise? She knew nothing of him, found not only his uncertain temper but his very presence unsettling. But…she trusted him. And he intrigued her. 'Yes, thank you,' she said with an uncertain smile. 'I'll go and get dressed.'

'I'll get Jamie to fetch you some hot water,' Calumn said, suiting action to words with a bellow which would have awoken the dead.

With the hot water, Jamie brought a letter which had just arrived. When he had washed and dressed, Calumn broke the seal reluctantly, his frown deepening to a scowl as he scanned the closely crossed sheets of his mother's elegant hand. *Father weaker… demise imminent…factor requiring constant supervision…your return required urgently.* All the usual phrases, although the bit about the attack on the western lands was new. *Revenge by a Jacobite clan…to be expected given the Munroes' stand,* his mother wrote. Calumn's stomach clenched in anger as he read this paragraph more closely. Bad enough the mess the Rebellion had left in its wake, now they must be feuding amongst themselves! If they were to survive in the Highlands, the clans must stick together, could they not see that!

Beg of you to return. Your father…not likely to live much longer. If his father died, the lands would be his. His to change and to renew, his to care for and nurture rather than work to exhaustion, his to

do all the things he'd thought about and planned
during the last few years. But they weren't his yet,
nor likely would be in the near future. His father
might be weak, but his grip on life was a lot more
tenacious than his mother gave him credit for. And
anyway, what was the point in dreaming, when the
fact was he couldn't go home. Not now. Maybe not
ever.

The usual feelings of frustration and anger and
pointless railing at fate, roiled in his gut, making him
nauseous. Calumn crumpled the letter up in disgust
and threw it into the empty hearth just as Madeleine
rejoined him. She raised her brows, wondering what
could have inspired such fury, but seeing the deep
frown which marred his face, chose wisely not to
comment. He was dressed in breeches and top boots
teamed with a dark coat, the clothes expensive and
well cut. He had shaved and tidied his hair, though
it was not tied back but swept away from his brow,
curling almost to his shoulders. It was unusual for
a man of his obvious standing to go without powder
or wig, but Madeleine thought it becoming.

Calumn gave himself a shake, pressing his thumb
into the furrow of his brow as if to smooth away the
thoughts which formed it. 'Come on, then,' he said,
holding open the door for her, 'my stomach thinks
my throat's been cut.'

They made their way down the stairs, out of the
dark close and into the Lawnmarket, which was now
teeming with hawkers and traders. Vendors vied for
supremacy in the calling of their wares. Horses and

carriages clattered on the cobblestones. Chairmen shoved and pushed their precarious way through the hordes thronging up Castlehill and down the High Street towards the Parliament buildings and the solid hulk of the Tollgate prison. The appetising scent of fresh bread, strong cheese and the dry, fusty smell of the many bales of cloth fought a losing battle with the stench from the sheughs, the steep gutters running either side of the street.

Madeleine paused, wide-eyed, in the close entranceway, waiting for a gap in the heaving crowd. Calumn took her arm. 'Hold on tight to me.'

She needed two steps to keep up with his one. The crowd seemed to part for him like magic as his long legs strode effortlessly through the busy market. Madeleine clung to his arm for dear life, with her free hand keeping a firm hold on her small supply of money through the slit in her petticoat where it was tucked into one of the embroidered pockets tied securely around her waist.

Noticing the trepidation on her face, Calumn pulled her closer. 'I take it you're not from the city?'

'I'm Breton, from a place near the town of Roscoff on the coast.'

'I've not been to Brittany, though I've been to France. So you're a country girl, then?'

'Absolument.'

He had not slowed his pace. They took the steep road down West Bow, Calumn leading the way unerringly through a warren of dark closes and narrow wynds to an inn on the Grassmarket where he greeted the landlord by name and demanded breakfast immediately. They were ushered into a dusty back parlour, away from the curious group of ostlers, coachmen and passengers awaiting the public conveyances, and shortly were served thick slices of bacon, eggs and blood pudding. Though Calumn ate heartily, Madeleine was more cautious, deciding against the heavy black pudding after a suspicious sniff.

'Tell me about this Jacobite you're looking for.' Calumn pushed his empty plate aside.

'He came to Scotland with a battalion called the *Écossais Royeaux*.'

'The Royal Scots. A mix of French and Scots, and a fair few mercenaries too. Under Drummond's command, am I right?'

'Yes. How do you know all this?'

He ignored her. 'All the French were pardoned, you know, rounded up and packed off home long since. How can you be certain this man of yours is still alive?'

She traced a pattern on the scarred wooden table with a fork. 'I just am. I can't explain, but if he was dead—well, I would know. I would feel it.'

Rory's dead, Calumn. It's been almost six months. He's dead, we have to accept that, all of us. Heronsay is yours now. His mother's words echoed, making him close his eyes in an effort to block out the painful memory. His own reply floated into his mind, so strangely reminiscent of Madeleine

Lafayette's. *He's alive. If he was dead I would know. I would feel it.*

Calumn blinked, and found that same Madeleine Lafayette's big green eyes watching him with concern.

'Is there something wrong?' Instinctively, she reached out her hand to his.

Her fingers were long, the nails well cared for, buffed and shaped. He laid his other hand on top of hers, noting the stark contrast between her smooth and creamy-white skin and his own, rough and tanned. Her hand felt good nestling there, fragile yet resilient. He twined his fingers into hers, liking the way her fingertips grazed his knuckles, fitting so perfectly, though she was so much smaller than he. He remembered then, last night, how the rest of her body felt, pressed close to his, fitting just as snugly, feeling just as right. It was as if he knew her. Had known her. Which was ridiculous. He dropped her hand, sat back and shook his head firmly. 'There's nothing wrong. I know what you mean, that's all, when you say you're sure he's alive.'

Just for a second he had looked lost. Vulnerable. 'You've obviously felt the same about someone,' Madeleine prompted carefully.

A door slammed shut. His eyes refocused. 'So who is he, this Jacobite of yours?' Calumn asked brusquely.

'His name is Guillaume, the Comte de Guise.'

'A nobleman. That should certainly make it a bit easier to track him down.'

'*Oui,* that's what I thought,' Madeleine agreed with relief. 'That's why I wanted to talk to the other Jacobites at the castle. I know it's unlikely, but I have to start somewhere.'

'It's highly unlikely, especially after all this time. Why have you waited so long? It's been over a year since Culloden.'

'You think I don't know that!' Madeleine's lip trembled. 'A whole year of trying everything in my power to find out what has become of him, but no one will tell me anything. I've written countless letters to the authorities and to the army, but all they will tell me is that Guillaume is not on any list, either of men who have been sent back, nor of any of the—the fallen, or the men who have been executed. It is so out of character for him not to get in touch. I don't understand it—where could he be?' Huge eyes swimming with unshed tears gazed up at Calumn beseechingly. The strain of the last year, the ordeal of the last few days, were beginning to take their toll.

'Do you not think, *mademoiselle,* that the time has come to accept that he is—'

'No!' Her gaze was fierce, her rejection absolute. 'No,' she said again more quietly, though no less resolutely, 'I won't listen, you sound just like everyone else.'

The accusation stung. Once again, Calumn was reminded of a similar scenario not six months ago, his own no-less-vehement rejection. His hand clenched into a fist. He had held out, held on, waited, but he could not forget the doubts. He had not been so steadfast in his belief as this woman was. Though he had held fast in public, in private he had questioned. Was not this certainty simply the guilt of the survivor? A stubborn unwillingness to confront the truth? He had survived his wound because fate, ill fate, had placed him on the side of the victors. Rory, who had chosen to fight with his kin, had most likely not been so fortunate. Yet still Calumn had waited, because not to wait would be to admit the inadmissible. The price he had paid, would continue to pay, for his own choices, was high enough without that.

'I'm sorry, I should not have been so rude.' Madeleine's voice broke into his thoughts. She was gazing at him searchingly. Too searchingly.

'There's no need to apologise,' Calumn replied gruffly. 'What you believe is not for me to question.'

She smiled tentatively. Whatever was going on in that handsome head to make his tempter so volatile, it was more than the after-effects of whisky. 'I know Guillaume is probably dead, I know that it's irrational of me to think otherwise in the circumstances, but I still find it impossible to accept. You understand, I think. It's the lack of certainty.'

His nod was reluctantly given, but it was eventually given all the same. 'What is this man to you?' he asked sharply.

'Guillaume and I are—friends.'

'Friends! You've come all this way, after all this time, for a friend? He must be a very particular friend.'

Piercing blue eyes, disconcertingly penetrating, searched her face. Madeleine returned to playing with her cutlery. She was strangely reluctant to tell him the truth. She put the fork back on the table and forced herself to meet Calumn's gaze. 'We have known each other since childhood. Guillaume is my best friend.' That, at least, was true.

Calumn raised his eyebrows sceptically. 'And how came you to be here in Edinburgh alone?'

'Everyone else thinks Guillaume is dead. No one will listen to me, I had no option but to come.' The truth was, she had run away, but if she told this man the truth she doubted he would help her. More likely he would insist on packing her back to her father, and she could not risk that, not when she had already risked so much just to get here.

'Won't you be missed?'

She shrugged, deliberately offhand. 'They will guess where I am.'

'I see,' Calumn said drily, thinking he did, now. She was obviously in love with the missing Comte, in all likelihood had been his mistress, and had equally obviously been abandoned. If he was not dead, this Guillaume de Guise, he had most likely taken up with another woman. Calumn had seen it himself many a time with his own men, stationed far from home for months on end, falling for a pretty local girl and abandoning all thought of the one waiting for them back home. Whether her swain was dead or unfaithful, Madeleine Lafayette was doomed to disappointment.

Callous bastard, not even to have the guts to tell her! If Guillaume de Guise had been one of his men! Calumn sighed and shook his head. 'You're probably on a wild goose chase, you know,' he said gently.

A film of tears glazed her eyes, but Madeleine shrugged fatalistically. The defensive little gesture touched his heart more than her tears. He did understand, of course he did. He'd been the same, all those months when Rory was lost to them. Calumn felt in the pocket of his waistcoat for his handkerchief and handed it to her. Wild goose chase or no, she'd been very brave to come here like this all on her own, so determined and so steadfast in her belief. He, of all people, could not but admire her for that. She deserved to find out the truth, even though she was heading for heartache. Why not help her?

He took her hand in his again, enjoying the feel of it again. 'I'll see what I can do,' he told her. 'I'm not promising, but I think I can get you into the castle, if you're set on it. And I have a friend here in Edinburgh who can check the records, make sure de Guise's name isn't on any of our lists for deportation or—or anything else.'

'I knew you understood,' Madeleine said softly.

The intensity of her gaze made him uncomfortable. Calumn threw some coins on to the table. 'Come on, let's see what we can do about finding this precious Guillaume of yours.'

Chapter Two

Calumn set off at a brisk pace with Madeleine hurrying along breathlessly at his side, buoyed up by the prospect of making progress at last. The Grassmarket was the disembarkation point for most coaches coming in and out of Edinburgh. At the far end stood the gallows, and towering high above it, perched on its plug of volcanic rock, stood the castle.

'Everything here is so tall.' She gazed up in wonder at the lofty buildings climbing four, five, some six storeys high. To one whose experience of a metropolis was limited to the small Breton market town of Quimper, the Scottish capital, with its crowded thoroughfares and bustling populace, was like an alien world. The houses were packed so tightly against one another it seemed to her that they, like the people on the street, were jostling for space and light. Inns and coaching houses took up most of the ground-level accommodation, separated from each other by the narrowest of alleyways. The skyline was a jumbled mass of steeply gabled roofs and smoking chimneys, with washing lines strung out on pulleys from the tenement windows, fluttering like the sails of invisible ships. 'So many people living on top of each other, I don't know how they can bear it. It's like a labyrinth,' Madeleine said.

'Aye, and a badly built one at that, down in this part of town,' Calumn replied. 'Some of these wooden staircases are treacherous. The problem is there's too many people and nowhere to build except up, because of the city walls.' He pulled her adroitly out of the path of a dray loaded with barrels of ale.

'Where are we going?'

'To see a friend of mine.' He led the way through a wynd, which rose sharply between the two streets it connected, then turned left into a small courtyard where more rows of laundry took up most of the cramped space, flapping on lines stretched between poles across its width. 'Mind these stairs. See what I mean about treacherous?'

The staircase wound up the outside of the building, almost like a wooden scaffold attached rather precariously to the stone tenement. Madeleine lifted her petticoat and climbed nervously, relieved when they stopped at the first floor.

'Jeannie,' Calumn called, rapping briskly on the door.

A young woman answered, her pretty face lighting up with pleasure when she saw the identity of her visitor. 'Calumn, what a surprise.'

Her vibrant red hair was caught up in a careless knot on top of her head. Her figure was lush, with rather too much of her white bosom on display through her carelessly fastened shift, Madeleine decided prudishly.

'I brought Mademoiselle Lafayette to meet you. Madeleine, this is Jeannie.'

'Good day to you, *mademoiselle,*' Jeannie said, bobbing a curtsy. 'Come away in, the pair of you, before we have the rest of the close wanting to know our business.'

Despite the fact that she was obviously not a respectable female, Madeleine warmed to her. Jeannie ushered them into a room which seemed to serve for living, sleeping and eating all at once. A huge black pot simmered over the fire, suspended on a hook which hung from a complicated pulley-and-chain device inside the chimney breast. A large table and an assortment of chairs took up most of the space, all covered with piles of neatly folded clothing. In the far corner a recess in the wall, like a cupboard without a door, was made up as a bed. Jeannie bustled about clearing some chairs and bade them sit down. 'I'm sorry about the clutter,' she said to Madeleine.

'Jeannie takes in laundry,' Calumn said, leaning comfortably back on a rickety wooden chair, clearly quite at home in the crowded room. 'She washes my shirts and I give her young brother fenc-

ing lessons in return. She also does the washing for
some of the prisoners up at the castle.'

'Those that can afford it, any roads. I'm up there
most days. It's a sorry sight, I can tell you. Some
of those poor souls have been locked up there for
years.'

Realisation finally began to dawn on Madeleine. 'You mean you can talk to the prisoners,' she
exclaimed.

'Aye, of course.'

'Mademoiselle Lafayette is looking for someone
who may be held there,' Calumn said, responding
to Jeannie's enquiring look. 'A Frenchman called
Guillaume de Guise.'

'What does he look like?'

If only she possessed a miniature! Madeleine
screwed up her eyes in an effort to picture Guillaume's face, but after so long without seeing him it
was as if his image had blurred. She could remember things about him—his smile, the way he strode
across the fields, the sound of his voice calling to his
dogs—but she couldn't see his face clearly. Instead,
she described his portrait, taken for his twenty-first
birthday and a good likeness. 'Tall, though not as
tall as Monsieur Munro. Slimmer too, with dark
hair, though he usually has it cut short, for he wears
a wig. Blue eyes, though not like Monsieur's either,
paler. And he is younger, he will be twenty-three
now.' She looked at Calumn, lounging with careless
grace on the chair next to her. He had such presence,
an aura of power, of—of maleness—that she could

not imagine ever forgetting what he looked like. In contrast, the memory of Guillaume appeared boyish, disappointingly ephemeral.

Jeannie shook her head. 'I'm sorry, I can't recall having seen anyone like that.'

'Wait a bit though, did you not say that Lady Drummond's being held in the Black Hole?' Calumn asked.

'Aye, she's there with her two daughters, and a damn shame it is too, to see such a proud woman brought so low. I have some of their shifts to take back today. Beautiful stitching on them.'

'Lord Drummond was the commander of the *Écossais Royeaux,* the regiment for which de Guise fought,' Calumn explained. 'He was executed some months ago now, but they don't have the right to send his wife the same way. She'll be worth talking to.'

'You can't expect me to take her there, Calumn, it's a terrible place.'

'I'm not afraid,' Madeleine declared determinedly, 'and I would be very, very grateful if you would help me. Will you, please?'

Jeannie pursed her lips disapprovingly. 'We'll have to do something about those clothes of yours, they're far too fine for a laundry maid. I'll give you an apron to put over them, and you can wear a cap, but you'll need to keep your hands out of sight. Anybody with a wheen of sense can see those have never done a day's washing.'

'Thank you!' Madeleine leapt to her feet and

impulsively pressed a kiss on Jeannie's cheek. 'You have no idea how much this means to me.'

'Don't be daft, I just hope you know what you're letting yourself in for. Away with you just now. Meet me at the bottom of Castlehill at two.'

'She's nice, I like her,' Madeleine said to Calumn as she once again found herself executing a little running step to keep up with his pace. 'She's your *chère-amie,* isn't she?'

Calumn laughed. 'Lord, no, Jeannie's a grand lass, but she's a friend, that's all.'

'And what does it mean, to be a grand lass?' Madeleine asked, articulating the strange phrase carefully. 'Am I one?'

They had reached the close which was the entranceway to Calumn's rooms. Smiling at her lisping attempt at the Scots tongue, he pushed the gate open and ushered her through into the courtyard. As she moved past him, the swell of her hip brushed his leg, and he remembered last night again. Her body had been so soft and pliant, on top of his own. He thought of the way her hand felt so at home in his after breakfast this morning too, and before he could stop himself he wondered if her lips would fit his in the same way.

She had stopped to wait on him as he shut the gate. As she made to walk to the stairs he caught her arm and pulled her towards him, startling himself almost as much as her. 'You are far too pretty to be called a grand lass,' he said. 'You, Madeleine Lafayette, are a captivating wee witch.'

'I am not a witch,' Madeleine said, flustered and indignant. She could feel the heat of his body, though they were hardly touching.

'No? Maybe a fairy then,' Calumn said, wondering fancifully if she had indeed cast a spell on him. Mere foolishness, but he hadn't come across her like before, and he didn't seem to be able to make himself stop what he knew he shouldn't be doing, for he wanted, suddenly, urgently, to kiss her. He leaned closer, and caught a trace of her scent, remembered that too, from last night, like the wisps of a dream.

'What are you doing? Let me go.' Madeleine's lungs seemed to have stopped working. Her heart was pumping too hard. Calumn's eyes sparkled blue like the summer sea. *He looked as if he was going to kiss her.* Surely he would not dare? Surely she would not…

Calumn kissed her. It was the softest of kisses, just a touch of his lips on hers. A warmth, a taste, a curl of pleasure inside her, and it was over. *'Oh!* You should not—'

A hooting noise interrupted her. It was Jamie, standing on the bottom step, a dog comprised mostly of terrier wriggling in his arms. 'Me ma says to remind you that this is a respectable close.'

'As if she would ever let me forget,' Calumn muttered, straightening up. 'Here, go and put your washerwoman's apron on. I've a bit of business to attend to. I'll be back in time to escort you up to the castle.'

He handed Madeleine the key to his lodgings. Madeleine took it, trying not to imagine what kind of woman Jamie's mother must be imagining her, to be caught kissing in public, even though *he* had kissed *her* without the slightest bit of encouragement! They would think her the same type of woman that Calumn obviously imagined her to be! For the first time since she had arrived, she was glad to have the North Sea between herself and her home. If her father had—but he had not seen, and would never know, and she would make sure it didn't happen again, so it was pointless to worry. 'There's no need to come back for me,' she said to Calumn, thinking that perhaps the less she was in his company the better, 'I know the way now.'

His lips thinned. 'You'll do as I say,' he said implacably.

It would be a waste of breath to argue; besides, she had much more important things to do right now. Madeleine nodded her agreement and made her retreat.

An hour later, her transformation to laundry maid was complete. She had tucked her petticoat and shift up at the waist, exposing her ankles in the way she noticed all the women did here, for the very practical reason of keeping their clothes from trailing in the stinking gutters. The closed robe she wore, the only one she had with her, was of cerulean blue with a darker stripe, and though the material, a blend of wool and silk, was of excellent quality, the long starched cotton apron Jeannie had given her covered much of it. She'd taken off her saque-backed jacket, and made sure that the frills of her shift showed at the neckline of her dress and at the hems of her tight sleeves, which she had pushed up to the elbows.

'Well, do I look the part?' Giving a little twirl before curtsying low in front of Calumn, she unwittingly granted him a delicious view of her cleavage.

He had thought her slender, but her curves were now clearly revealed. She had a delightful body. The slim arms emerging from the fall of lace at her elbow were white, the fragile bones at her wrists and ankles, and the elegance of her long, tapering fingers, her neck, all were somehow emphasised by the changes she had made to her clothing. The soft mounds of her breasts had the lustre of pearls against the white of her shift. Her mouth, with its full lower lip, was pink and luscious.

'You look more like a princess playing at dressing up. Here, let me.' He carefully tucked her hair back under the cap, giving her a marginally less just-got-out-of-bed look. Up close she smelled as sweet as she looked. Lavender and sunshine. 'I'm not so sure it's such a good idea after all, letting you go to the castle like this. Can you not pull the neckline of that dress a bit higher? You'll have half the garrison lusting after you.'

'I'll be with Jeannie.'

'Exactly. I should never have introduced you to her. I don't know what I was thinking.'

Madeleine giggled. 'You weren't thinking very much at all. You had the headache from all that wine—no, I forgot, whisky—last night. You shouldn't drink so much.'

'If you had to live in my head, you'd know I can't drink enough,' Calumn flashed angrily.

Taken aback at the acrimony in his voice, she flinched. 'And does it work?'

'What do you mean?'

Resolutely, she held his gaze. 'Mostly, people drink to forget something.'

'I am not most people.'

No, he most certainly was not. But he was trying to forget, none the less. Madeleine decided it was probably best not to say so, however.

They arrived at the bottom of Castlehill to find Jeannie waiting with two large baskets of laundry. She surveyed Madeleine and shook her head doubtfully. 'They'll have you for breakfast if we're not careful.'

'That's what I've been telling her,' Calumn agreed, picking up both the baskets, carefully stacking one on top of the other.

'Don't speak to anyone unless I tell you to,' Jeannie said, setting off up the hill towards the castle at a pace which rivalled Calumn's. 'And don't catch anybody's eye, especially not Willie MacLeish, the head gaoler, he's a lecherous old devil.'

Madeleine struggled to keep up in more ways than one, for Jeannie spoke as quickly as she walked, in a broad lowland dialect that she found difficult to follow. She was reduced to nodding and smiling as

Jeannie continued to rap out instructions and advice, concentrating all her efforts on keeping abreast of her two companions. By the time they reached the entrance way to the castle she was out of breath and panicky.

'I'll wait for you here,' Calumn told her. 'Just do what Jeannie says, she'll keep you right. *Bonne chance.*'

Madeleine smiled bravely, wishing desperately that he was coming with her. He had an air of authority which she was horribly conscious she lacked. Without him she felt strangely bereft and extremely nervous.

'Stick close and you'll be all right,' Jeannie said reassuringly and set off apace. The guards at the portcullis nodded them through, casting a curious glance at Madeleine, but making no attempt to stop her. They hurried on up the spiralling incline to another gate and finally entered the heart of the castle. A company of soldiers were being drilled in the courtyard. The distinctive clang of metal on metal came from the armoury in the far corner. A group of Redcoats lazed idly in the afternoon sunshine. To Madeleine's relief there was no sign of her attackers from last night. Already it seemed like a lifetime ago.

The familiar scent of horse was strong. She wondered if Perdita, her own faithful white mare, was missing her daily outing. She wondered what Calumn was doing. He was a strange mixture, that one, as fiery as the whisky he consumed to escape his devils. As golden in appearance, too, and, she suspected, every bit as addictive. A pleasure to be paid for with a sore head—or a sore heart, maybe.

'Auld Willie MacLeish.' Jeannie's warning voice intruded on her thoughts. A middle-aged man with wispy tufts of hair looking comically as if they had been glued on to his pate and a complexion like porridge awaited them at the entrance to the castle vaults. 'Keep behind me,' Jeannie hissed. She dumped her laundry basket in front of the man, neatly preventing him from coming any closer, and did the same with the basket Madeleine was carrying. 'Here you are, Willie, I hope your hands are clean.'

Willie's toothless grin was like a dank cave. He proceeded to rake through the neatly folded linen, causing Jeannie's displeasure when he shook out a shirt and threw it back in carelessly. 'Aye, that all seems to be right,' he said eventually. 'I see you've help with you the day, Jeannie—who's this wee thing?'

'She's just a friend lending a hand.'

'And what's your name, girlie?'

Madeleine shrank back as the full impact of Willie's body odour hit her.

'Do you think we've got all day?' Jeannie said sharply, poking the man in the ribs. 'I've plenty other customers to see to after this, you know.'

Willie cackled. 'I bet you have, Jeannie Marshall,' he said with a leer, but to Madeleine's relief he led

the way towards a heavily studded door and began
to apply his keys.

Though she had been warned, Madeleine
was appalled by the conditions, unprepared for
the human suffering which confronted her. Her
admiration for Jeannie grew as she watched her call
out cheery greetings before producing an astonish-
ing assortment of goods from the capacious pockets of her petticoats, including tobacco and some
flasks of whisky. Many of the prisoners were
Jacobites, but some were common felons awaiting
the gallows. With Jeannie's help Madeleine spoke to
any who would listen to her, but none had anything
to say about either the Royal Scots or Guillaume,
the Comte de Guise.

Deeper down the cells were much smaller, the
prisoners manacled and the requirement for laundry sparse. It was with relief that Madeleine followed Jeannie back to the main door. 'Have you
known Calumn long?' she asked as they waited for
the gaoler to return and let them out.

Jeannie drew her a knowing look. 'I met him
when he came back to Edinburgh after he left the
army. He'd been a Redcoat, even been stationed
here at the castle once, so he told me. My brother
Iain has ambitions to join the army too, so I asked
Calumn if he could give the boy a bit of a head start.
That's when he offered the sabre lessons. Calumn's
good company, we have a bit of a laugh and a joke
together, but that's all there is between us.'

'He was a soldier?'

'A captain, no less. He doesn't talk about it, mind, I'm not sure why. It's a touchy subject with him.'

'Did he fight in the Rebellion?'

'I don't ken. I told you, he doesn't talk about it, and if I were you I wouldn't go prying. Calumn Munro's not someone who would take kindly to your poking your nose into his business.'

'What about his family?'

Jeannie shrugged. 'They've lands somewhere in the Highlands. He doesn't talk about them either. Calumn has been a good friend to me and my brother, but you'd be wise not to get any ideas about him. He's what we call a charmer.' She picked up her basket at the sound of the key grating in the lock. 'That'll be Willie. He'll take us to Lady Drummond.'

The Black Hole was above the portcullis, so that the prisoners held there were under almost constant surveillance by the sergeants of the guard. The conditions in the other vaults were unhealthy, but the Black Hole was positively inhumane. Lady Drummond, a tall, thin woman with a Roman nose and piercing grey eyes, shared the small space with her two daughters. She greeted Jeannie in a friendly manner, but, seeing Madeleine, immediately looked suspicious. 'And who are you?' she asked in a cultured voice with the lilt of the Gael.

Madeleine dropped a curtsy. 'Madeleine Lafayette, *madame*. I've come in search of news of someone who fought under your husband.'

'A Frenchman? They've all been deported, so I'm told.'

'Yes, but Guillaume has not come home.'

'Guillaume?'

'Guillaume de Guise, the man I am searching for. Do you know of him?'

'The Comte? I remember him, certainly,' Lady Drummond conceded. 'May I ask what he is to you?'

Quickly, Madeleine told her. 'Please, if you know what became of him, I beg of you to tell me.'

Lady Drummond's face softened marginally. 'You must understand, *mademoiselle,* that the little I do hear I cannot be certain of. Rumours reach me, it is true, and I have my own means of communicating with the outside world, but—knowledge can be a very dangerous thing, in times like these. If I am discovered…'

The door at the foot of the stairs was opened and Willie MacLeish's voice bid them hurry before they got him into trouble. Despairingly, Madeleine picked up her basket. 'You've lost everything because your husband chose the Prince. I'm trying to prevent the same thing happening to Guillaume.'

Lady Drummond pursed her lips. 'There is something. It surprised me, for it did not sound like the de Guise I knew, but—there is no saying what war will do to a man, and there cannot be two men with such a distinctive name. I can't promise anything, *mademoiselle,* but if you'll give me a little time I think I can find out his whereabouts. I'll send a message through Jeannie, one way or another. Tomorrow, the next day at the latest.'

'Thank you, *madame,* thank you so much,' Madeleine said fervently, kissing Lady Drummond's hand and dropping a deep curtsy before she hurried down the steep stairs. The temptation to look up as she passed under the portcullis was strong, but she resisted.

Calumn was waiting near the top of Castlehill. Madeleine and Jeannie made a pretty picture as they approached, striking enough for most men on the busy thoroughfare to take a second glance. Jeannie sashayed confidently through the crowds, casting flirtatious sidelong glances to the left and right, the deep red of her hair glinting in the sunshine like a summons. Beside her, Madeleine's fey looks and flaxen hair were ethereal, her step as graceful as a dancer's. 'I take it your visit was a success then,' he said when they came into earshot.

'I'll know soon. Lady Drummond has promised to send me a message through Jeannie.'

They were at the junction of West Bow. Jeannie stopped to take her baskets from Calumn. 'This is where I leave you. I'll be in touch once I've had word from her ladyship.'

'Remind your brother to expect me on Wednesday,' Calumn said.

Jeannie glanced over at Madeleine. 'Aye, provided you don't get distracted,' she said with a teasing smile, heading off down the hill.

Back at his lodging, Calumn steered Madeleine towards the settle in the reception room. 'I've asked

Jamie's mother to serve us dinner. I've told her you're a distant relative, on your way to London to take up a post as a governess.'

'A governess!'

'I had to think of something to save her sensibilities,' Calumn said, 'though God knows, you look no more like a governess than a laundry maid. You can use my spare room again tonight, it will save you the hunt for other lodgings.'

'You are very kind, but I don't think it would be right.' It would most definitely be wrong. Once again, Madeleine thanked the stars for the cold grey sea which, she sincerely trusted, would protect her hitherto spotless reputation. There would be questions when she returned, but she was relying on Guillaume's presence and her father's relief at their safe return to plug any gaps which her own imagination could not fill. It grieved her to think of deceiving Papa, but really, it was his own fault for not believing.

'I could ask Jamie's mother to recommend somewhere,' she suggested, strangely loath to do so. Because she was tired, she told herself, not because she actually wanted to stay here.

'You could, but you've seen how crowded the city is, you'd likely have to share.'

'I didn't think about that. But it wouldn't be right for me to stay here. People would think—they would say that—it wouldn't be proper.'

Calumn laughed. 'I've told you, they think you're

a distant relative. Anyway, isn't it a bit late to be worrying about the proprieties after last night?'

She stared into those perfectly blue eyes of his, searching for his meaning. *Did he remember?* Madeleine folded her arms nervously across her chest, realised how defensive the gesture was and placed her hands once more in her lap. 'You're right. I should have thought about it before. I shouldn't have stayed here last night.'

'Why not?' Calumn sprawled in the seat, but he was looking at her with unnerving penetration.

She twisted her hands together, suddenly nervous, and moved to the large chair opposite him. 'I should have told you before. I'm not what you think I am. In fact, I am Guillaume's betrothed,' she confessed baldly.

Calumn looked remarkably unperturbed. 'I guessed it must be something like that, even though you did your best to lead me into believing you were just his mistress.'

'You guessed!'

'You're not a very good liar. That vagueness about your family, and when I saw you with Jeannie—it was obvious you were gently bred,' Calumn explained matter of factly. 'Then there was the fact that as de Guise's discarded mistress you can't have had much to gain in coming looking for him, whereas if you were his affianced bride—it had to be something like that to make you run away, which is what I presume you've done?'

Madeleine stared at him in astonishment. 'Yes, but…'

'And why should you tell me the truth, after all?' Calumn continued in a musing tone. 'You're in a foreign country, you've been attacked by three drunken soldiers and we have known each other less than twenty-four hours. Frankly, I'm impressed that you've had the gumption to get this far without a fit of the vapours.'

Madeleine smiled weakly at this. 'Thank you.' She fell to pleating the starched apron Jeannie had lent her. 'I won't go home. You won't make me go home, will you? You know what it's like, don't you, the needing to know what happened? You know what it's like to have to wait and wait and wait, and all the time everyone is telling you that you're wrong?' Her big green eyes had a sheen of tears. 'You do understand that, don't you, Calumn?'

For the second time that day, her words evoked memories he spent most of his waking hours suppressing and much of the night time reliving. The months of waiting, the guilt of the survivor gnawing away at his guts, adding to the agony of the betrayal he had been forced into and the lingering pain of his slow-to-heal scar. He did not want to remember. Calumn ran his fingers through his hair. 'We're talking about you, not me. What family have you back in France?'

'There's just Papa and me. I'm an only child—my mother died last year.'

'Just Papa. Who will no doubt be insane with

worry. Did you say you left no word of where you were going?'

'No,' Madeleine whispered, shrinking from the thought of the upset her disappearance must have caused, 'but he will guess where I am.'

'You left his care without telling him and you left it alone. He will be imagining all sorts, any father would be,' Calumn said sternly. 'You must write to him, put his mind at rest, as soon as you have word from the castle. What possessed you to do something like this after so much time has passed?'

'Guillaume's cousin has started legal proceedings to have him declared dead. If he succeeds, all Guillaume's lands will pass to him—a man who has spent all his life in Burgundy,' Madeleine said contemptuously. 'Guillaume loves La Roche, it would break his heart to lose it. Papa would not listen to me, he said I should forget Guillaume, that coming here to look for him would be too painful, but I couldn't stand by and let La Roche fall into a stranger's hands.'

'Ah. So it's about land.'

The sudden change in Calumn's tone made Madeleine wary. 'And Guillaume.'

'An arranged match, I assume?'

'We were betrothed when I was five years old, and certainly it is the dearest wish of my papa to see me settled so close, for our estates share a border and a son of mine would be able to inherit where I cannot, but—'

'Very touching, but it's still an arranged match.'

'Guillaume is my best friend. I know him as well as I know myself. He is like the son my father never had, and—I don't need to justify my marriage to you. Yes, it is an arranged match, but I am very happy with it. It will make me happy.'

'How does it make you happy?'

'What do you mean?'

'De Guise gets you and, through your son, your father's lands. Your father gets to keep his estate in the family and his daughter next door. But what about you, what do you get out of it?'

'Get out of it?' He did not sound angry, but there was a tightness about his voice she could not understand. 'You make it sound like a business transaction. It is what I want.'

'Really? 'Tis not my experience that fulfilling the expectations of others leads to happiness. You'd have done better to stay at home. At least that way you'll avoid being shackled to a man you are marrying only to please your father.'

'You know nothing of the situation,' Madeleine said indignantly. 'Of course I want to do this for Papa, but I am not just doing it for him, and I am certainly not being forced into doing something I dislike. In any case, what is wrong with wanting to do what I know will make others happy?'

'Nothing at all, unless it makes you unhappy.'

'Why should doing what I know is the dearest wish of those nearest to me make me unhappy?' Madeleine asked in bewilderment.

'You subscribe to the view that duty is its own

reward, do you? Aye, well you're right in one way. In my experience duty *is* always rewarded handsomely. By misery. You're fooling yourself, Madeleine. You're not in love with Guillaume de Guise.'

'Guillaume is the dearest person in the world to me since Maman died.'

'Like a brother, maybe, but are you in love with him?'

'I've known him since we were children, of course I love him.'

'Love, not in love. That's not the same thing at all.'

She stared at him wordlessly, feeling out of her depth. She could not read his face. He did not seem angry, but he had a look in his eye she did not trust, a tightness about the mouth she was wary of. He was watching her too closely. His coat hung open, the full skirts trailing on either side almost to the floor. He crossed one long leg negligently over the other, so casually, yet there was something about him that was most definitely not casual. He was baiting her. Setting a trap for her, if only she knew what it was.

'Answer the question, Madeleine.'

Unexpectedly perturbed by the turn the conversation had taken, Madeleine got restlessly to her feet, tugging Jeannie's cotton cap off her head. Several long strands of her hair unfurled, curling over her cheeks and down her neck. 'Love, in love, it's the same thing,' she said with a certainty she was by no means feeling. 'I love Guillaume as my friend. When we are married I will love him as my husband. I will love him *because* he is my husband, and because in making him my husband I know I am making both him and my family happy.' She said the words like a catechism, as if by articulating her feelings in this way they would acquire more heft. Tugging impatiently at the bow which held her apron in place, she managed to pull it into a tangle.

'Come here.' Calumn sat up. 'Let me do that.'

She stood with her back to him. His knees brushed the sides of her petticoat. His fingers pulled at the bow. 'Closer, it's worked itself into a knot,' he said, tugging her nearer, so that if she leaned back just the tiniest fraction their bodies would be touching. He bent his head and it brushed against her back.

'There,' Calumn said and the strings of Jeannie's apron unravelled.

He turned her round, putting his hands on her waist. Then he stood up, still holding her, giving her a look that could be mistaken for a smile, a curl of his mouth that seemed to reach up inside her like long fingers, squeezing her, slowly squeezing the breath out of her in the most curious way. Her lips were level with his throat. If he kissed her again, she would have to stand on her tiptoes. Not that she was going to kiss him. Or allow him to kiss her. *What on earth was she thinking?*

Calumn's voice, softer now, interrupted her thoughts, which seemed to have strayed far beyond the bounds of what was decent. 'Being in love is a different matter entirely from feeling affection for someone. The fact you don't understand that tells me you're not. And just to prove it, Mademoiselle Lafayette, I'm going to kiss you again.' He tilted up her chin.

'No,' Madeleine whispered.

He put his arms around her.

'No.' Her heart raced, as if she had been running. Calumn leaned towards her, and a long lock of hair, bright as new-minted gold, fell over his cheek. She gazed into his eyes as he lowered his lips to hers, knowing she should move away, but something contrary and stronger in her kept her there, because she wanted to know what it would be like to be kissed by him. Properly. Just so she would understand what he meant.

She couldn't move. She gazed at him like one mesmerised, her lips parting just the tiniest fraction, the movement so small she was not even aware of it.

Calumn hesitated. She should not be here. He should not be doing this. Not even to prove her wrong.

But her mouth was made for kissing. He hadn't thought of much else since that tantalising taste of her earlier in the day. She felt as if she were made for him, though who would have guessed it to look at her, so fragile compared to his own solid bulk. His hand tightened on her waist. He should not, but how could he resist when she was looking at him, unblinking, with her bewitching eyes, as if she saw into his soul? As if she was luring him towards her, exactly as mermaids do to sailors. She wanted him to kiss her. And it was for her own good, was it not? He could not resist. He simply could not. So he kissed her.

He kissed her and Madeleine sighed, the sound of the dying wind playfully ruffling a sail at sunset. Calumn's mouth was warm as before. Soft as before. Gentle as before. It fitted over hers perfectly, his lips moulding themselves to hers, sipping on hers, as if tasting, encouraging her to do the same. She twined her fingers into his hair, relishing its springy softness, and pressed her lips against his, relishing the different softness and now the taste of him. She felt her blood heat. He kissed her and she kissed him back, liking the way his breath came just a bit faster, the way his fingers clenched just a bit tighter on her waist, the way his excitement fuelled her own. His tongue touched hers, turning warm into scalding hot. His fingers tangled in her hair. His tongue on hers again, a flash of heat that made her insides quiver and an answering surge in him, for she could feel the hardening of his arousal nudging against her.

She sighed and this time it sounded like a moan. She thirsted for more. His kiss became less gentle and she liked that, too. She pressed, mouth to mouth, breast to breast, thigh to thigh, flesh to muscle, her softness against his hardness. His hand slipped up from her waist to cup her breast. No one had ever kissed her like this. No one had ever touched her so intimately. No one. Not even—*what was she doing!*

Madeleine wrenched her mouth away. *'Non!'* She wriggled free of his embrace. Heat turned to cold in seconds, as if her blood had been flushed with ice, though her lips were burning. She tried to cool them against the back of her hand. She forced herself to meet Calumn's gaze. His eyes were glazed, his hair in wild disorder. A dark flush suffused his cheek bones. His breath was coming in short, shallow gasps. Shamed, she realised she probably looked the same.

Calumn shook his head, pushing his hair back from his forehead. 'No,' he agreed, 'you're right, that was more than enough to prove my point.'

'What point?'

'You would not have kissed me like that if you really were in love with de Guise.'

Madeleine blushed furiously. 'It is none of your business how I kiss Guillaume, and none of your business to be kissing me. You should not have done so. I told you to stop. I said no, I—'

'You're deluding yourself, *mademoiselle,*' Calumn said with infuriating calm. 'You wanted to kiss me, just as much as I wanted to kiss you.'

Madeleine stared at him in consternation, desperate to contradict him, but instinctively knowing that to do so would be foolish. 'I…'

Just then, there was a soft rap on the door. 'Your dinner's here, Master Munro,' a female voice called.

'Saved,' Calumn said with an infuriating smile as he left the room to relieve Mrs Macfarlane of her loaded tray.

Chapter Three

Mrs Macfarlane's plain but excellent repast eased the tension between them. As they ate their way through chicken stew served with a dish of peas and greens, Calumn directed the conversation to less personal matters. Perhaps he felt he had made his point, perhaps he wished simply to enjoy his food without further contretemps; whatever it was, Madeleine was happy to follow his lead. Banishing the whole kissing episode to the back of her mind, she regaled Calumn with a highly coloured version of her two days at sea in a Breton fishing boat. It made him laugh, and encouraged him in turn to recount some of his own—carefully edited—traveller's tales. His description of a meal of pig's trotters he had eaten in a Paris café encouraged Madeleine to recall the plate of pig's fry she had been presented with as a child, after attending the ceremonial slaying of the said pig by one of her father's tenants.

'It was an honour, you know,' she said with a grin, 'but I was only about five, and I said to Papa, I don't like worms.'

'Did you eat it?'

'Oh, yes, Papa would not have his tenants insulted. It didn't taste of anything much.' The clock on the mantel chiming the hour surprised them both. 'I didn't realise it was so late,' Madeleine said in dismay.

'You'll stay here, then? It's far too late for you to go looking for somewhere else now, and at least if you're here I'll know you are safe.'

Though he phrased the words as a question, his tone indicated that he would brook no argument. Madeleine was inclined to dispute this assumption of responsibility, but common sense and an inclination to spend more time in his rather-too-appealing company made her keep quiet. 'Thank you. I would like to stay, if you're sure.'

'I'm sure.' Calumn pushed back his chair. 'I'm going out for a while. Have you everything you need?'

She was disappointed, but realised he was being tactful. 'Yes. And thank you, Calumn, you've been very kind.'

'Until the morning, then.' The door closed behind him, leaving the rooms resoundingly quiet. Loneliness threatened. To keep it at bay, Madeleine tried to think about what she would do when—no if, it must be if—Lady Drummond sent her a message with Guillaume's whereabouts. But that set her into a panic about how she would do whatever she had to do, so she took herself to bed, and despite being absolutely certain she would lie awake all night worrying, Madeleine fell into a sound sleep.

The company at the White Horse was thin, and Calumn was not in the mood for gambling. Returning early, he lay awake, all too aware of Madeleine in bed next door.

Her situation was abominable. He knew too well what it felt like, that wanting to know. If de Guise was alive, the bastard deserved a whipping for not having the guts to face her. He did not deserve her, any more than he deserved to have her save his lands, for he must have known his cousin would claim them in his absence. In fact, de Guise seemed altogether too careless with all his property. Of a certainty he didn't deserve it. Unless of course he really was dead, which, the more Calumn thought about it, seemed the most likely thing.

Except that Madeleine seemed so sure. Just as Calumn had been, against all the odds. What if he'd given up, as his mother had begged him to? How would that have looked, on top of everything else? Angrily, he closed his mind to that path of thought. Betrayal was betrayal. A matter of degree made no difference.

Back to Madeleine, an entrancing enough diversion. Such a shame it would be for such a lovely one as she to throw herself away on someone who didn't deserve her. Her response to his kisses had taken him aback. His own response had been equally surprising. Calumn was not a man accustomed to losing control, but there was a depth of sensuality in her which was obviously yearning to be released.

Releasing it was absolutely none of his business, Calumn told himself. None, no matter how tempting the idea was. Misguided Madeleine might be in choosing to marry for the sake of her family, but at the end of the day, it was her decision. And as to seducing her just to prove a point—no! No matter how attractive the proposition was, it was strictly against his own rigid rules of conduct. But that did not prevent him from thinking about it.

Madeleine awoke the next morning to an insistent tapping on the door of her chamber. Still befuddled with sleep, she tumbled out of bed and opened it, wearing only her shift. Calumn stood on the other side, already dressed, filling the small room with his presence. 'What's wrong?' she asked, gazing up at him in bewilderment.

He reached down to twist a long coil of her platinum hair around his finger. 'You look even more like a mermaid than usual, with your hair down like that.' His eyes widened as he took in her state of undress. The neck of her shift was untied, revealing the smooth perfection of her breasts.

She caught the direction of his gaze and blushed,

placing her arms protectively over herself, trying to bat away the hand which toyed with her hair. It was a nice hand. Warm. The fingers long and tapered. Not soft but work-roughened. He had not the hands of a gentleman, but nor were they of a common labourer. He had interesting hands. Realising she had been holding on to one of them for far too long, Madeleine dropped it.

'It's a bonny day,' Calumn said. 'I thought I could show you a bit more of Edinburgh while you wait on her ladyship getting in touch.'

'That would be lovely, but I'm sure you must have business to attend to.'

'Nothing that can't wait, and at least if you're with me I can be sure you're not getting into any trouble.' He smiled down at her. 'Don't look like that, you know perfectly well you shouldn't be going about a strange city on your own, and you know perfectly well you don't really want to. Allow me to be your guide. I want to.'

The clank of a pail heralded Jamie's arrival with hot water. It was an appealing idea charmingly proposed. After clearing the air last night, and spending such a pleasant dinner, Madeleine could think of no reason to refuse it. 'Thank you. I'd like that,' she said, with a smile she tried hard to restrain.

'We'll go out by the Bow Port,' Calumn said, taking her arm at the gate of Riddell's Court half an hour later, 'then we can walk through the royal park. I'll show you where Prince Charles Edward stayed in the lap of luxury while he was in Edinburgh—and where his men were forced to camp in less salubrious conditions.'

They proceeded in their usual fashion through the Edinburgh streets, Calumn striding with graceful ease through the crowded thoroughfares and maze-like wynds. 'Thank you for taking the time to show me around. Despite what you said, I am sure you have other things you should be doing,' Madeleine said, clinging to his arm.

Calumn cast her a shrewd glance. 'Are you fishing?'

Her dimples peeped. 'A little. You don't strike me as a man who would be content to be idle. Jeannie told me you'd been teaching her brother how to fight with a sword.'

'Did she now? And no doubt she told you I'd been in the army too?'

Remembering Jeannie's warning about Calumn's reticence on the subject, Madeleine nodded warily.

To her relief Calumn seemed not to take offence. 'I joined up at sixteen. 'Twas my father's idea. I was in need of some discipline, he said, and to be honest I was relieved to get away from him—I was just beginning to see that what he called the old ways were more or less tyranny. We were forever at outs. A couple of years' service is all he intended, enough for me to learn how to do as I was bid, then I was to come home and do as *he* bid.' He smiled ruefully. 'But the army made me; my regiment was more like a family to me than my own blood. After two years, though my father ordered me home, I stayed on. Two years became six, the rift between us became a gulf, but the more he created the less inclined I was to obey and as for him—even now he's on his last legs, there's no give in him.' Calumn's face darkened, then he shrugged. 'I was a good officer and I worked hard to earn the respect of my men. There's any number of wee laddies in these parts like Jeannie's brother who think to escape as I did, though what they're running from is poverty rather than despotism. I spend a fair bit of my time teaching them the tricks of the officer's trade. Not that any of them will be able to afford a commission, mind, but if they know how to use a sabre and a foil, if they have some education and understand the basic rules of warfare and command, it will give them an advantage in moving up the ranks.'

'I imagine you are an excellent teacher—though with that temper of yours, I would not envy the boy who gets it wrong.'

Calumn laughed. 'Aye, it suits me fine, being able to vent my spleen on a roomful of waifs and strays. Believe me, they give as good as they get.'

'And does it work?'

'As I said, it gives them a start. The idea proved so popular, we set up regular classes. I suppose it's grown into a sort of school. The day-to-day business is in the charge of two men who served under me for many years, and our old regiment is more than happy to take recruits trained by them—and to give them a bit of financial support, too.'

'I wish I could see it. Do you spend a lot of time there?'

'Not as much as I did at first. Truth be told, they don't really need me now.'

'So you're looking for something else to do?'

They were approaching the imposing gate in the city walls. 'I'm supposed to be showing you the sights,' Calumn said, making it clear he had answered enough questions. He pointed out a large house. 'That belongs to Archie Stewart, who was Lord Provost of Edinburgh in 'forty-five when Charles Edward was here. They say that he gave a party for the Prince, and up at the castle they got wind of it, but Archie's house is riddled with secret stairs and passageways, so Charlie escaped, which is more than can be said for poor Archie. He was taken south as a prisoner, charged with abusing his position. Luckily for him they sent him back to Edinburgh for trial, and the good citizens here decided to find him not guilty.'

'You don't like the Prince much, do you?' Madeleine said, risking a glance upwards to check Calumn's countenance.

He frowned. 'No.' His tone forbade further probing.

Since it was a beautiful day and Madeleine did not wish to spoil the mood, she made no further comment but instead gave one of her little Gallic shrugs and smiled sunnily at him, pleased to see his frown fade. They passed through the Bow Gate and headed away from the walls of the city,

towards the outskirts of the royal park belonging to
the Palace of Holyrood. A steady stream of traffic
jammed the road, dray carts and carriages belonging to the better off competing for space with mud-
spattered public coaches drawn by sweating teams
of horses. Laden mules, equally laden tradesmen and
farmers with their wares formed a never-ending
queue to pass through the gates. Calumn kept Madeleine clasped close to his side until they could leave
the road and take one of the paths which headed
towards the immense green space of the park.

He was an entertaining companion, knowl-
edgeable, with a dry twist to his humour which
exactly correlated with her own. As she did, he
enjoyed inventing histories for the people they
passed on the road; unlike Guillaume, who was more
often than not puzzled by her tendency to exagger-
ate and embroider in order to entertain, Calumn
was amused by her wit and did not once ask her to
explain herself. By the time they reached the park-
land, Madeleine was as relaxed in his company as
if they had been friends all their lives.

Looking about her, she was astonished to find
they were in what appeared to be the depths of the
countryside, though they had not come so very far
from the great city. The Palace of Holyrood sat in a
little valley of its own, surrounded by formal gardens, with a chapel clearly visible. To her right a
group of hills rose up surprisingly high, looking
almost as if they had been lifted from the Highlands

and plopped down carelessly in the flat lowlands. 'It's very beautiful here.'

'We'll walk round by the palace and you can see where the Prince first greeted the people of Edinburgh when he arrived.'

'I read in the newspapers at the time that the Prince and his army were well received.'

'I suppose it's true enough, they were all for Charlie—or, more accurately, they were all against the Crown. It was hard times here just before the Rebellion, people were starving. They were looking for a champion and they didn't mind who he was,' Calumn said cynically. 'It helped, mind you, that Charles Edward is a fair-looking man. The ladies loved him.'

'I didn't,' Madeleine said with conviction.

Calumn was startled. 'You've met him?'

'When he returned to France after Culloden. His boat landed not far from my home.'

'You must be one of the very few of your sex to dislike him. The lassies here were hurling themselves at him, from what I heard.'

'Hurling?'

'Throwing.'

'Well, I didn't do any of this hurling. I thought he was arrogant and conceited and rude.'

They had reached a junction in the path they had been following. Ahead lay the palace, but Calumn led Madeleine to the right, to a sheltered spot in the lee of the hills. It was warm. He stripped off his coat and laid it down on the ground. 'We'll rest here a moment, it's a pretty view.'

Madeleine knelt down on Calumn's jacket. He sprawled beside her, propping himself up with his elbow on the grass, careless of his pristine white shirtsleeves. A light breeze ruffled his hair, which in the strong sunshine was streaked with touches of red, like flames. They were in a slight hollow, completely hidden from passers-by. She was suddenly incredibly aware of his presence, as if her skin was reaching out for him. 'It's very beautiful here,' she said, trying to focus on the scenery and not on the man at her side. 'I can hardly believe the city is so close.' As she spoke, she felt a prickle of awareness which she tried to ignore, keeping her gaze fixed on the horizon.

'I think it's very beautiful here, too,' Calumn said softly, and she gave in to temptation and turned to look at him. It was a mistake. 'Very beautiful,' he said, tugging at her wrist so that she tumbled off balance, falling on top of him.

She knew she should move, but it was nigh on impossible to bring herself to do so. It was as if she were drugged. Or mesmerised. Or simply mindless. She lay on top of him as she had done that first night, pressed tight against him, chest to chest, thigh to thigh, only this time Calumn was fully conscious and his hands were doing the most delightful things, running down the curve of her spine, moulding themselves to the roundness of her bottom, as if he were learning her contours through her clothing. It was shocking to be touched in this way. And exciting.

She became aware of his arousal hard against the inside of her thigh. 'I shouldn't,' she managed, but what it was she shouldn't, she did not want to put into words.

She made no move to pull away—though he waited, and knew he should wish she would. 'Madeleine?' She dropped her gaze, as if abdicating from the whole difficult question. 'We should not be doing this,' he murmured.

'No,' she agreed.

'No,' Calumn whispered. Then his lips met hers and there was no going back, for when they kissed, it was as if they had always been kissing. As if they had only just left off kissing. As if kissing was what they were made for, and rules—rules simply did not apply.

Delight and danger. Madeleine knew it, but she didn't care. His kisses made her feverish, made her thirsty for more, made her care for nothing except more. Where Calumn led she followed, echoing what he did, nibbling on his bottom lip while he sucked on her top, softening when he pressured, opening when he pushed, taking what he gave and giving more. Allowing him, encouraging him to master her with kisses that reached down inside her to ignite her very blood.

She was driven by a need she could not define. Her fingers coiled into Calumn's mane of golden hair, relishing the springy, silky texture of it. His hands were on her face, rough fingers on the soft area of her skin, stroking her eyelids, her ears, loosening her hair from its pins, combing through it, spreading it out behind her, his mouth leaving hers to nuzzle on the lobe of her ear, the hollow in the nape of her neck. He felt so solid. Solid chest. Solid thighs. And a different kind of solid hardness between his legs. She wanted to feel all of it pressed into the softness of her own flesh. As if he could imprint her with his shape, like a shell on the sand.

He whispered something in a strange language, something lyrical that curled like his smile around her, melting her bones. His mouth, soft and warm, kissed into the slope of her breasts at the edge of her shift, making her gasp with pleasure and alarm. Her nipples bloomed, crying for attention. 'Calumn,' she whispered, a question, a caution, which could too easily be mistaken for incitement.

He looked at her, smiled, heavy-lidded, watching her face with a fierce concentration as he shifted position to undo the fastenings of her robe. Watching for any sign that he should stop. That she wished to be released. Or perhaps that she wanted to encourage him. *Which?*

She was distracted. Pleasure. This must be what he meant. The very word was horribly enticing. Pleasure. Calumn gave it a whole new currency of meaning. Pleasure. Not something light and airy, but more deep-rooted. No longer the colour of sunshine, but the dark and beating colour of a creature he had conjured.

Her robe fell open. The ribbons of her shift were untied, the shift eased down over her shoulders to expose the startling whiteness of her breasts to the sunlight. It would seem the decision had been made, though she surely had not made it! Another of those addictive shivers rippled through her, making her skin tingle. Her nipples puckered and darkened as blood rushed to them. Calumn licked the tip of his finger and ran it over first one, then the other. Exquisite. A touch as gentle as a breeze. Warm, then cool. Rasping pleasure. She whimpered. Calumn licked his finger again. He looked at her, his eyes speaking to her, telling her something both mystifying and arousing. He touched her again. So new. So strange. For something so illicit, so unexpectedly wonderful.

He took her nipple in his mouth. A gentle sucking made her squirm. A tiny nip made her moan. A slow languorous licking made her gasp. His hands stroked the contours of her breasts. Feathering touches. Moulding hands. Warm, licking, sucking mouth. Tracks of sensation shot out from where he touched her, connecting with the heat that was building lower down. A thrum of vibration like the strings on a harp being tuned. Instinctively Madeleine prepared to resist whatever it was, though she had the strangest premonition that it would prove irresistible. She tensed.

He noticed the subtle change in her immediately. Astonished at the depth of her response, taken aback by how quickly it had happened, how close he was to forgetting himself and all his resolutions,

Calumn sat up. One thing to dream of seduction. Quite another to suit actions to words.

He tore his eyes away from the vision spread in front of him, her hair almost white in the sunlight, her skin so perfect, slight traces of his touch blossoming like petals of passion on her breasts. She was intoxicating. He shifted uncomfortably, for the weight of his erection was thrusting against his breeches. He was unbelievably hard. He had not meant things to proceed so far, so quickly. He swore in Gaelic, the language he always returned to at times of emotion. 'I didn't mean this to get so out of hand.'

He forced himself to move, to create a distance between them, though his body screamed in protest. Calumn pulled Madeleine's shift back up over her shoulders. 'Cover yourself, for the love of God, before I lose sight of the little control I have.'

Madeleine did as she was bid, fumbling fingers making hard work of the ties and fastenings of her clothes. She felt like an instrument tuned too tight, stretched to screaming point, her strings taut with music they could not release. The glimpse she had had of something—something white hot, something liquid and pouring, something to drown in—was fading slowly as her body cooled. Had she disgusted him? Of a surety she had shocked him almost as much as she had shocked herself. *What was happening to her?* She barely recognised herself in the wild creature she had become under Calumn's tuition. Why had not Guillaume ever...?

Guilt racked her. It did not matter what Guillaume had not done, the point was what she had! Kissed a man who was virtually a stranger! Allowed him to touch her most intimately. No—*be honest, Madeleine*—*encouraged* him to touch her most intimately, wanting him to do things to her she had never before dreamed it was possible to want.

Shame washed over her. She could not meet Calumn's eyes, but sat frozen, plucking at one of the buttons on his coat, which she was still sitting on. 'What must you think of me? I don't know what came over me, I can assure you I have never, ever…'

He put a finger to her lips. 'Look at me, Madeleine,' he commanded, forcing her to do so. 'You did nothing to be ashamed of. You're a lovely creature, remarkably responsive, and I got carried away. What you're feeling, it's not wrong. It's not shameful. It's perfectly natural. Or at least it is when people are attracted to each other as you and I are, at any rate.'

She thought carefully about that. 'You mean to imply that I am not attracted to Guillaume in that way?'

Calumn shrugged. 'I didn't say that.'

'You didn't need to, but you're wrong. It's just that he's never kissed me as you did.'

'Why not?'

'I don't—he has not—because—it is none of your business.'

'No, it's not.' *It was not! And he shouldn't have started this.* But now that he had, he couldn't leave it alone. 'What about you, Madeleine? Have you never wanted to be kissed as we just did? Have you never dreamt of your wedding night? The bliss to be found in the union of the flesh. Love making. Pleasure, not procreation. Desire, not duty.'

'*Stop it.* Of course I haven't.'

'*Of course you haven't.* Listen to yourself. Betrothed to a man you claim to love, and you have never imagined making love to him!'

'You will be saying that I am in love with you next.'

He laughed at that, amusement curling on his mouth, where the bottom lip was slightly swollen from their kissing, she noticed. 'No, what we have between us is something much more earthy. Craving. Passion. Lust. All the things you don't feel for your future husband. And all the things I'm damned sure we should not be indulging in, no matter how tempting.'

'Marriage is not about passion and—and craving. It's about much—much worthier feelings,' Madeleine said defensively.

'Worthy!' Calumn sought relief in Gaelic, cursing long and fluently under his breath. Then he gave a deep sigh. 'All right, have it your own way. If you are content with worthy, who am I to argue with you!' He pulled her to her feet. 'It's too nice a day to argue. Let's forget it. All of it. It won't happen again.'

She managed a tremulous smile, telling herself she should be relieved, perfectly well aware that she was as much to blame for what had happened as he was, and too shocked at herself to do much more than walk by his side, listening with half an ear as he told her more about the Queen of Scots who had also been, for such a short time, the Queen of France. He told the tale with his own peculiar brand of cool irony, and eventually made her laugh.

At ease again, they skirted the grand Palace of Holyrood, taking the path out to the nearby village of Duddingston. 'You never did tell me about your meeting with the Prince,' Calumn reminded her.

'It was in September last year, when he landed in France after he escaped capture from the British army. He was spending the night at a château close to our home, friends of my father's, and they gave a party for him. I went because I wanted to find out about Guillaume.'

'And what did Bonnie Prince Charlie have to say for himself?'

'He pretended to remember Guillaume, but he did not. He told me he would not have left such a pretty betrothed behind, and then he tried to kiss me. I don't understand what people see in him. I don't understand why they followed his cause. He's an arrogant, conceited pig, and I would not follow him in to dinner, never mind into battle.'

'Bravo, Mademoiselle Lafayette. Would that others held your opinion. Scotland would have been saved a lot of heartache, and you would have been spared your journey.'

And she would not have met Calumn Munro. She didn't know what to make of that thought.

They had arrived at Duddingston. The little village was built beside a small loch, with the kirk set on a promontory stretching out on to the water. It was very pretty, calm in the warmth of the afternoon, with the colours of the trees reflected on the still of the water. 'Charlie's men camped here before the Battle of Prestonpans,' Calumn said.

'It's so strange to think that Guillaume may have been here. It's so peaceful too, not a place for an army.'

'Are you hungry? There's a howf here, the Sheep Heid. They'll run to some bread and cheese if you care for it?'

'I'd love it. I'm starving,' Madeleine said with a grin.

The inn was a simple stone building with a skittle alley built on to the side. It was quiet, for the locals were all at work, so they had the taproom to themselves.

'Tell me more about your life in Brittany,' Calumn said, once they were seated.

Madeleine took a reviving draught from her small tankard of beer to wash down the crusty bread she had been chewing on. 'It's very different from here. The air is full of the sea, it's like it's heavy with the salt. My family has an estate not far from the village of Roscoff. We grow wheat, and artichokes, too. But our biggest crop is apples, which we grow for the *cidre*, and also for mead. Then there are the dairy cattle for the butter and cheese so creamy and soft—not like this cheese which I think must come from sheep—and of course many of Papa's tenants are fishermen as well as farmers. Most days I ride out with my father to oversee whatever needs done, and I also do the accounts and manage the dairy.'

Calumn smiled. 'You really are a country girl.'

'I can't imagine a life spent living in the city, or languishing like a lady of fashion with nothing to do all day except needlepoint and gossip. Which, now I come to think of it, are very similar pursuits, for one involves embroidering tapestry, the other the truth.'

Calumn laughed. 'You certainly have a needle-sharp wit.' He took a long draught of ale. 'In many ways Brittany sounds a lot like my own home.'

'Tell me a little of it. You know so much about me, and yet you've given away very little about yourself. It's hardly fair.' She kept her tone teasing and was careful not to sound overly interested, but she was determined to satisfy her curiosity.

'I come from a place called Errin Mhor in the Highlands, north-west of here. My family also has a large estate with tenant farmers. We're situated on the coast too, so most people both fish and farm. In Scotland we call it crofting.'

'What do you grow?'

'Oats, barley, neeps, potatoes, kale. The winters in the Highlands can be long and harsh, the soil is shallow, not nearly as fertile as your homeland. But the fish—I'll wager it tastes even better than what you're used to.'

'Is it beautiful, this place Errin voe—what did you call it?'

'Mhor. It's very beautiful. I don't think there's anywhere more beautiful on earth—but I'm prejudiced. It's surrounded by mountains that seem purple in the summer with the heather. Then in the autumn, when the weather's on the turn, they have all the shades of brown you can imagine—golden and amber when the sun rises over them, glowing russet and auburn in the sunset. And in the winter their peaks are white with snow and ice, glittering like diamonds. Our land lies in the lee of the mountains, grazing for the sheep in the lower slopes, farm land on the flat shelf that runs out to meet the sea. We've beaches of the whitest sand, and there's lots of little islands just off the mainland where the water is shallow at low tide, and you can fish for the biggest crabs you've ever seen in your life.'

He stopped talking, gazing off into the distance with a smile on his face.

'When I was little we used to race the crabs across the sand.'

Calumn dragged his mind back from his homeland to the dark, smoky interior of the howf, the enchanting woman facing him over the scarred wooden table. 'We did that too, me and my friend Alasdhair.'

'Do you not miss it?'

He was about to shrug, as he always did when asked this question, as if to dismiss Errin Mhor as a place of the past, but then he stopped. Of course he missed it. Errin Mhor was a part of him, a hole in his being that nothing else could fill. 'There's not a day goes by I don't think of it.'

She had been granted a confidence and was immensely touched, for she knew it was a rare thing. 'I would love to see it.'

'You'd like it. We've much in common, us Highlanders and you Bretons. We're both Celts, after all.'

'And you and I, we're both farmers at heart.'

'So my mother would have me believe. According to her, no one is fit to manage Errin Mhor except me, now that my father's health is failing. She's appointed a factor, but she's sure the land will go to rack and ruin unless it's overseen by a Munro by birth.'

'But that's true, Calumm, your *maman* is right,' Madeleine said enthusiastically. 'When you are born to it, you have *l'affinité* which no one else can have. Why do you stay here in Edinburgh when you are needed at home?' she was emboldened to ask. 'You said yourself that you have nothing to keep you here. What are you running away from?'

'Running?' He stared at her long and hard. Emotions flitted across his face. Anger. Sadness. Bitterness. Resignation. 'I'm not running. I can't go home, that's all. I don't have the right any more.'

The anguish of his expression made her wish to put her arms around him, but she knew instinctively he would interpret any such gesture as pity. He was not a man who would take to having his hurt exposed. She had thought him a rich philanderer with too much time on his hands. Philanderer he was, and a very, very charming one, but he was not a man devoid of belief or honour. He was a man stripped of it.

There was a tiny thread of a scar under his left eyebrow which she had not noticed before. 'How did you get that?' she asked, tracing the slight pucker of the healed skin with her fingertip, the contact in some way assuaging the need to give him comfort.

'A childhood injury. I got in the way of an arrow at a hunt when I was eight or nine. 'Twas my own fault for not paying attention. The pain from the arrow was as nothing, believe me, to the beating my father gave me afterwards.'

'Your father beat you?'

Calumn shrugged. 'He warned me to stay at the back, but I didn't listen. I was shot at for my stupidity and beaten for my disobedience. My father is the laird. He expects to be obeyed in all things.'

'Just like you,' Madeleine said, softening her words with a smile.

Calumn got to his feet. 'You'd do well to remember that.'

The walk back was accomplished in silence, though it was not an uncomfortable one. As they neared the city walls and the traffic, mostly heading away from Edinburgh, grew heavier, Madeleine fell to wondering if Lady Drummond had left her a message. But when they arrived back at his rooms she was disappointed on two counts. Lady Drummond had not been in touch, and Calumn announced that he would be dining out. The truth was, he did not trust himself in Madeleine's company alone, but being unaware of that, she chose to be insulted, and was consequently aloof to the point of rudeness when he departed, dressed in his evening attire.

She spent a lonely few hours, dining off mutton broth and rabbit stew cooked by Mrs Macfarlane and leafing through a well-thumbed book of poetry which she found on the floor beside the chair in which Calumn usually sat. Though the long walk should have given her an appetite, and Mrs Macfarlane's cooking smelled delicious, Madeleine could not do justice to it. She retired early, and lay for what seemed like hours in the dark trying to plan her next steps, in reality listening anxiously for the sound of a key in the lock.

What was he doing? Who was he with? She was struck by the illogic of her feelings. What cause had she to be jealous, when he was nothing to her? No cause, and no right, but Madeleine prided herself on her honesty. She was jealous, none the less.

She could not understand it. Did jealousy then go hand in hand with the other emotions he had awakened in her this afternoon? Desires which she had not even been aware she could possess. Desires which, now they had been roused, would not let her be. Her body seemed to have acquired a distinct mind of its own. One which, she could almost convince herself, had nothing to do with her. It distracted her now, forcing her to remember this afternoon, to wonder how it would have been had Calumn not called a halt. To wonder, knowing that whatever she imagined, it would not be anywhere close to the reality.

Such *distracting* thoughts. Madeleine tried to summon up Guillaume's slim figure, but it was like attempting to replace flesh and blood with smoke and glass. Though Guillaume's hand had held hers a thousand times, though she had swum with him, danced with him, ridden out almost every day of her life in his company, it was as if all her memories of his touch, his scent, his looks, had faded.

Calumn's face swam back into her mind. She had no difficulty at all in recalling his particular scent, the contours of his body, the way his skin felt against hers. The way her body felt against his. *It meant nothing.* But even so, frustration and desire kept her awake, tossing and turning until the lumpy mattress upon which she lay felt as if it were a bed of hot coals.

Finally she heard Calumn's quick, light step on the stairs of the close and listened alertly as his key turned in the lock and the heavy door was carefully closed. He paused in the hallway just outside her door. She heard him sigh. Heard the door of his own bedchamber open and close. Gently. He was not in his cups tonight. The muffled sounds of him undressing and the vivid images her mind dreamed up as he did so ensured that any notion of sleep had fled. She lay in the quiet darkness of the night, listening to her own sighs and unable to stop thinking of the man lying naked on the other side of the bedroom wall.

* * *

The man in question was indeed naked, lying on his stomach, pillow pulled under his chin, the dappled moonlight playing on the long ridge of his back, his taut buttocks and muscled legs. An onlooker would be forgiven for thinking that a classical statue in all its smooth, firm and sculpted perfection had been splayed across the bedcovers.

Calumn, however, was wholly oblivious to the picture he made. In search of diversion he'd joined a group of friends in a game of cards, but his mind was not on the game. All he could think of was Madeleine. Madeleine laughing. Madeleine spread out underneath him on the grass. Madeline's faraway look when she talked of home. Madeleine's mouth. Her breasts. He liked the way she tucked her arm into his. He liked the way she fitted so snugly by his side.

Unable to concentrate on anything else, he had at least had the sense to lay down his cards before his losses were too heavy. Not even whisky appealed any more. But without whisky, he dreamed.

What are you running from? She was a mite too perceptive, Madeleine Lafayette. Her ability to see through him was unsettling. Describing Errin Mhor to her had brought back just how much he missed home. Depression draped like a heavy black cloak on his shoulders. Who was he to preach happiness to anyone? He, whose only aim in life these days seemed to be to avoid further pain. He, for whom happiness now would be forever out of reach. He had not the right to happiness, any more than he had the right to go home.

Calumn closed his eyes and pulled the sheet around him, trying to settle down to rest. But he was almost certain it would elude him.

He awoke the next morning, feeling as if his head had been stuffed with cotton. When he finally dressed and entered the reception room, he found Madeleine already sitting at the table with the coffee pot, looking quite at home. As she said good morning and handed him a cup, he found himself wondering what it would be like to see her like this every morning. Irritated with himself, he pushed the thought away and sat down opposite her. But the truth was, dammit, she'd made him realise he'd been lonely as well as homesick. 'I have things to do today, I'll be out most of the morning,' he said brusquely.

There were dark circles under his eyes. She had heard him shouting in the night; a bad dream. She had listened at his door, wondering whether to wake him, afraid that to do so would be an unwelcome intrusion. Now, faced with his dark mood, she was glad she had not, though she was longing to know what had aroused such violent emotions. 'That's all right,' Madeleine said brightly, 'I'm hoping to hear from Lady Drummond. I thought I could go and wait on Jeannie returning from the castle.'

'You'll never find your way on your own. Jeannie

will call if she has news, best to wait for her here.'
His tone brooked no argument.

'I sense I'm in danger of overstaying my welcome.
I'm extremely grateful for your hospitality, but I've
imposed on you far too much already. Hopefully it
won't be for much longer.'

'You haven't imposed. I'm just tired, that's all.'

'Did you not sleep well?'

Had she heard him shouting? As he often did
when he did not want to answer, Calumn chose to
ignore her question. 'I'll be back by two, then we
can discuss your plans.'

Madeleine clattered her cup on to the saucer.
'Don't worry about me, I'll be all right,' she said
haughtily.

'I know you will.' He looked at her meaningfully.
'So long as you stay here and do as you're told.'

'So long as you stay here and do as you're told,'
Madeleine repeated as the door slammed behind
him. The arrogance of him! Gone was the delightful man from yesterday, and in his place this forbidding stranger who was obviously determined to
keep a distance between them. Very well! But that
did not mean she had to obey his every command.
Madeleine muttered to herself angrily, lacing her
boots and tying her tippet. 'The arrogance of him!'
She would not sit here meekly twiddling her thumbs
waiting on Jeannie to call. Calumn Munro was not
her lord and master!

But as she stood on the edge of the Lawnmarket, watching the bustle of the traders, she had to

work hard to suppress the urge to turn tail and do exactly as she had been bid. Nervously, hitching her skirts clear of the cobblestones, she made her way into the throng.

Chapter Four

Three hours later she returned to Calumn's rooms to find them still empty. She was unwrapping her purchases in her room when a light tap on the door heralded Jeannie's arrival. 'You have news,' Madeleine asked anxiously, after greeting the woman with a kiss and leading her into the parlour.

'Aye. Is Calumn not here?' Jeannie asked, seating herself on the very edge of one of the large chairs by the fireside.

'No, though he should be back soon. Never mind Calumn, tell me please, what did Lady Drummond say.'

''Tis good news,' Jeannie said with a smile.

Madeleine gave a little squeal of excitement and clapped her hands together. 'She knows where Guillaume is?'

'You're to make your way to a place called Castle

Rhubodach. She says you'll be expected, and he'll find you there.'

'Castle Rhubodach, where is that?'

'Goodness, I don't know. It must be in the Highlands somewhere, for she says Calumn will know.'

'Calumn! How does Lady Drummond know we are acquainted?'

Jeannie looked embarrassed. 'That was my fault. She asked me to tell her more about you yesterday, and I said that you were Calumn's guest. I'm right sorry I told her now. I thought it would help, him being a Highlander and all, and gentry too, just like her. But it was a terrible mistake.'

'Why so?'

'It turns out Lord Munro, Calumn's father, is a staunch supporter of King George. Lady Drummond was almost spitting blood when she said his name; it seems the families are old enemies. I was quite taken aback by her reaction, let me tell you—I'd have thought Calumn would have warned me. She said she wouldn't put her trust in a Munro if he was the last man alive.'

Madeleine leapt to her feet, a bright flush of anger flying like a banner across her cheeks. 'How dare she! She doesn't even know Calumn.'

'No, of course she doesn't, but these Highlanders and their clans, they're terrible ones for bearing grudges.'

'What does she think Calumn will do to Guillaume, for God's sake—murder him?'

'Most likely she thinks I'll have him brought to

justice, which amounts to the same thing,' a voice said from the doorway.

Both women jumped as the man in question entered the room.

'You shouldn't be eavesdropping at the door,' Madeleine said, flustered by his sudden appearance. 'It's rude.'

'It's my door, and it's just as rude to talk about your host behind his back. I don't like to be gossiped about.'

'We were not gossiping, we were just—Jeannie was just telling me…'

'That Lady Drummond doesn't trust me. I heard.'

'She doesn't know you,' Madeleine said, glowering at the other woman.

Jeannie shook out her apron and straightened her cap, eyeing Calumn apologetically. 'Who cares what that old snob thinks? I'll be off now, I've sheets on the line, and it looks like rain.'

'Then this is goodbye, Jeannie,' Madeleine said. 'Thank you, I am truly grateful for your help.'

'Och away, it was nothing,' Jeannie protested, though she swiftly pocketed the coin Madeleine proffered. The door closed softly behind her.

'It's good news then, I take it,' Calumn said.

She had seated herself back on the settle, but it was a mistake, for she had to crane her neck to look into his face. He looked tired, and his hair was dishevelled. She had an urge to smooth it down.

He leaned his broad shoulders against the mantel. 'Well, cat got your tongue?'

'Calumn, what Lady Drummond said about your family, I—'

'I don't want to discuss it.'

'But—'

'Did you not hear what I said?' he thundered, lowering over her like an avenging angel in a way that had her recoiling in her chair. 'I will not discuss the matter further.'

Though she had seen flashes of his temper, this was something very different. She knew him well enough, though, not to pursue such an obviously touchy subject and waited in nervous silence for him to calm down, which he did surprisingly quickly, taking a few paces round the room before resuming his position leaning against the mantel. 'So, what *did* the good Lady Drummond say then?'

'I am to go to a place called Castle Rhubodach and wait for Guillaume to get in touch.'

'So he's definitely alive, then?'

Amazingly, this single, vital fact had not truly sunk in until now. Madeline's smile dawned slowly. 'Yes. You're right. Guillaume's alive! He must be, mustn't he? You don't think it's some kind of cruel joke? Or a trap perhaps,' she asked anxiously.

Calumn sat down on the settle beside her and put his arm around her shoulder. 'Regardless of what Lady Drummond thinks of me, I don't think she's the type to lie. If she says he'll be in touch then she must have cause to believe he will. So, yes, it looks like de Guise might be alive after all.'

Madeleine slumped heavily against his side. 'I

can't believe it.' Tears, hot tears of relief, welled up in her eyes. 'I'm sorry. It's just such a shock.'

'I know.' He remembered as if it were yesterday the day Rory appeared out of the blue at Heronsay. Word had reached him on the island an hour or so in advance, but he would not credit it. Not until he saw him standing there on the beach. Until he heard his voice, until he could actually touch him, would he believe that his brother really was alive. He closed his eyes. It was a happy day. About the last happy day he could remember.

Madeleine burrowed her face into Calumn's chest, the woven fabric of his waistcoat rough on her skin. He felt so solid. He smelled so good. She felt as if she belonged there. A very foolish thing indeed to think. Guiltily, she eased herself away. 'Do you know where this Castle Rhubodach is?'

'It's near a place called Aberfoyle. Quite a bit west of here, in the Trossachs.'

'Oh,' she said blankly.

'You're none the wiser, are you? You'll need horses. You'll not be able to go by carriage, there are no roads, only tracks.'

'Oh,' she managed again, trying not to feel daunted by the prospect. Being completely ignorant of the terrain, she had not actually contemplated the mechanics of her journey. 'I'm used to riding. I hate being stuck in a carriage,' she managed bravely.

'It's wild country. Mountains and lochs are the least of your worries. Most likely you'll have to spend a few nights in the open. And you'll be hard put to find anyone who speaks English, they all have the Gaelic. You'll be lost unless you have a decent guide.'

'A decent guide. Of course.'

'Someone who knows the lie of the land. A native.'

Just as she was beginning to question her sanity in contemplating such an undertaking, an idea came to her, so audacious she wondered if she had the temerity to suggest it. She had no right to ask, no right to expect, yet—surely he would see it was the perfect solution. She cleared her throat nervously. 'Calumn, I don't suppose—no, it doesn't matter.' She laced her fingers together in her lap, trying to summon up the courage, wondering if to do so was wise.

'What is it? It's not like you to be so reticent.'

She couldn't help it, the idea was so perfect. Despite her best attempts to contain it, an excited smile spread across Madeleine's face. 'Oh, Calumn, would you?'

'Would I—you expect me to accompany you?' He stared at her incredulously.

Madeleine's smile withered like a vineyard grape in the merciless glare of the sun. 'I thought—yes.'

His lips thinned. 'Completely out of the question. I cannot return to the Highlands. I told you that.'

'Yes, but you did not give me a reason.'

'What, you think I am answerable to you now? *How dare you!* Who are you, a chit of a lass set upon her own ruination, to demand that I explain myself?

I have reasons. Very good reasons. But they are my business and no one else's.'

Though his anger appalled her, the task which lay ahead of her was even more intimidating. What's more, she was fast coming to the conclusion that whatever his reasons for avoiding the Highlands, Calumn should be forced to confront them. It was this thought which gave her the courage to challenge him. 'You are a hypocrite, Calumn Munro,' she flung at him. 'You are so certain you know what is best for me, but you are determined that no one but you knows what is best for you! Who are you to talk to me about happiness, when it is quite obvious that you are miserable? I asked you yesterday what you're running from and you didn't answer. Why not? Are you afraid as well as unhappy?'

Calumn turned white, though whether it was anger or some deeper emotion Madeleine could not tell. She held her breath, willing herself to refrain from retracting her words, for she had hurt him, and she had not meant to do so, only to provoke him into action. Even as she thought it, she knew she was being unfair. Selfish, even, for it was not just that she wanted him by her side as a guide, but that she was not ready to say goodbye. 'I'm sorry,' she said contritely, her shaky voice breaching the silence which threatened to overpower her. 'You are quite right, it is none of my business. I should not have asked such a thing of you, especially when you had already made your feelings on the matter plain.'

Her tone, more than her words, eased the tension.

Calumn realised his fists had been clenched, so close to the bone had her accusations been. Far too perceptive, Mademoiselle Lafayette. Most definitely, he did not like it. 'Why are you even contemplating such a difficult journey? Why must you find de Guise, when he has obviously no inclination to be found?' he asked, made callous by his need to redirect her thoughts.

Madeleine flinched. 'You know why. It's not just our betrothal, it's Guillaume's land. La Roche is his inheritance. I can't bear to see it taken from him.'

The hurt in her voice made him feel like a monster. 'The Highlands can be an inhospitable place to a stranger. I don't want you to come to any harm,' Calumn said in a more gentle tone.

'Then I'll hire a guide as you suggested.'

'You'd be an innocent abroad. How would you know who to trust?'

'I trusted you, didn't I? Are you telling me that was a mistake?'

They glared at each other in silence. Calumn drummed his fingers on the arm of the chair. 'We'll send a messenger to Castle Rhubodach on your behalf with a letter asking Guillaume to come here.'

'No, I need to go myself. Lady Drummond said—'

'Lady Drummond is not here. You're in my house, and you'll do as I tell you.'

She could tell by the way he clenched his jaw that he was fast losing control of his patience, but the words were out before she could retract them. 'I don't take orders from you, *Captain Munro.*'

He took a hasty step towards her, then stopped. *'Don't call me that!* You'll do as you're told!' Taking a deep breath, he tried, not entirely successfully, for a more conciliatory tone. 'It's for the best, Madeleine, you'll be far safer here, where I can keep an eye on you.'

A desire to get to the bottom of the matter made her bold. 'You could keep an eye on me if you came with me to Castle Rhubodach. Why won't you come with me? Please, won't you tell me? You are an honourable man, I know you are, I can't believe you've done anything terrible.'

'You wouldn't understand,' he said bleakly.

'Then explain it to me.'

A wash of tiredness swept over him. 'It's too sad and sorry a tale to sully your ears with, and anyway we've strayed a long way from the point. Trust me, it will be best if I you do as I suggest. Write a letter to de Guise asking him to come here. I've promised Jeannie's brother some extra tuition. I'll arrange for someone to take your letter north when I get back.'

He had that set look on his face that told her his mind was made up. She knew there was no point in arguing, though she was absolutely certain that he was wrong. She must go to Guillaume herself, Lady Drummond had been quite specific about that. And reluctant though she was to bring their acquaintance to a premature end, she thought that perhaps it was best after all to remove herself from Calum's presence. He disturbed her. He led her thoughts down a perilous path. How perilous a path it was, she did not want to explore. 'Maybe you're right,' she said meekly, though she hated to deceive him.

Calumn looked relieved. 'Good. I'm glad you're finally seeing sense. I'll see you in a wee while.'

He would not, though he did not know it. Best get it over with quickly. Best not to think about it. She swallowed hard. 'Calumn?'

He paused in the doorway.

'Thank you for—for everything. I'm sorry if I spoke out of turn.'

'Forget it. I'll be back soon,' he said, and left.

Alone, Madeleine fought the urge to lie down on the bed and weep. Instead she threw herself into action, for if she gave herself time to reflect, she suspected she would lose courage. She wrote not one note but two, the first a letter to her father, informing him of her whereabouts and intentions, which she trusted Calumn would post for her. The second was to Calumn himself, begging his pardon for deceiving him, thanking him for his hospitality, pleading with him to return home himself to right whatever wrong he felt he had done. Exactly what that was, she could not imagine, nor could she believe him capable of anything heinous. A tear fell on the words, leaving a tell-tale blot, but she had not the time to copy the letter out again. She folded it, propping it up in front of the clock on the mantel, where he would be sure to see it when he returned.

With a heavy heart, she dressed herself in the clothes she had purchased in the Luckenbooths near St Giles's earlier that day. The plain cotton shift, or sark, as the woman in the market stalls had called it, was similar to her own, though of coarser quality. Over it she donned a petticoat of pale blue, and a shorter skirt of blue-and-gold stripes. She kept her own stays, boots and stockings, but abandoned her saque-backed jacket for a simpler arrangement, a garment of blue wool like a man's waistcoat, with wide sleeves laced into it. Her own clothes were bundled together into her Breton tippet, then she picked up the plaid, or *arisaidh,* a double length of striped worsted, and concentrated hard on tying it as the woman had shown her. First, she fashioned the long strip of material over her skirts like an apron. A slim leather belt held this in place, then she pulled the remainder of the plaid up over her shoulders like a cloak, its folds hanging like pockets down over her hips. A pewter brooch held the whole thing in place, fastened at her breast, leaving enough of the soft wool on her shoulders to pull up like a hood over her head to protect her from the weather. The operation took her some time, but she was much taken with the effect. With the hood to cover her give-away fair hair, she believed even her father would be hard put to distinguish her from a native Scots woman.

It was time to go. At some point in the future she hoped to be able to look back on these last few days fondly, but for now it was with a heavy heart that she closed the door firmly behind her. She would never know if Calumn heeded the advice in her letter. She would never know, either, the sensual pleasures his body had promised. Nor must she ever allow herself to think of them again, for to do so would be to take the first step along the path of acknowledging their significance. She must will herself to forget. Without Calumn's distracting presence, that would surely be a simple enough thing.

Madeleine stepped out into the afternoon sunshine and hurried down to the Grassmarket. She had checked while out shopping, and knew the coach for Falkirk left from the White Hart in half an hour. From there, she could hire a guide and horses—at least she hoped so, not having planned that far ahead. Head down, *arisaidh* covering her hair, clutching her small bundle of belongings, she scurried away down the Edinburgh streets.

Calumn arrived back at his rooms later than he had anticipated. He knew she had gone the moment he closed the front door behind him. The quality of silence betrayed her. He could sense her absence like an animal senses the loss of its young. The note caught his eye immediately, his name written on it with a flourish in an elegant copper-plate hand.

Fury possessed him as he read its contents. He flung it into the hearth. Took a turn about the room. Picked the note out of the hearth and scanned it again. Screwed it up into a ball and hurled it at the window. Rude, headstrong, stupid, stupid girl with no sense of the danger she was like to encounter. *How dare she disobey him!*

A heavy crystal glass shattered satisfyingly on the hearth. For God's sake, she had not even an idea where she was going. No idea how to go about hiring a guide, nor to judge if he was trustworthy. At the mercy of every shyster and villain who wandered the highways and byways looking for just such easy prey! She would be lucky if she ever made it to the Highlands, never mind track down her cursed Guillaume. *Damn the pair o' them!*

Calumn picked the note up once more, smoothing it out and perusing its contents for a third time. *It is your home, where your heart is, and where your heart is, is where you belong.* The words were like salt in a wound, but he could not deny the truth of them. Edinburgh was not home. He was hiding here. None the less, that did not prevent him from wishing to make her pay for forcing him to confront such an uncomfortable truth. He had successfully avoided doing so for months, but now she had flung it in his face, he could run from it no longer. *The De'il take you, Madeleine Lafayette!*

Still clutching the note in his hand, Calumn slumped down on to a chair. But even as he reached for the whisky decanter, he paused. Whisky was a diverting companion, but a dangerous one. He needed a clear head.

By the time the coach arrived in Falkirk, Madeleine was feeling distinctly travel-weary. The small vehicle was extremely cramped inside, and she had been squashed into the greasy squabs beside a dour-faced minister who muttered passages from his well-thumbed Bible in a relentless droning monotone until the fading light forced him to stop. A large—very large—farmer who smelled quite distinctly of pig occupied more than his fair share of the seat on her other side. As the minister intoned his final amen, the farmer gave a grunt which may have been concurrence, but sounded uncommonly like something which would have emanated from one of his stock and fell immediately asleep. The assault on Madeleine's ears was then renewed, with a series of whistling snores impressive in their variety of tone and duration.

The roads between Edinburgh and Falkirk were deeply rutted from the recent dry spell, and the coachman seemed to have no notion of sticking to the published timetable, stopping to exchange friendly banter with almost every other vehicle they passed. Madeleine's head ached from the bumping and racketing and the minister's incessant mutter-ing, and her empty stomach had been gurgling in protest for the last ten miles.

She had had ample time to regret her hasty depar-ture and fret about the reception her note would receive. Ample time to doggedly refuse to give room to the persistent worry that Calumn's accusations about her feelings—or lack of them—for Guillaume had some grounds. Ample time to remind herself, with rather less conviction as each mile passed, that until Calumn sowed the seed of doubt in her mind she had been perfectly content.

Finally, exhausted by her own circular arguments, irked at her own inability to convincingly shore up the foundations of her future, she stopped thinking all together. Descending on shaky legs from the coach when it eventually pulled up in the bustling courtyard of the inn, she thought only of a meal and her bed.

'Mademoiselle Lafayette. We meet again,' said a very familiar voice.

She must be hallucinating. A man in full Highland dress who looked uncannily like Calumn stood before her, large as life and even more unfairly handsome. Madeleine swayed on her feet. The ground rushed up to meet her. For the first time in her twenty-one years, she fainted.

She came to in a private parlour in the inn. Opening her eyes, she gazed around, for a few seconds completely disoriented. She was sitting on a chair. There was a fire crackling in a grate. A pair of long, muscled legs stood in front of the fire. She blinked. Looked up. Blinked again. 'Calumn?'

His soft laugh was unmistakable. 'Didn't you recognise me?'

She sat up. It was him, it really was Calumn Munro, but a Calumn she barely knew, so breathtakingly different did he look. It was as if his heritage as a Scottish laird was stamped on his bearing. A mantle of authority seemed to have descended on him, power and lineage emanating from his very stance, the aristocratic profile, even the curl of his fiery hair. Highland dress seemed designed to emphasise Calumn's height and muscular frame. It seemed, in fact, to Madeleine's admiring stare, to have been designed specifically with Calumn Munro in mind.

He wore two separate plaids made from lengths of the same tartan wool, red interwoven with very dark blue and gold. The *filleadh beg,* or belted plaid, was held at his waist with a large leather belt, the buckle of silver embossed with the Munro coat of arms, the motto *Dread God* in Gaelic on the hilt of his dirk, the long, lethal knife he wore sheathed at his waist. The *filleadh beg* stopped just at the knee, showing his long muscular legs in their woollen hose to perfection. The dusting of golden hair, glimpsed on his thigh and the top of his calves as he turned, the pleats of the plaid swinging tantalisingly out behind him, matched the darker gold on his head. Madeleine realised he must be naked underneath. She dragged her eyes upwards, lest her face betray the stirring in her blood.

A dark blue worsted jacket, the skirts much shorter than the fashionable length, was worn over his white shirt, and over that was the second plaid, the *filleadh mòr,* which served to keep out the cold at night, but was during the day fixed to his shoulder with a long silver pin engraved with Celtic symbols, topped with a large emerald. He did not wear the traditional bonnet. His hair, loose and tumbled, golden and amber, looked somehow wilder, much more of a mane, its vibrant, luxuriant life symbolic of the heart of the man. His eyes seemed a deeper blue, like the colour woven into the tartan he wore. His whole being seemed taller, wider, more solid, and rough hewn. She could not say how, but it was so. 'You look *magnifique,* but also—I don't know, as if you have a new skin.'

He should not have been surprised at her perceptiveness. Calum smiled, flattered but disconcerted, for he was aware of the change himself. The tartan had been woven by his mother. The stockings were her work, too—she was, despite her noble birth, a skilled needlewoman. The dirk had been a present from his father for his sixteenth birthday, the pin a baptismal gift from his maternal grandmother. It felt as if he was wearing his ancestry. It felt almost like a homecoming and just as bittersweet. 'You think I've come out of hiding?'

Madeleine looked uncomfortable. 'I didn't say that.' He smelled of wool and leather, an earthy combination which added to the elemental look of him. He had a leather pouch attached to his waist, some sort of purse it must be, finished with fur. 'What do you think of my outfit?' she said in an effort to distract her thoughts. 'Do I pass muster as a Scots lass?'

'Very nice. It suits you surprisingly well. I take it you went out behind my back to purchase it?'

She decided to take a leaf out of his own book

and ignore this question. 'What are you doing here, Calumn?'

After much soul-searching, he had finally been forced to admit that Madeleine was right. Such an established thing it had become in his mind, the belief that the north was closed to him, but over the last few days, she had pushed open the room in which he had locked both his pride and his spirit. Her flight had forced his hand, but once he had calmed down he found he had not the will to incarcerate them again.

It was time to take the first steps towards confronting his demons.

And then there was Madeleine, so charming before him in her Highland dress. If he must face up to reality, then so must she. *Quid pro quo.* Such a foolish thing as she had done, taking matters into her own hands and expressly disobeying him. She was a feisty piece, but she must learn there was a price to be paid for nerve. By the time she was reunited with de Guise, he would make sure she entertained no more thoughts of marriage to the man. Would make very sure that she knew the difference between affection and passion. The prospect made him smile in anticipation.

'What's so amusing?' Madeleine's voice brought his reverie to an abrupt halt. 'You haven't answered my question—I asked what you're doing here. And now I come to think of it, how did you know where to find me?'

'As to finding you, it was a straightforward

enough matter. I sent Jamie off to the Grassmarket to make enquiries. I wasn't expecting the Highland dress, but fair-haired foreigners, especially pretty maids, are not exactly common. You were seen boarding the Falkirk coach. Travelling alone on horseback, 'twas an easy enough matter to get here first. As to why I'm here—I think I should be asking that of you. Did I not tell you to wait? Have you any idea how foolishly you've behaved?'

'How I behave is none of your business.'

'You may be nigh on two-and-twenty years old, but you are still a naïve young woman alone in my country, and a foreigner to boot. I am responsible for you. How do you think I'd feel if you came to harm? Did you honestly think I'd let you go off on your own like this?'

'I knew you would be angry, but I never thought you'd come after me. I didn't do it deliberately to make you follow me—you don't think I did, do you?'

'No,' Calumn conceded. 'You're headstrong and willful, but you don't strike me as the manipulative sort.'

'I'm sorry to have left without telling you, but if you've come all this way to try to persuade me to go back, you've wasted your journey. I won't go.'

Calumn smiled wryly. 'There's an old Scottish saying—*save your breath to cool your porridge*. It means don't waste your time on unwinnable arguments. I haven't come to persuade you to come back, I've come to take you myself.'

'You'll come with me?' With a squeal of delight,

Madeleine leapt to her feet and threw her arms around him. Relief and gratitude soon gave way to a prickle of conscience, however. 'Are you sure it's what you want to do? I am grateful—more than grateful—but I don't want to force you into coming with me just because you're worried about my safety.'

'You're not forcing me, I'm coming because I want to. I'll take you as far as Castle Rhubodach and no further. After that, God help him, you are de Guise's responsibility, are we clear on that?'

She nodded, only too happy to agree to any terms, if they meant he would accompany her.

'One more thing, Madeleine,' Calumn said softly. He put his finger under her chin, forcing her to look up, to hold his gaze. The look in his eyes sent her pulses racing, a peculiar combination of threat and promise. 'I'll not be accused of cowardice. Not by you, not by anyone. I don't have to prove that to you, but I will. And it's not the only thing I will prove.'

Her mouth was dry. Somehow she knew he was about to make the ground shift under her feet. 'What else?' she said, her voice more croak than anything else.

'I will show you the true route to happiness and you won't find it in obedience.'

'You think to make me fall in love with you,' she said incredulously.

'Oh, I won't go that far. But I know I can make you want me. Enough to give yourself to me.'

'Why must you see my betrothal as a personal

challenge? You won't do it, though I realise that you will see these words too as a challenge. I am committed to Guillaume. If I am not in love with him now—at least, in love as you describe it—then I have no doubt that love will follow once we are wed.' If truth be told, she was, in fact, beginning to doubt that very thing, but now was not the time for telling the truth. Now was most certainly not the time to be allowing Calumn Munro to see any chink at all in her defences.

'We'll see,' Calumn said with a soft laugh.

She tried to formulate a response which would penetrate that infuriating confidence of his, but could not. In the end, she wrenched herself from his grasp and gave her little Gallic shrug. 'Yes, we will,' she said.

'And I very much look forward to it,' Calumn added, claiming the last word, as ever. 'But not tonight,' he continued, turning to more practical matters. 'I have taken the liberty of bespeaking rooms—have no fear, separate rooms—for us. I suggest we discuss our route over dinner, and then retire betimes since we've an early start, and must make sure we have adequate provisions with us for the journey.'

'You make it sound like a military exercise.'

'As an officer I would remind you that I'm used to giving orders—and, I might add, having them obeyed to the letter. Dinner will be served in fifteen minutes,' Calumn said, trying not to smile.

She could not but respond to the challenge in

his voice. Madeleine drew herself up to her full height, stood solemnly to attention and performed an extravagant salute. *'Oui, mon capitaine,'* she managed before fleeing from the room. As she ascended the stairs, she was gratified to hear the sound of deep masculine laughter reverberating in the air.

They set off just after daybreak the next morning on the well-trodden road to Stirling. It was as if they were retracing the Rebellion in reverse, for it was at Stirling that Charles Edward's Jacobite army had been involved in another ineffective siege of a castle, prior to the Battle of Falkirk. Madeleine was struck by how similar the two fortresses looked, Stirling and Edinburgh, built high and impregnable on their plugs of rock, as if the earth had thrust them up ready made from its core. If anything, Stirling Castle, perched on its heavily wooded escarpment, looked even more dramatic, surrounded as it was by completely flat farmland. They decided to avoid the busy town, stopping only to purchase food before carrying on north towards the Trossachs and the start of the Highlands.

The landscape shifted before Madeleine's eyes, the roads narrowing to tracks, the land rolling and rising on both sides of her as they travelled through glens enclosed by hills, the mountains of the southern Highlands looming in the distance. Lush green grass gave way to the dark of fern, the vibrant yellow of late gorse in flower, and the purpling of the heather. In the glens, streams ran plentifully, icy

cold and sparkling from the mountains, the ground
springy, sometimes sodden under the horses' hooves.
As the afternoon faded into evening, Madeleine
caught glimpses of tiny roe deer gazing thoughtfully out from the cover of the ferns.

'We'll stop here for the night,' Calumn announced
as they came to a small clearing near the head of a
glen. 'It's plenty mild enough to sleep in the open,
and there's no sign of rain,' he said, scanning the
cloudless sky, pale in the evening sun.

Madeleine slid gratefully out of the saddle, leaving Calumn to tend to the horses, removing their
tack and hobbling them, while she set out their
provisions. They ate hungrily, the fresh air having
given them both a hearty appetite. Afterwards, as
they lazed on the grass, Madeleine became aware
of the sound of running water. She removed her
arisaidh, boots and stockings and went to investi-
gate. It would be good to wash off the dust of the
journey. The stream gushed and burbled along the
flat, boulder-strewn valley floor, forming pools in
the rocks. Madeleine picked her way to one of the
pools, tucking her skirts up into her belt.

The water was crystal clear. Taking a deep breath,
she pushed up her sleeves, cupped some of it in her
hands and splashed it on her face. Droplets spattered on to the neckline of her sark, her sleeves, her
neck, her breast. She cupped and splashed more,
gasping as the icy water fell on her skin. As she bent
over again, her foot lost its hold on the smooth stone

underneath and she wobbled, only just managing to steady herself, avoiding a fall at the last minute.

Laughing to herself, she looked up to find Calumn by the bank watching her. He, too, had stripped to wash, and was wearing only his shirt and his *filleadh beg*. His legs and feet were bare. His shirt was open to the throat. It was not that she had forgotten, but, taken up with the journey, the scenery, the newness of everything, she was struck afresh with how incredibly attractive the man was.

Water was surely her element, Calumn was thinking. It darkened her hair to tarnished silver, sheening on her skin, making the sleeves of her waistcoat, and the frill of her sark, cling provocatively to her. He imagined how it would feel to lick every delicious droplet from her damp body.

'All yours,' Madeleine said, stepping daintily up on to the bank, suddenly embarrassed at the intimacy of the moment. Resisting the urge to look over her shoulder, she wandered back to where they had left their belongings in a little hollow hidden from the track by a high bank of gorse and fern.

Calumn stripped off his shirt and waded into the stream, where he washed quickly and efficiently. Throwing his shirt back over his dripping torso, he rejoined Madeleine. She had spread out their two plaids on the ground and was sitting on one, combing her long hair. It was unbound and flowing down over her shoulders. The ends were damp and curling. Her bare toes peeped out from under her skirts. She had removed the sleeves of her waistcoat and placed them to dry over a gorse bush. Her waistcoat bodice was unlaced, revealing the white skin of her throat, the soft mounds of her breasts.

Alerted to his presence, she looked up. The expression of elemental lust on his face was unmistakable. She dropped her comb, her heart pounding. She was afraid—not of what he would do, but of her ability to resist. It was wrong, but she knew that it would feel right. Worse, shamefully worse, she wanted it.

Calumn's magnificent body was damp under his shirt, the contours of his muscles tantalisingly revealed through the wet folds of cloth, his strong legs planted before her. He was staring intently down at her like a ravenous predator. She knew she was his prey, for she felt spellbound and helpless.

But still, 'No,' she whispered as he knelt down beside her. 'I can't.'

'Yes, you can, if you want to. No one will ever know.'

She was intrigued, as he had known she would be. 'But how?'

Calumn's soft chuckle was filled with knowledge and certainty. 'There are many ways to take pleasure without risk. I can show you.'

'You mean we wouldn't—you wouldn't…'

'You'll still be a maid. But a sated one.' His eyes were a deep, mesmerising blue. As beguiling as the sea on a hot summer's morning. Eyes to dip into. Eyes demanding that she do so.

'Sated,' Madeleine repeated, feeling the word

trickle down her throat, tempting and heady as illicit liquor.

'Sated,' he whispered huskily in her ear. His breath was like a warm caress. His fingers twined in her hair as if they would weave magic spells. 'Trust me,' he said.

Tantalising little kisses on her eyelids. *Trust me.* She did. But she did not trust herself. Calumn nibbled on the lobe of her ear. A shiver like quicksilver made her bite her lip.

'Don't you want to know, Madeleine, how it feels? Don't you want to know what it's like, to let go?'

Nibbling kisses on her mouth now, following the line of her lower lip. 'Let go?' Even as she spoke the words in an odd, breathy voice, she remembered it, that tuned-too-tight feeling. Recalled, too, the way it had ended, leaving something unfinished. Her breathing quickened with the memory and the allure of Calumn's promise. A flush stained her cheeks. Inside, deeper down, she felt another flush begin to pool.

He saw the moment she decided from the way her bewitching green eyes darkened with passion. 'Let go,' he said again, only this time it was a command he knew she would obey.

He smiled at her, a slow, seductive, certain smile, watching its reflection in her eyes, feeling a tightening coil of desire in the pit of his stomach. Beneath his plaid, his manhood unfurled and stiffened. He prayed for restraint. His own. For Madeleine he wished the opposite. The urge to be naked on top of her was almost overwhelming. He gave in to it partway, tugging his shirt over his head.

Madeleine drank in the view of his torso, as unfamiliar to her as the Highland landscape and just as magnificent. Still-damp skin tinged with golden hair, smelling of mountain water and male muskiness. Her eyes traced a path across the breadth of his shoulders and down his arms with their muscles like whipcord. Back along the valley of his chest and down to the dip of his ribcage, the concave of his stomach, where a vicious scar curved in a crescent shape, disappearing like a question mark, beneath his belt buckle. Where did it finish? How had it happened? She would have liked to trace its path with her fingers. She wanted to touch him, but was afraid to.

When he removed the bodice of her waistcoat, she neither resisted nor aided him. He unlaced her stays, then the ties of her sark so that her breasts were exposed to his touch. The urge to cover herself from his gaze was instinctive, but he gently removed her hands, replacing them with his own. His touch was quite different, moulding their shape in his palms, the abrasion of his roughened skin on her own softness making her nipples bud and peak. His mouth now, kissing, licking, sucking on her nipples, making her breathe fast then slow, light then heavy, as pleasure-coated needles of feeling surged through her. Her body arched like a bow being readied.

She was hot, heated from within, as if a brazier had been set alight, low down inside her, licking flames into her blood, out to her pulse points. More flames where Calumn touched her, licked her, stroked her, as if he were lighting fuses, separate but connected, all tracking a path to the heat which was building between her legs. His hand on her flank now, under her petticoats, on the soft skin at the top of her thighs.

As his fingers brushed the damp of her curls he felt her instinctive resistance. He cupped her, waited, delicately kneaded her, coaxing, cajoling, until she relaxed and he felt her wet, enticingly wet, against his hand. With a heroic effort, he gathered up the shreds of his self-control and stroked lightly, gently, then teasingly, flitting around the edges, careful not to tumble her over the precipice too soon.

Madeleine moaned, her fingers clutching and digging into the ground on which she lay. She could feel her muscles gathering and clenching. A heady tightness. She tried to steady herself, but his touch kept her off balance. A trickle of perspiration ran down her back. Everything he did, every touch, whatever it was he was doing—she didn't care what it was—stoked the heat, bound her tighter. A delicious light-headedness combined with the tightness. Too hot. Too bright. Too much. Almost too much. She writhed, as if she would escape his touch, but all she wanted was for it to go on and on.

'Let go,' Calumn whispered urgently.

For a split second she had a vision of herself, lying exposed and dishevelled on the ground, allowing herself to be intimately caressed by a semi-naked man she barely knew.

'Madeleine, stop thinking.' His kiss gentled her, soothing her as if she were a frightened animal.

She closed her mind to the conflicting messages her brain was attempting to formulate. She stopped thinking. Allowed one hand to drift over his heated skin. Relished the so-different feel of him. She kissed him back. Kissed him back again. Felt heat surge as his tongue tangled with hers and his fingers worked their magic.

Like a gathering storm it was, inside her. Clarity like a lightning fork, and she knew what he meant. She let go. Swelling. A quickening and surging, gathering force like an avalanche of heat, and just as unstoppable. She cried out as it caught her, took her, flicked her into the air and sent her tumbling to earth in a free fall, her breath escaping in a series of little panting cries.

Sated. Lying with her eyes closed, drowsily wallowing in a wholly new sense of well-being, she wondered if this was what Calumn had meant. Sated. She forced her eyes open, for it was as if her lids were weighted down. He was sprawled beside her, propped up on his elbow. Watching her. In his smile she could see triumph writ quite clearly. She could not grudge him it. She smiled back. A surrender, albeit a temporary one.

Beside her, Calumn lay equally content. Not because he had taken another step towards making his point. Strangely, that thought did not occur to him. His feelings had rather more primitive roots. The satisfaction of a man who knows he has given his woman pleasure.

Chapter Five

Madeleine awoke in the soft light of the morning. A majestic stag was grazing in the clearing just a few feet away. As she stirred he looked up, his nose twitching, staring at her imperiously for long seconds, his antlers looking impossibly heavy for his head. She blinked and he was gone, the white of his scut disappearing over the brow of the hill.

Madeleine sighed. After last night, it was no longer possible for her to fool herself. She was wading into deep water with Calumn Munro. Whatever were her feelings for Guillaume—and she was no longer so sure of those, either—what she felt for Calumn was fast becoming irresistible. The notion that she could keep the two separate was, she had to admit, not only naïve, but perhaps even untenable. The point was fast approaching where she must put an end to things if she were not to jeopardise her future. The problem was, she was no longer sure that the future she was protecting was the one which she wanted.

In many ways nothing had changed. She still loved Guillaume. She was still certain that her marriage to him made sense. In every way but one. Somewhere along the way, between landing at the docks of Leith and last night, she had begun to doubt that it would make her happy.

What did make her happy? It was a question she had never asked herself. *This,* came the unwanted thought. The fresh of the Highland morning air cool on her face. The contrasting cosy warmth of the rest of her body, covered in Calumn's plaid. Being cradled against Calumn's chest. His arm draped lightly around her waist. His chin resting on the top of her head, feeling his breathing. *This.*

She wanted more. She knew it was what Calumn intended. More. To make her see his reason. Which she was beginning to see for herself. Tempting. Illogically tempting. And potentially fatal. But still, she wanted it. More. Wanted it enough to be able to believe for just a little longer that it didn't preclude a way back.

Beside her, she felt Calumn stir. 'Up with you,' he said, putting paid to her reverie, rolling away from her and pulling the plaid away at the same time. 'We've a long day's journey ahead of us.'

By the time they had breakfasted and saddled the horses, the dawn chill had melted away, giving the promise of another mild Scottish summer day. They made good time, reaching Aberfoyle just after noon. The little town lay right on the edge of a stunningly dramatic shift in scenery, as if north and south of it were two different worlds. Behind Calumn and Madeleine lay the gently rolling hills of the Campsie Fells, with Stirling Castle still discernible in the far distance. Ahead of them lay the rugged grandeur of the Highlands. They stopped to rest and water the horses, partaking of a simple meal at an inn on the High Street. Suitably refreshed, they resumed their trek north.

The terrain was becoming increasingly difficult. Mountains rose sharply out of the landscape, their lower slopes shielded by ancient forests. Above the tree line, heather and bracken lent purple and amethyst, burnt umber and tawny shades of brown to the palette of colours, and higher still were peaks stony and grey with scree or dusted white with snow. The ranges receded on and on into the horizon like a painting, stark against the pale blue of the sky.

They followed the path along the river which tumbled down to Aberfoyle, zigzagging along the contours of the hillside to Loch Awe, a sheen of deep blue dotted with islets, the mountains and hills reflected in its depths. The air here was sharper, for summer came much later in the north.

By the banks of the loch, Madeleine reined in her horse and sat staring, overcome by the sheer majesty of the terrain spread out in front of her. 'I've never seen anything like it,' she whispered, her eyes following the effortless gliding of a huge bird of prey riding high on the thermals above the water.

'A golden eagle,' Calumn told her, following her gaze.

They sat in silence for a while, watching the eagle search for a fish to pluck from the water. Though Madeleine continued to feign interest in the bird of prey, her attention was in reality focused on the man by her side. He fitted perfectly here, his planes and contours, rolling muscle and sinew in harmony with the land of his birth. She remembered the stag this morning. Majestic was a word quite as suited to Calumn as he sat astride his horse, his hair glowing like a halo, clearly master of the landscape. A shadow flitted over his face, a grim sadness, reflected in the tightening of the muscles in his cheeks, his throat, his shoulders, the straightening of his spine. His gaze remained fixed on the distant horizon, his thoughts lost deep in a place she could not imagine and could not reach.

As if sensing his change of mood, Calumn's horse snickered nervously, reclaiming his attention. His eyes refocused. Madeleine hurriedly lifted her own skywards, only to find that the eagle must have already swooped down successfully on its prey, for it was no longer anywhere to be seen.

'Where is Castle Rhubodach from here?' she asked. 'Is it far?'

'It's over there.' He pointed to the head of Loch Awe. 'Beyond the peak you can see, Ben Venue. The track skirts round the base of the mountain. It's a fair way yet. We won't make it before nightfall.'

'It's so beautiful here. Could we not spend the night on the shore of this lake and finish our journey tomorrow?'

'It's a loch.'

'Lock.'

'Loch.'

'Lochchchch,' Madeleine repeated, laughing at her own abysmal attempt to imitate the soft sound.

Calumn grinned. 'It is a bonny place, right enough. Come on then, let's find somewhere to camp.'

The shores of the loch had several small sandy bays. Trees grew down almost to the water's edge in places, and on some of the tiny islands too there was a sparse scattering of the distinctive Caledonian pines, looking as if they were growing out of the loch itself. Calumn found a shallow cave which would provide shelter from the elements later, and here he stored the horses' tack, their saddle bags and provisions. The water was calm, the sun at its zenith in the sky, and there was not another soul to be seen. They sat together at the mouth of the cave, drinking in the silence which surrounded them.

Madeleine removed her boots and stockings, enjoying the gritty feel of the sand between her toes. The deep calm of the water looked unbelievably tempting. 'Is it safe to swim in the…' She hesitated, concentrating furiously on trying to form her mouth into the right shape to pronounce the word, a performance so endearingly comical that Calumn had difficulty containing his laughter. 'Loch,' she managed finally, looking inordinately pleased with herself at the result.

'Can you swim?'

'I've swum in the sea all my life. Maman taught me.'

'Your mother!'

'*Mais oui, bien sûr.* Maman was not well born, you know? She was the only daughter of a fisherman, and she had two brothers, both fishermen also. Believe it or not, Breton fishermen think it's unlucky to learn how to swim, they think it tempts fate, but Maman believed it was rather tempting fate not to be able to swim.'

'Fishermen are a superstitious bunch, it's the same here.'

Madeleine's dimples peeped. 'But you are not a fisherman, are you? Swim with me, Calumn.'

He shook his head. 'Not a good idea. It'll be freezing.'

'I'm used to the Atlantic Ocean. It can't be any colder than that.'

'I think you'll find it is, but go on,' he said, 'see for yourself.'

Unable to resist the implied challenge, Madeleine got to her feet and picked up her skirts, making her way to the water's edge. Tentatively putting one foot into the water, she gasped with shock, for it was icy, even colder than the mountain stream she had bathed in last night. Behind her, Calumn roared with laughter. Determinedly she put her foot in again, thinking she would grow accustomed to the temperature, but if anything this time it felt even colder. Head held high, she walked the short distance back over the sand towards him.

'I told you,' he said, grinning up at her.

His teeth were white and even. His mocking eyes were blue, drowning-in blue. Deep and tempting, like the waters of the loch. Though warmer. Much warmer. He was sitting in his shirt sleeves, his brogue-clad feet planted firmly in the sand, the folds of his *filleadh beg* draped between his legs. His hose were tied below the knee. He had nice calves, she thought, muscled yet shapely, clearly defined under the woven stockings. 'You were right, I admit it, you were right. I would freeze.'

She looked so adorable, standing over him like that, the breeze whipping tendrils of her hair around her face. He wanted her. More than he had ever wanted any woman before. 'Forget swimming,' Calumn said, 'I can think of a much better way to amuse ourselves.'

Before she could stop him, his hand on her wrist yanked her down on to her knees before him, like a supplicant. He looked at her in such a way as to make his intentions unmistakable. Now was the time to exercise the caution she had urged upon herself only this morning. Now was the time to put an unequivocal end to Calumn's assault on her mind. On her senses. *Now!*

Madeleine flicked a strand of hair from her eyes, and in doing so set herself off balance. Reaching out for something to stop herself from falling over, she encountered Calumn's leg. Warm skin. Rough hair. She froze.

Calumn watched her as a hunter will when trapping a wild thing. Unmoving. His eyes on hers, unblinking. Waiting. Enticing. She pulled her hand away.

'Coward,' Calumn said.

She licked her lips. She did not feel afraid, though she knew she should, for she was without doubt on the brink of something irrevocable. She felt uncertain. Which way to jump? *Which way?* Frantically she wished he would decide. At least then she would not have to.

'What are you afraid of, Madeleine?' Calumn said with that annoying habit of his of asking her questions she did not want to answer. 'Admitting defeat?'

'Defeat,' she repeated, confused by the word. Which way was defeat, surrender or retreat? She was in no doubt of what she wanted. Did surrender really have to lead to her defeat? Could it not somehow go hand in hand with victory? Why must she have one and not both? She knew she could not, but it was what she wanted. Right now, more than anything, she wanted Calumn. She felt so strange. Nervy. Agitated. Excited.

Keeping her eyes fixed on his face, as if her actions were naught to do with her, she ran her fingers up under his plaid, from his knees to the top of his thighs. The lightest of touches. A touch which could mean nothing or everything. A touch which could easily be continued, and just as easily withdrawn. Calumn's eyelids fluttered briefly closed. She moved her hands to the back of his thighs, her fingers fluttering from there down to the crease at his knees. He made no attempt now to dissuade her. She could see from the darkening of his pupils, like a storm brewing, that desire already had him in its grip.

She could stop. Now would be the time.

'It's me you want, Madeleine,' Calumn whispered, uncannily echoing her thoughts. 'You know that. Admit it.'

'I want you.' The truth. Or *a* truth. She could not think straight. No longer cared to think. Not with him so close. So distractingly near. Temptation personified. Who was she to resist? 'I want you, Calumn,' she said again, testing the words for their veracity, finding them solid.

Triumph lit up his eyes at her admission, but it was not due to the defeat of her betrothed. That contest was far from Calumn's thoughts. It was his name on her lips, the winning of her for himself which mattered. With a low growl he pulled her closer to him.

She would have overbalanced, were it not for her hands on the outside of his thighs. His plaid had become dislodged, moving higher up his legs, so that she could see almost up to where she held him.

Heat flared inside her like a warning beacon, but already she was beyond heeding it.

Her lips were so perfectly formed for kissing. Her kisses were more addictive than any whisky. Calumn needed no urging. He kissed and was kissed. Still kissing, he discarding her bodice and loosened her stays, freeing her breasts to his touch. She responded by tugging at his shirt. He stopped kissing her only to pull it over his head. Her hands on his skin set him aflame.

'Slow down,' he whispered raggedly, the instruction intended as much for himself as for Madeleine. He gentled his kisses, positioning her so that she faced him, their spread legs intertwined, their lower bodies still clad. He pulled her into his embrace so that her nipples brushed against his chest when he kissed her. He could feel them peaking against his skin. It was delicious. He moved, so that they grazed the hairs on his chest, the tiniest of movements sending hot pulses of feeling down to his groin, and he knew from the way she gasped, from the way she clutched his back, that it was having the same effect on her.

He ceased his plundering of her mouth to watch her as he touched her, his fingers tracing the line of her neck, her shoulders, the tender flesh on the inside of her arm, then the mounds of her breasts, the indentation of her waist, watching her, seeing her eyes darken, her skin respond to his caress, watching and silently encouraging. He saw the moment her instincts kicked in, the little flick of her tongue on to the full pinkness of her bottom lip, the glance up at him for reassurance as she started to mimic his actions.

He prayed for control. Wondered, for the first time, if he would be able to stop at the point where he must. He had never had cause to doubt himself before, but this was different. Fleetingly, it occurred to him that everything about Madeleine was different. Then he closed down his thoughts and focused on what was here. And now.

She was acutely aware of him watching her. Not where his hands touched, but watching her face to see how she felt when his hands touched, so she did the same. Watched his face as she ran her fingers over the line of his jaw where there was the faintest trace of stubble, down the column of his throat to the little hollow at the base. His shoulders were broad, a complex pattern of muscles underneath his skin, which rippled as he moved. The blades seemed not so sharp as hers, which were nearer the surface. More layers of muscle from the top of his arms to his elbow, where his flesh became sinewy, the hairs on his forearm downy, the skin lightly tanned. There was a pulse beating at his wrist. The skin on the inside of his arms was soft, vulnerable. She could feel a tiny scar there. Her fingers traced its shape.

His chest was all valleys and rolling hills. She smoothed her palm across his breast, feeling the flatness of his nipple, sucking in her breath when in return he rolled her nipples between his fingers. Without thinking, she leaned forwards and licked him, allowing her teeth to graze where his fingers pinched, tasting the slightly salty tang of him, smooth skin and rough hair and puckered male nipple, and then she looked up and felt a surge of pleasure when she saw the effect of what she had done on his face.

Then a resounding surge of response from her as his mouth enveloped her breast, licking, sucking, tugging heat from her. Her hands ran down his torso, the vee-shape to his narrow waist, the curve of his ribcage, counting her fingers over the muscles of his abdomen. She traced the curve of his scar, then kissed it, pushing him back so that her tongue could run over its ridges, so that she could flutter kisses over it, as if she were the answer to the question it asked, as if her kisses could fill the void it had obviously left, as if she could heal him. For he needed to be healed. She knew that much.

The ornate buckle of his belt grazed her chin. Her fingers struggled with the fastenings until he managed it for her, casting it to the side.

She wriggled closer to him, and he pushed her skirts up around her thighs, positioned her legs over his, so that her feet were gripping the sand behind his back, her calves brushing his waist. *What now?* Panic threatened. It must have shown in her eyes, for he kissed her slowly, holding her steady, stroking her hair, brushing her sensitised breasts against his chest.

Seconds of stillness. Aeons of stillness. Then he kissed her again, pushed her skirts high up around her waist so that she was spread in front of him, but also nestled in to him. Then he tugged at the front fold of his plaid, pulling it apart.

He took her hand and placed it on his erection, wrapping her fingers around its girth. Hard and smooth. Unexpectedly smooth. He guided her wrist so that her circling fingers moved up to the tip. Back down again. Finally, she dropped her gaze and allowed herself to look. A ripple of sensation, like water flowing over stones, made her muscles contract as she gazed in fascination. Her fingers pale against the dark of his shaft. The surprising size of him. The knowledge that she had caused this, that it was for her, that this was her hand on the very core of his being, was intensely sensual. He encouraged her to stroke him again. She saw from the way his stomach clenched that what she did he liked. She felt her own stomach clench.

'We don't look the same, but we feel the same,' Calumn whispered. 'When you do that to me, this is what I feel.'

His fingers slipped easily inside her, slid up slowly, easing her apart delicately, then retreating. He did it again and instinctively she gripped him. Again, and this time she echoed him, doing to him what he did to her, and again, slowly, again, her breath coming faster as she felt, and saw what she felt reciprocated, and so felt more. Again.

Calumn stayed her hand, placed her fingers on the tip of his erection where the skin was darker. 'And here, when you touch me here,' he said rather jaggedly, as if he was struggling for breath, 'this is what I feel.'

His touch between her legs became the caress she remembered from yesterday, slipping up to stroke; fluttering touches where she was hot and swollen, where each touch sent lightning-bright sparks. With the tips of her fingers she touched the tip of his erection, dancing, flitting touches, circling when he did, stroking when he did. The first caresses had lit the smouldering embers of a fire. Now it was as if a bellows had been applied, for the flames shot up and out and burned and licked at her as they had done yesterday, only more intensely because already her body was welcoming and not resistant and because she could see that Calumn was feeling the same.

She felt him thickening in her hold. She heard the tempo of his breathing change. She felt herself swelling under his touch, and that swooping, diving, tumbling crashing sensation as he touched her exactly where she needed to be touched, and when she felt his fingers slip inside her again, plunging in to muscles eager for him she knew to resume the sliding, stroking movement on his shaft. And although she closed her eyes because she could not keep them open—so intense was the first wave of her climax that she dug her heels into the sand and arched her body up—she knew she had been right, for she felt him too, pulsing in her hand, hardening, swelling, the wave travelling up his length. Then she heard his groan, dragged from him, and felt him explode hot and wet in her hand, as she was hot and wet in his.

She slumped into his arms, her body pressed against his heaving torso, clutching tight as she fell back to earth, then hugging into him as she landed, feeling his breath on her hair, floating on a cloud of sensation, her limbs heavy, as if she had been drugged. Different from yesterday. More. The pleasure of giving as well as taking making it much more. Her body hummed.

She searched her mind for guilt, but found only a sense of rightness. Though she knew what she had done was without doubt a betrayal, still she could not see it in that way. Calumn had awoken this wanton in her. Calumn, whose scent was on her now, whose body was wrapped around hers at this very moment. Calumn, whose breath matched hers, whose mouth seemed to have been made to fit hers.

It was then that guilt struck her. Not for what she had done, but for what she had been trying to avoid. The truth stared her in the face. She glanced at it, then looked away as the foundations of her world tilted. Not yet.

They tarried by the banks of Loch Awe the next morning. When Calumn suggested they postpone their journey another day, Madeleine eagerly agreed. She was happy here with him. She did not want it to end. Was not yet ready to face what the ending would involve.

They ascended the slopes of Ben Ann, one of

the smallest of the surrounding mountains, nestling egg-like against the skyline, an easy but rewarding climb. The views from the summit were panoramic, back to the lowlands and north-west where the true peaks of the Highlands could be seen snow-capped and stark.

'Mountains and lakes—lochs,' Madeleine hastily corrected herself, shading her eyes from the sun. 'There are no towns, I can't see any people, no farm land, just us and some sheep. In Brittany it is either sea, or orchards and crops, so very different.'

'It's only the flat land in the glens, by the lochs or the shores that can be cultivated,' Calumn replied. 'That's why sheep are so important. And cattle, too. All these tracks you can see, they're mostly drovers' roads, though beef is too expensive for the Highland folk to eat themselves.' He was staring off in the direction of his own home, Errin Mhor, which sat near the coast, far out of view. Up here on the peak of Ben Ann, the landscape spread before him and plucked at his heartstrings in a way he could not ignore. His yearning for Errin Mhor was primitive and instinctive, an ache in his very bones that he had grown adept at suppressing. Now it came to life like a creature which had been hibernating inside him, filtering into his blood, so that standing here looking west, it was as if Errin Mhor called to him and he must answer.

'Which direction is your home?' Madeleine asked, as if she could read his mind.

He directed her to a distant valley. 'That way and west, in the land that lies between there and the sea.'

'Is it far?'

'Two or three days from here.'

His tone was bleak. She did not know what to say. All her instincts told her that he should go there. Everything she had seen of him here, so at one with nature, served to convince her that her instincts were right. But she knew that to press him was to invite his resistance.

'Over yonder,' Calumn said, pointedly changing the subject, 'on the other side of the glen, that's Castle Rhubodach where your destiny awaits.'

He was silent on the way down the mountainside, walking in front of her where the path was narrow and steep, ready to catch her should she fall into one of the many streams—burns, she corrected herself—that traversed the mountainside, making the way boggy, though the heather flourished. She enjoyed his protectiveness, the way he made her feel that she was something precious and delicate, feminine. An unusual sensation for her, who would normally assert her independence.

'It was always I who decided what we would do,' she said, grasping Calumn's hand to clamber over a fallen tree trunk which barred their way. 'When we were younger, I mean, Guillaume and I.'

'That doesn't surprise me.'

'He didn't mind. Guillaume's always been very good-natured.'

'Not quite so biddable a year or so ago, though,' Calumn reminded her caustically.

'That's true.' She had been angry, but now she was glad, for if he had not run off, she would not have met Calumn. Wisely, she kept this thought to herself.

'Has it never occurred to you to wonder why he hasn't come home?'

'Of course it has. It's obvious something must have prevented him. He's been ill, or imprisoned or—or something of that nature,' she finished lamely. 'What is it? What are you thinking?'

'The most obvious thing—assuming he's not dead—is that he's found someone else.'

'But we are betrothed,' she said blankly.

'Madeleine, when I was in the army I saw it happen often,' Calumn said, taking her by the hand. The path on the lower slopes which wound through the forest to the loch was wide enough for them to walk side by side. 'Young men fall in love very easily.'

'But even if he did, he would not just forget all about me.' Though she had not thought of it before, now the idea had an awful appeal. Unfortunately, knowing Guillaume as well as she did, it had not the ring of authenticity.

'So, even if he has taken another woman, you won't mind,' Calumn persisted.

She searched inside herself for some emotion, but drew a blank. 'I've never thought about it,' she said, nonplussed by her own lack.

'If you loved him, you'd be able to answer that question straight away.'

'You mean I should be jealous.' She tried again, but still there was nothing. Wondering if she were immune, she thought fleetingly of Calumn with another, and struggled to conceal the resultant surge of something black and vengeful. Not immune. Furious with herself, she turned on Calumn. 'This is absurd. How can I be jealous when I don't even have any grounds to think that he has met someone?'

'It's absurd to think he hasn't, in all this time.'

'Well, if Guillaume has—has some experience, then he will not mind that I have too,' Madeleine said, clutching desperately at straws.

Calumn gazed at her in astonishment. 'Do you really think de Guise will want his wife to have been tutored by another man?'

'No, when you put it like that, but—what I mean is—well, *you* would not mind, would you?'

'You're quite mistaken. *If* I was ever inclined to take a woman to wife—which I never have been— but if I was, I'd want to know I was the first man and the last to make love to her.'

'So you would expect her to be faithful and true while you are not. That is so unfair!'

'On the contrary. If I was in love, that's exactly what I'd be. If I was in love, I would have no desire at all for another. That is what being in love is about. I believe I've pointed that out to you before.'

'Then in your eyes I am ruined.'

'Ah, but I've taken great care not to ruin you. De

Guise will never know, provided you are prepared to lie to him, which you obviously are.'

'What do you mean?'

'If you marry him, you will be living one big lie and you know it.'

She did, she thought wretchedly, she knew it very well, but why did he have to throw it so mercilessly in her face! She glared at him, struggling in vain for some reply which would put him down and answer his question without embroiling herself in subterfuge, but none came. 'Let's not argue, Calumn,' she said finally. 'Whatever has happened to keep Guillaume here, I know it is not another woman. He would not forget his promise to me. More importantly, he would never abandon La Roche.'

'More importantly? You think his home is more important than you are?'

'Well, yes, La Roche will still be there long after I am dead. Do not you think the same about Errin Mhor?'

Calumn frowned heavily. ''Tis what my father thinks. What I've been raised to think, that I should marry for the sake of the lands. I suppose I used to think that, too.'

'And now?' Madeleine prompted. They had reached the tree line by the loch. Wandering over to the water's edge, they sat down together on the sand. The surface was choppy from the light breeze which had blown up offshore.

'Now? No. I have lost the right to love Errin Mhor. And even had I not, I would not marry for the sake of the land. Such marriages as you contemplate provide cold comfort. The children they produce are valued only for their ability to inherit. If I married, I would want a wife who would love me, not my possessions. Soil and earth, no matter how richly cultivated, do not keep you warm at night. Bairns should be a blessing, not a bargaining tool or a weapon.'

His bleak tone pierced her heart. 'You sound as if you're speaking from bitter experience,' she said compassionately, putting a hand on his arm.

To her surprise he shook it off angrily. 'I am, but at least I've learned from it. Would that I could teach you the same lesson. You want me. I know you want me, yet still you carry blithely on with your plans to wed another man,' he said savagely.

'Calumn, I don't...'

He shook her hand away from his arm. 'Have you really thought about what that will mean, my sweet Madeleine? How it will be when you lie cold and unmoved beneath him, enduring his caresses for the sake of your precious heir. Will you remember how it was between us? How I make you feel? The places I can take you to? Will you regret that you and I did not do out of wanting what your husband must do to you out of duty?'

Her eyes were heavy with unshed tears. She knew he meant to hurt her, but she could not grasp why, for surely his stubborn need for her to admit he was right did not merit such a vicious attack. She had thought he cared for her in some way. Now, the way he was looking at her made her doubt that, too, on top of all her other doubts. The urge to confide in him fled. She could only stare at him wordlessly.

'What, have you no answer for me?' Calumn continued in a brutal tone which made her shiver. 'No, for though you'll tell yourself any number of lies, you know better than to attempt the same with me. The truth is, Madeleine, that every time you make love to your husband, you'll be wishing it was me. Even though you and I have not actually made love. Fool that I am, I thought I was doing the honourable thing. Perhaps I was wrong.'

She found her voice at this. 'What do you mean?'

'You want to. I want to. What's the point in my behaving so honourably, when you are thinking so dishonourably? It seems a shame to deny you such a sweet memory.'

The very idea of her with another man made the bile rise in his throat. At least this way he would leave his mark upon her. He would be her first. He would be the one she thought of. Always. The fierceness of the need to possess her took hold of him like a raging fever. He pulled her to him suddenly, holding her hard against him, locking her tight with hands that were demanding. 'What do you say, *ma chérie?*'

She was dazed. Lost. Hurt. And appallingly excited. Wanting gripped her so fiercely it squeezed the breath out of her. She clung to the only certainty left to her as a drowning sailor will cling at the wreckage of his ship. Her need for him. The rightness of that need. 'Yes,' she said huskily.

For seconds he stared at her, as if unwilling to believe what he had heard. Then he kissed her and she kissed him back, hard, passionately, furiously, as if her own temper had been tightly leashed and was now let go, and when he tried to pull away from her, she dug her nails into his arms to punish him for his cruel words. Possession. The need to possess. To take. And to give. Something unstoppable had started.

Passion lit higher and brighter, surging more violently than before. Hands and lips demanding, bodies responding more fiercely from knowing each other, more fiercely still from a deeper need as yet unsated. This was passion borne of need, need which must be satisfied, not pleasured. A hunger held them in its grip, so immense it was as if they had been fasting. A need which was a punishment too, for saying the unsayable, for forcing on the other a glimpse of the unseeable.

Clothes tugged and ripped and pushed hastily aside. Kisses, starving kisses, hands clawing and bruising, touches on the edge of pain but not felt enough. Nothing would be enough except that most intimate touch. That most intimate plundering. That most intimate possession. Nothing would be enough until they were melded, welded together, seared and burned together, spent together.

Her lips were bruised from kissing, but still she clung, desperate for more. She lay beneath him now on the sand, her skirts around her waist, his hand cupped around the heat and wet between her thighs, and she pushed shamelessly against him, moaning, saying his name over and over again. Her hand reached for him, hard, hot, pulsing in her grip, and she heard him moan too, heard him say her name. He inched her legs apart so that she was embracing him with her knees. She arched up against him. She could feel him nudging between her thighs, so close, the tip of him touching her. She dug her nails into his back. He gripped her bottom, tilting her up for him and she held her breath, for it seemed that she had been waiting for this moment since she was born.

And she waited. But it did not happen.

'No!' Calumn let her go. He sat up, pulled her skirts around her legs, his eyes closed as if he was in pain, and in truth he was in agony. He got to his feet and pulled her with him. 'Not like this. I won't take you like this.'

Madeleine shook her head as if the motion would clear it of the whirling from the force of their passion. 'Why not?' she asked baldly, already raw with the pain of his rejection.

He looked like a devil, standing before her, his body glistening with sweat, his eyes glittering dark with something fierce. Something which made her recoil. The look he threw her was like a flaying. 'My honour is all that I have left to me. I won't allow you to strip me of it, nor will I permit you to use me as your excuse. You are a very, very desirable woman,

Madeleine Lafayette, but I won't take you. Not on these terms.'

Not flayed, stripped bare to the flesh and bone. And not by Calumn, but by the truth. The extent of her own dishonourable behaviour shocked her. She stood rooted to the spot for a moment, staring at him, then instead of righting her clothes suddenly pulled them all off, discarding them in a frenzy, leaving them in a muddle on the damp sand, angrily slapping at Calumn when he tried to prevent her, pushing him away from her when he tried to hold her back, set only on escape and release as she had always sought it before. Naked and furious she plunged into the icy-cold waters of the loch.

She did not hear him call her name. She did not see how he waded in after her, stopping short, thigh deep, on the steeply shelving bank, his eyes searching anxiously for her. She swam under water, emerging some distance from the shore, her hair streaming behind her, arms and legs synchronising to power her out, away, beyond his reach, beyond her own thoughts, letting the cold and the resistance of the current, and the slap of the waves and the soothing action of each stroke of her arms and paddle of her legs use up all her energy.

Only when she felt her breath come sharply, her limbs become heavy, did she turn back, clambering out over the jagged rocks to the sandy shore where Calumn was waiting anxiously to wrap her in the comfort of his *filleadh mòr,* rubbing her dry, blowing heat into her fingertips and toes with his mouth, seating her, silent and shivering, in the mouth of the cave while he lit the fire and prepared a meal. She ate silently. She wanted to cry, but she felt she did not deserve to feel sorry for herself. And she was afraid that if she did she would not be able to stop.

As the moon rose in the velvet black of the sky, they lay by the fire wrapped in their separate plaids listening to the lap of the water, the contented whickering from the horses, the rustling in the nearby woods of the various night creatures. Each in their own way shocked by the force of their feelings, they had not spoken, save for common courtesies, since she had returned from her swim.

Madeleine lay motionless, aching for the feel of Calumn's arms around her, knowing she had not the right to ask, for the terms of their relationship had altered fundamentally. If only she could turn back the clock. But to do so would be to lose the best part. What she really wanted to do was to obliterate the past. To have been able to step on to Scottish soil unencumbered. To wipe the slate of her life clean and start afresh. If only she could. Instead, she must face a bleak future indeed. Now tears did fall, silent and painful, like pinpricks.

'Come here.' A comforting arm around her shoulders pulled her close. Warm fingers stroked her hair. Words, strange words in a beautiful language were whispered in her ear. She asked what they meant, but Calumn only hushed her and told her to sleep.

'I can't.' She felt as if she would never sleep again.

As if she should not. For to sleep was to dream. She did not want to dream.

'When I was a child,' Calumn said, 'a bairn really, about two or three years old, my mother used to tell me the fairies would take me away in the night if I didn't go to sleep. Wicked things, fairies. You'd be amazed the lengths you have to go to just to keep them at bay.'

His voice was warm and crooning with a hint of irony. He spoke to her like a child, and like a child she was soothed by his presence and his tone. 'What sorts of things?' she asked.

'When a bairn is born all the mirrors in the house must be covered lest his image is taken by the fairies. They've a terrible appetite for bairns, the little creatures have—we call them kelpies. 'Tis thought if they are not kept away from the birth by a cross of rowan, they will steal the child and substitute a changeling of their own. Salt, or earth in the bairn's mouth as soon as he has had his first cry, and the father's dirk in his cradle, will ward them off.'

Madeleine snuggled closer. 'Poor fairies; in Breton folklore they get a very bad name, too. *Les Dames Blanches* are particularly evil. There is one, Melusine, who disguises herself as a woman, but every week, on a Saturday, she has to take her real form as a sea serpent.'

'We have that legend, too. A selkie is a seal who takes a woman's form. Old Shona MacBrayne, the local fey wife, was always full of tales of selkies.'

'What's a fey wife?'

'In the village some call her a witch—and I'm sorry to say, so does my mother. A woman who knows about healing, herbs and potions. The old ways. One of the cunning folk who can talk to the fairies, maybe even cast spells. When I was wee it used to be a great game, chapping on her door and running away.'

Madeleine gave a watery chuckle. 'The further north we travel, the more you sound Scottish. It's lovely, but I have to work very hard to understand the words. I wish I spoke your Gaelic. It sounds like Breton—do you want to hear some?'

'Go on then, lass,' Calumn said. She could feel the smile in his voice like a warm posset.

She thought for a moment, then recited something. 'It means, wait for the night before saying that the day was beautiful.'

'It's night now.'

'Yes.' She realised he was waiting for an answer. 'I wish the day had not been quite so beautiful.'

The sweetness of her answer was painful. 'Go to sleep, Madeleine.'

'I can't sleep.' But she was yawning.

'Hush. Just try,' Calumn said, pressing a kiss to her brow. 'Hush now,' he said, stroking her hair. And Madeleine slept.

As the night sky thickened and the moon made its ghostly way across the heavens, Calumn lay awake, cradling Madeleine in his arms. Tomorrow they would reach Castle Rhubodach, and he must hand her over to her fate. He did not want to let her go. Not to de Guise. Not to anyone.

She was his. He felt it like he felt the call of Errin Mhor when they were on top of the mountain today. Madness, for what did he have to offer anyone? These last few days, he had come close to a happiness which he had not thought possible. When she was gone, he knew he would be lonely. She had awoken such longings in him, had been the instrument of his homecoming. She could very well prove the instrument of his downfall, if he were not careful. Or perhaps his saving grace?

She stirred in her sleep and he pulled her closer, tenderly tucking the plaid under her chin. Frustration, that's all it was, this possessiveness. Frustration, and of his own making, too, for she had been as intent on giving as he had been on taking. A noble frustration then, he thought, mocking himself. Calumn fell into a troubled slumber.

Chapter Six

'Traitor.'

Madeleine's eyes snapped open.

'Traitor,' Calumn mumbled. He was dreaming. A nightmare, by the sounds of it. He had pushed her away, was lying in his shirt, sweating and tossing his head from side to side.

'Calumn,' she said gently, shaking his shoulder. 'Calumn,' this time more firmly.

He started, sat up, gazed unseeing at her. 'Rory?'

'It's Madeleine.'

'Madeleine.' His eyes were blank. 'I've a terrible drouth.'

'Drouth?'

'Thirst. I'm thirsty.'

She scrabbled for the pewter drinking cup and filled it quickly from one of the many burns which fed the loch. He drank deeply from it, then opened his eyes properly, focusing his gaze on her.

'I woke you. I'm sorry.'

'You were dreaming. Do you want to talk about it?' She pulled the plaid back over them both, stroking his hair, damp with sweat, from his temple.

He stared at her in the half-light, still dazed from the horror of his dream. 'No.' His denial was instinctive.

Madeleine ignored it. 'Is it linked to your scar?' she asked, laying her hand fleetingly on his stomach. 'I know you were in the army. Did you get this in battle?'

'Culloden,' he said, the word harsh and clear in the night air. She had the right to know. He wanted her to know, he saw that now, stripped of his defences by the ferocity of the dream. He wanted there to be some truth between them.

Madeleine inhaled sharply. 'You fought at Culloden? Against the Jacobites? *Mon dieu.*'

'I took a blow from a claymore. I was lucky not to die, they told me. I sometimes wish I had.'

'Don't say that!' She wrapped her arms tight around his waist, placing her cheek on his shirt where the question mark of his scar was, feeling the heat of his skin through the soft material. She held him thus, comforting him like a child, her own mind racing. It dawned on her almost immediately. She sat back so that she could look at his face. 'You

fought opposite Guillaume. That's why you didn't tell me. You thought I would hate you for it.'

'Don't you?' His voice seemed drained of emotion. He spoke as if he were far away, behind a barrier she could not breach.

'Of course I don't.' She shook him by the shoulder in an effort to penetrate the wall he seemed to have erected around himself. 'Calumn, I could never hate you, please don't think that. Even if by some monstrous co-incidence Guillaume had died at your hand, it would not be your fault. He chose to be there.' She made no attempt to disguise the bitterness in her voice, nor her long pent-up anger at Guillaume, which she had never until now acknowledged. 'It was his choice, his decision to leave me and La Roche to fight for that—that popinjay prince.'

Calumn was forced to smile. 'Don't go speaking about Bonnie Prince Charlie in that tone when we get to Castle Rhubodach, it'll not find favour.'

'Anyway, it's not really about Guillaume, is it?'

Calumn's smile faded.

'It's because you fought against your own people that you stay in Edinburgh—that's why you've given up what you call the right to call yourself a Highlander, isn't it?'

'Aye. Partly. Maybe.' Calumn dropped his head into his hands. 'You don't understand.'

'Then tell me. Make me understand, Calumn,' Madeleine said earnestly. 'Please. Tell me what it is, this black thing you carry around inside here.'

She laid a hand gently on his scar. 'I really want to know.'

Though the habit of silence was a strong one to break, the temptation to unburden himself was immense. He wanted her to know. To be his confessor and his judge. For some reason, he trusted her, as he trusted no one else, to do both wisely.

'Tell me about the dream, Calumn,' Madeleine prompted. 'Do you have it often?'

'Too often.'

'And whisky helps keep it away.'

'It does, if I take enough of it.' He frowned, trying to clear his head. 'Are you sure you want to hear this?'

She nodded. Her face was alabaster white in the moonlight, her mouth set in a determined line, her eyes gazing unwaveringly into his own. She gripped his hand tight and he told her it all, finally let it all come pouring out of him like poison from a wound. The battle. The noise. The smells. The driving rain and sleet. The boggy moor. The terrible fear that when the word came to advance he would not be able to, that his men would think him a coward. And when he did advance, the worse fear of killing his own kin.

'I felt as if I was being split in two,' Calumn said, his voice raw. 'My men relied on me. In battle, especially when you're in the middle of battle, you have to trust absolutely that your comrades are on your side. Always, until that point, I had been, without question, but never until that point had I been asked to fight with my own against my own. It was like attacking myself.'

He broke off to stare into the distance. Beside him, Madeleine sat listening intently, moved by the raw emotions she could see flitting like lost souls over the sculpted planes of his face.

'I didn't have a choice,' Calumn continued bleakly, 'but I still had to choose. Join the Jacobites? But I didn't believe in their cause. Desert? I thought about that, but it was just opting out. I chose to fight, to fight with the regiment that was my life, to save the Highlands from the consequences of the Young Pretender's grasping self-interest. He didn't care about Scotland, all he cared about was the crown. He didn't care either that he was splitting his own country asunder in trying to take it. So I faced my own people across the battle lines while I stood side by side with my own men. I shouldn't have had to choose. If it wasn't for that bastard Charles Edward, I wouldn't have had to. If it wasn't for him, none of us would have had to. Do you see now why I hate him?'

Madeleine pressed his hand. 'Yes, I do see. And Rory? Who is Rory?' she asked gently.

'Rory is my brother.'

'Your brother! *Mon dieu,* you mean he was there, on the Jacobite side?' The full horror of his predicament hit her. 'You faced your brother in battle?'

'My half-brother, and any number of his kin, who are some part my kinfolk.'

'I can't imagine, I can't even begin to imagine—no wonder it haunts you.'

'I saw him, or thought I saw him, just before I was wounded. In my dream, that's when I always wake up.'

'Is he—did he die?'

'I thought he was dead. For six long months I thought he was, and our mother was certain of it. But, no, thanks be to God, Rory is alive.'

'That's why you understood about Guillaume straight away. I knew you did, I felt it.'

'When Rory didn't come home they all assumed he'd died on the battlefield. Of the few of his men who survived, some said he'd been wounded, others that he'd been taken prisoner. You have to understand, a battle like that, it was chaos—and a rout, for the Jacobites were vastly outnumbered.'

'But when it was over, if your brother had been one of the dead, surely his body would have been identified?'

'This was no ordinary battle. The Duke of Cumberland, our Commander in Chief, is a vicious man. He wanted to punish the Highlanders for putting him to the inconvenience of having to fight,' Calumn said bitterly. 'He's a brilliant military strategist, but he's also an arrogant, cruel sadist. After the battle, he ordered that the Jacobites be shown no quarter.'

She hardly dared ask, 'What does that mean?'

'Cumberland ordered his men—my men—to—to make sure no one was left alive. He had them murdered, the wounded and dying. Bayoneted. And not just the Jacobites, but their women and some children too, who had come on to the moor to tend to them. All of them were killed. Can you imagine it? As I was lying face down in the bog, clutching my stomach to prevent its contents from spilling out, I heard them. The screams and the cries, the calls for mercy. And I saw them, too, when they finally carried me off on a stretcher, women throwing themselves on top of their men to save them, the look of bloodlust on the faces of the Redcoats, and of disgust on a few. Too few. So you see it was possible, more than possible, that if Rory had been wounded he would have been killed.'

'But he hadn't?'

'No. And though my mother would have it that he had, I refused to believe that. He's a tall man, as tall as me, and we've the same hair, which makes us stand out a bit. On top of that, he's the laird. His clothes, his belt and his weapons would have proclaimed his status. As soon as I could leave my sick bed, I went to the isle of Heronsay where he has his lands, and I waited.'

'What happened?'

'He'd been taken prisoner by the Campbells. Rory is a Macleod, not a Munro. His father died when he was just a bairn, and my mother remarried within six months. Not wanting a Macleod cuckoo in his nest, my own father made her leave Rory on Heronsay. I didn't even know of his existence until I was ten. Anyway, after Culloden, the Campbells took the opportunity to punish him for an old grudge against

a long-dead Macleod relative. Rory escaped from
their dungeons and made his way home eventually.
He brought a lowlander with him, he'd taken her
hostage—so they claim, the two of them. Jessica,
her name is, and she's a very pretty piece. So pretty
Rory wouldn't let her go. They're married now, it's
a very romantic tale.'

'And you were there on—what did you call it—
Heronsay?—when he arrived?'

'Aye. I couldn't believe it. Nor could he, mind, he
thought *I* was dead. 'Twas quite a touching reunion.'
His tone was light, but she knew by the strength of
his grip on her hand that his feelings ran deep.

'So it was a happy ending, then?'

Calumn shook his head despondently. 'We're
brothers, but we fought on opposite sides. Rory lost
many good men in the Rebellion, and some of the
clans who are my neighbours lost many more. I survived because my wounds were tended. Had I been
on the other side, I would have been slaughtered
where I fell. Do you not see? I have that blood on
my hands, the blood of my fellow Highlanders, as if
I had carried out Cumberland's orders myself—as I
might have done, had I not been wounded.'

'I don't believe you would have. You said you
fired into the air,' Madeleine said fiercely, 'you
would not have done anything so barbaric, under
orders or not.'

'Maybe not, but the habit of obedience is strong.'

'The habit of knowing what is right and what is
wrong is stronger. You would not have done such a

thing, Calumn.' A couple of deep breaths, and she was a little calmer, though anger at the perpetrators of the atrocities, also the source of Calumn's pain, bubbled furiously inside her. 'You were not the only Highlander under Cumberland's command, were you? There were other Scots who fought against the Jacobites.'

'A good few. 'Tis the Sassenach press who chose to portray it as the English against the Scots, but the truth is that a deal of the clans were agin' the Stuarts.'

'Including the Munroes?'

'Aye. Though my father's reasons are more to do with protecting his own rather than protecting the Crown. The Highland lairds were a rule unto themselves and my father wanted it to stay that way. He didn't want Charlie stirring things up.' Calumn laughed bitterly. 'As it turns out, with the English wreaking their revenge for the Rebellion, the old ways are done for anyway. Though we fought on the same side, myself and my father's men, he does not see it so. I chose my regiment over him, is how he views it. Another grudge he bears against me.'

'And Rory? Does he still bear a grudge against you?'

'He says not, but the truth is I haven't seen him since he returned to Heronsay. I left the Highlands then. Do you see now, Madeleine? I betrayed the army in failing to fight. I betrayed my kin by trying. Maybe I even betrayed my father, who sent me off for a Redcoat in the first place all those years ago—I don't know. He wanted me to lead the clan, you see, but I chose to lead my own men instead. I tried to do my duty, and in trying I was torn in two. I have not the right to be here. I have not the right to call myself a captain, nor the right to call myself a Highlander, and I have no right to the lands which I've always thought one day would be mine. I should not be here. Do you see?'

'I see now how you have come to think all this. I don't believe you are right, though,' Madeleine replied.

Calumn smiled wearily. 'That's progress, at any rate.'

'You should try to sleep now.' She felt heartsore at the tale he had unfolded, but she felt too that she was beginning to understand him. 'Thank you for telling me.' She kissed his cheek. 'I can't imagine the horror of what you've been through, but I do know, what I already knew, that you're a very brave and a truly honourable man. I knew it from the moment I met you, and what you have told me tonight has made me quite certain. For if you were not,' she said, preventing him speaking by putting her fingers over his mouth, 'if you were not honourable, you would not feel guilt, and you would not have these nightmares. Do you think the real perpetrators of this mess, this Duke of Cumberland and Charles Edward Stuart, do you think they have nightmares? No, I think I can safely bet that they sleep easy in their beds. It is because you are such a good man that you suffer, do you not see that?'

The black creature on his shoulders shifted its weight. Though it still perched there, he could feel it spreading its wings as if it might take flight one day. Calumn's teeth glinted in the grey light as he smiled. 'You make a good case, lass. I'll think on it.'

She laughed. 'Lasssss. I like the way you say it.'

'Coorie in then, lass,' Calumn said sleepily, pulling her close. 'We've a long day ahead of us.'

When he awoke a few hours later, Madeleine was already up and had caught a trout for their breakfast, having fashioned a line with a hook made from a sharpened hairpin. The appetising smell of it cooking over the fire, with the last of the bannocks toasting beside it, wafted over to him on the morning air. In response to Calumn's frankly incredulous stare, Madeleine gave her Gallic shrug. 'I told you, my mother's family were fishermen. I don't know about you, but I'm ravenous.' Calumn needed no second bidding.

As they set out after breakfast on the steeply rising path at the head of Loch Awe which would take them through the next glen, a soft mizzle of fine rain began to fall. The day was overcast, in line with Madeleine's mood, the sky a uniform leaden grey, the waters of the loch white-crested and choppy.

In the soft light of dawn, as she sat on the edge of the loch with her hand-fashioned fishing hook, Madeleine had looked her future squarely in the eye. She could not marry Guillaume. She knew now, without a doubt, that she did not love him, nor would come to love him in any way other than as a friend. To marry him would be to deprive them both of the potential for happiness in the future, for even if Guillaume did love her, a marriage based on anything less than equal affection would undoubtedly be the road to misery.

Calumn was right. Though the pain her decision would cause squeezed her heart, she knew she must be brave enough to make it. She could not live a lie. She should be grateful to have found out in time that that is what she would be doing. But still, the dread of causing hurt made her flinch from the task, keeping her silent on this, the last leg of their journey.

She pulled her *arisaidh* over her head, draping its folds to conceal her face. As they rose higher, a patchy mist enveloped them. Above, mountain summits rose out of the grey like the mystical peaks in a fairy tale. Ahead, the forest on the lower slopes of the hills faded as the mist swirled eerily. Not a sound could be heard save the snorting of the horses, the soft clump and scrabble of their hooves on the scree which formed the path, the trickle of a burn somewhere to the right, and the soft plop, plop, plop, of rain drops dripping from the gorse onto the fern and bracken below.

She would tell Calumn, but only once she had seen Guillaume. To Guillaume she owed her first duty, and so he should be first to hear the news. Then Calumn. And then—but here, her mind skittered to a halt. She was afraid. Of the confrontation with her father which must ensue, but afraid, too, to probe further into her feelings. To hope, when most likely it would be in vain. To face this one, final thing, which was perhaps at the root of all. For now, she had enough to worry about.

Moisture dripped from her lashes and from the stray locks of hair which had escaped the cover of her plaid. The landscape, what she could see of it, took on a dreamlike quality, looming up suddenly as a patch of mist cleared, disappearing just as suddenly when the next one formed, so that she very quickly had no sense of time or distance, and would have felt horribly lost if it had not been for Calumn's reassuring presence just in front of her.

'Is it often like this?' she asked, when he paused to wait for her at a fork in the track.

'Up here, more often than not. It can swoop in on you without warning, like an eagle on its prey and just as dangerous. Are you soaked through?'

'I don't mind that. In Brittany it rains and rains and rains in the winter. Not soft like this, more of a deluge.'

'You get that here, too, and not only in the winter.'

'It's stunning, though, isn't it, even if it does feel as if we're the only people on earth.' Altitude had reduced the temperature significantly. When she spoke, her breath formed little puffs of air.

'We're actually not far from Castle Rhubodach. If the mist clears, you'll be able to see it from the top of this next rise.'

Sure enough, when they breasted the hill, emerging out into clearing skies from the narrow glen, they saw it. A tall, stern square building of some three storeys built in grey stone, with a steeply sloping roof and a turret at one corner. Four small lochans surrounded it, acting as a natural defence.

'They're called the four sisters,' Calumn told her. 'Aileen, Catriona, Johanna and Fiona. Named for ancestors of McAngus, whom legend has it squabbled so much that when they died they were interred, one in each lochan to keep them apart.'

'I wish I had a sister. Just one would have been nice.'

'Ailsa, my own sister, is much younger than me. She was a bit of a surprise for my mother, I suspect.'

'But it must be nice for her to have a daughter.'

'Sons are what are important to my parents.'

'Some things are the same the world over, then,' Madeleine said wryly.

On the flat land by the longest of the sister lochs, Catriona, she could make out signs of cultivation, ploughed fields and some crops, though the fields were much smaller than she was used to at home, more like strips of land forming a small patchwork. The demesne of the castle was marked by a low wall, and a small cluster of cottages was strung out from the gates along the banks of the loch. She could see the moving black dots which were the villagers, almost the first they had come across since leaving Aberfoyle. Smoke wisped lazily into the air from the chimneys of the castle and the roofs of the cottages.

A mournful lowing came to them through the mist, making Madeleine jump.

'It's only cattle,' Calumn told her, pointing down the track.

There were about ten of the beasts ascending the path accompanied by a drover, but they looked like no cattle Madeleine had ever seen, being small, with long shaggy brown coats and extravagant horns. She stared in amazement. 'They have fur,' she said, wondering if he was teasing her and they were not cows at all.

'They need it to get through the winter up here.' Calumn nodded to the drover, exchanging a few words in Gaelic with him. Madeleine listened to the lilting cadence of their voices, marvelling at the beauty of the conversation, which was like a song. The drover was a small lean man, dwarfed by Calumn's height and breadth, dressed in the *filleadh mòr* and *filleadh beg,* though the wool was threadbare, the colours faded, and he had no jacket. On his head he wore a brown bonnet rather like the beret worn by Breton farmers. Madeleine smiled at him and he doffed his hat, but said not a word to her.

'You're expected, apparently,' Calumn said. 'Lady Drummond seems able to maintain an effective network of spies, even from the dungeons of Edinburgh Castle.' As they started the descent to the castle, the horses skittered and slid on the treacherously wet rocks. 'Angus McAngus is a staunch Jacobite who lost a son at Prestonpans. He and Lord Drummond are old allies.'

She could see the people more clearly now, working the fields, men and women together, the men in plaids, some in trews and shirtsleeves, the women wearing long black skirts and aprons, their heads covered with a kind of handkerchief.

'A kertch,' Calumn said in response to her question. 'It shows they're married.'

A short distance from the hamlet, Madeleine reined in her horse. There was something wrong with the picture of rustic simplicity, but she could not at first work out what it was. Then she noticed that several of the cottages had no roof, standing open to the weather with their rafters blackened. 'Look, there's been a fire.'

In the far field a man was ploughing, sweating as he pushed the blade through the stony soil. 'Why is he doing that himself?' she asked Calumn. 'Have they no mule or horses? And the men, they are all old. Where are the young men?'

Calumn's face was as stony as the soil which was being planted. 'Retribution,' he said bleakly. 'Another of Cumberland's ideas. He ordered that Jacobite lands be forfeited or razed to the ground as punishment for the Rebellion. After Culloden he sent the army to rape and pillage their way through the Highlands. Murder and wholesale destruction—done by men I'd served with. This village has obviously been burnt out, see where the thatch on the roofs is new? There are no young men because they've all been taken—prisoners for deportation if they were lucky, but many, one in ten I heard, were executed. There will be a generation of Highland women now with no men. A generation of bairns with no fathers.'

'I had no idea.'

'They praised him for it in the newspapers, for subduing the wild Gaels. Cumberland is a hero in the lowlands, but here he's known as the Butcher, and you can see why. This is his legacy. My legacy, for I was part of it, part of the army which did his bidding.'

'But you had no part in this.' The set of his face worried her. He was retreating to a distant land where soon he would be beyond reach. 'Calumn, you can't take responsibility for this, any more than you can take responsibility for the Rebellion.'

'I can't take responsibility for you any more either.'

'What do you mean?'

Calumn's expression was grim and set, like an obelisk. 'This is where I must say goodbye. You knew that, it's what we agreed.'

Panic rose in her throat. It was too soon. Too sudden. This was not how she had imagined it. 'I thought you would come with me. I thought—we have so much—you can't go now!' She pulled her horse alongside his to clutch at his sleeve. 'We've come this far together. There are still things between us which need to be said. Please, Calumn.'

'Come on, Madeleine, you can't have it all ways,' Calumn said, made brutal by his determination to leave, his equal determination no longer to interfere. His overwhelming, completely contrary desire to stay, to shake her into submission, to ride off with her over his saddle. To do, and no longer to think. 'Surely you're looking forward to what lies ahead? The touching reunion with your sainted Guillaume, the equally touching reconciliation with your dear papa, marriage and happy ever after. What can I possibly add to all that?'

'It's not like that. It won't be like that, you know that. Calumn I—I can't—please,' she said desperately, 'please don't go. Not yet.'

'Madeleine, Angus McAngus will not welcome the likes of me into his home, and I don't blame him.'

Immediately, she was overcome with remorse. 'I'm sorry. I did not think. I would not expose you to the possibility of—indeed, I am sorry. It was wrong of me to ask.'

That she had taken his cruel jibes on the chin made him feel much worse than if she had cast them up at him. Now her contrition rubbed salt into the self-inflicted wound. He did not want to leave her. Surely facing up to the likes of Angus McAngus was exactly what he had come here to do?

Calumn's pride, a long-subdued animal, stirred in the depths of its cave. He was a Munro, after all. 'I'll come with you,' he said abruptly. 'But mind, it is for McAngus to say whether he will take me in or no.'

The immensity of her relief showed plainly on her face. 'Are you sure? I would not want to make you do anything you don't want to.'

Calumn laughed. 'Since when have you ever done that! I'm sure. Come.'

Calumn nudged his horse into a walk. Riding side by side, he and Madeleine went past the half-recovered village, through the wrought-iron gates in which the crest of the McAngus clan was worked, and up to the heavy, studded front door of Castle Rhubodach. It had not seemed to occur to Madeleine that de Guise might be waiting for her behind it. Now it occurred to him, he hoped he was wrong.

Angus McAngus was waiting to greet them— alone. He was another short, lean Gael, with a sparse head of hair which must once have been fiery red, but was now streaked with grey and faded to the colour of autumn leaves. The Scots were obviously a compact race, rather like the Bretons, Madeleine thought. McAngus was dressed in a plaid with a jacket, the material woven in shades of blue. His eyes were a faded blue of the same colour, though they peered at her brightly enough, and his smile, through his straggly beard, was welcoming.

'Mademoiselle Lafayette, *bien venue,*' he said in softly accented French, bowing and taking her hand in his bony one. 'Lady Drummond sent me word to expect you.'

'Monsieur McAngus,' Madeleine replied with a curtsy, 'it's an honour, and you speak very good French.'

McAngus chuckled at that. 'Better French than English, my dear. The auld alliance, as we call the friendship between our two countries, goes back long before the recent Rebellion.' He turned his attention to Calumn. 'And who is your escort? You have not the look of a hired guide, if you'll forgive my plain speaking, sir.'

'This is…'

'Calumn Munro of Errin Mhor,' Calumn interrupted her, bowing formally.

McAngus's expression broke into a broad smile. 'Ah! You must be Rory McLeod's brother. You're the living spit of your mother, boy, I see that, now I look at you. No mistaking that hair of yours. Aye, I remember now who you are. I've no seen you since you were a wee laddie, but I know your brother well. I've met that Sassenach wife of his, too. She's had a bairn, did you know?'

Calumn looked surprised. 'No, no I didn't.'

'A wee lassie, I heard, so you're an uncle now. Well, come away in the both of you, you must be hungry.'

'Sir,' Calumn said, remaining on the doorstep, 'you must know that I—before I can accept your hospitality, you must know that I served under Cumberland in the late Rebellion.'

He spoke with barely a falter, but Madeleine could see, from the way he held himself, the way he met the laird's eye not fearlessly but steadily, what the words cost him. He had not apologized; she was glad he had not, for she could not imagine him being abject. She had not seen much evidence of his pride, but it struck her now that pride in his lineage was—or had been—an integral part of him. How it must hurt him to feel it so damaged. She held her breath as she watched McAngus's smile fade, ready to leap to Calumn's defence if necessary, though she knew he would not appreciate it, for he was a man who must fight his own battles.

'I remember now, your father sent you off to be a Redcoat.'

'A fusilier. I was a captain.'

'Aye. So, you fought against us, did you? You're not going to tell me you had a hand in the Butcher's atrocities afterwards?'

Calumn's face registered disgust. 'I was badly wounded in battle. I left the army as soon as I recovered.'

'No need to get your dander up, you can't blame me for asking. Where did you see action, lad?'

'Culloden.'

'I lost a son at Prestonpans. Andrew, my youngest.'

'I heard that.'

'You must have lost a fair few comrades yourself. And now I mind it, that brother of yours, was he not given up for dead, too?'

'He was.'

McAngus turned to Madeleine. 'It's coming back to me now. 'Twas the talk for miles around when it happened. First they thought this one was killed on the battlefield, then he turned up like the walking dead, and they thought that Rory was done for. Did he tell you, lass, how he kept vigil for his brother?

Saved Heronsay from the Butcher, too, didn't you, boy?'

'No, he didn't think to mention that,' Madeleine said, looking up at Calumn with awe.

'Too modest, eh, lad?'

Calumn looked embarrassed, and shrugged dismissively. 'I see you have not been so lucky,' he said, indicating the husks of the damaged cottages.

McAngus looked grim. 'Aye, they were determined to make us pay, one way or the other. The Prince has a lot to answer for, if you ask me. Though I was for him myself, I can't help but wish now that he'd stayed put in France and saved us all a lot of heartache.' The old man shook his head sadly.

'Well,' McAngus continued after a moment's silence, 'it's all water under the bridge now as far as I'm concerned. What's important is that we Highlanders stick together, eh? They're out to destroy us, the English, they've been waiting a long time to take away the power of the clans. We did them a favour, rising with the Prince, gave them the opportunity they've been waiting for to come up here and wreak havoc. Come away in now, I don't know what we're doing still standing here on the doorstep. *Fàilte,* welcome to you, Calumn Munro, and you, *mademoiselle.* Come away in.'

He extended his hand, and Calumn took it in a strong two-handed grasp. 'I'm honoured,' he said gruffly, 'truly honoured.'

Looking down, Calumn was dazzled by the smile which lit up Madeleine's face. He had been aware of her, tense and silent, by his side, as he spoke to McAngus. Her obvious delight in his reception touched his heart. He smiled back unaffectedly. It was a strange feeling, to have one so determinedly in his corner. He liked it. Happiness burst on him like the sun coming out. Though it lasted only until he remembered why he was here. What lay ahead.

The great hall, which took up most of the ground floor of the castle, was a huge vaulted affair, with an immense stone fireplace on one wall in which a small wood fire was burning sluggishly, billowing smoke and emitting only the faintest trace of heat. A curved stone staircase decorated with gargoyles led to the upper storeys, and a small studded door on the right to the turret. The furnishings were all over-sized, made of ancient black oak, ornately carved. Shabby rugs were strewn randomly over the uneven stone slabs, and a worn standard hung above the fire-place.

Two deerhounds rose from their place next to the fire to greet the visitors, their long shaggy tails waving in a stately manner, their soft silky snouts snuffling at Madeleine's hands as she petted them. They were so tall their heads were on a level with her waist. 'We have dogs like these in Brittany,' she told McAngus. 'We use them for hunting.'

'They've the same use here. We've a stag hunt planned for tomorrow, so you'll see them in action then, if you want to join us.'

'What about de Guise?' Calumn asked.

The laird was tugging a bell pull at the side of the

mantel. 'He's expected any day now. No one knows when for sure, he's a man who likes to keep his own counsel. For very good reasons.'

'What do you mean?' Madeleine asked curiously.

'Well, his behaviour doesn't exactly endear him to the authorities,' McAngus said with a chuckle, 'though it's made him popular enough with some.'

'His behaviour? What has Guillaume done?'

'Do you not know? Lord bless us, lass, I thought Lady Drummond would have tell't you. He's a bit of a hero in these parts, your Guillaume. Like Robin Hood in the old English stories—only a mite more bloodthirsty.'

'Bloodthirsty! Are you sure we're talking about the same man?'

'Och aye, it's not likely there's two of them. He and a band of Jacobites are out to extract their revenge on the Butcher. Most of the troops are gone now, of course, but while they were here, yon de Guise led them a merry dance, and killed a fair few. Now, they pick on lands belonging to those who were against the Prince. Your father's lands, Calumn Munro, amongst others. Crops ruined. Houses burned.'

Calumn swore heavily in Gaelic. 'My mother mentioned it in one of her letters. She knew it was vengeance, my father made no secret of his beliefs, but she made no mention of de Guise. The bastard, does he not realise it is the poor who suffer cold and hunger because of what he does? The likes of my father are not so easily hurt.'

'Aye, you're in the right of it there. There's still some who think de Guise does a necessary job, but there's more, like myself, who think the time's come to call a halt.'

Madeleine sat down heavily on a large carved wooden chair, so big that her feet did not touch the ground. She was aghast. 'I can't believe what I'm hearing. Guillaume must have changed beyond recognition if he is committing such crimes. Perhaps the fighting has deranged his mind.'

'Madeleine, he sounds like a dangerous man. You'll not be going near him without me, do you hear?' Calumn said in a voice that would brook no argument.

'Guillaume would never hurt me.'

'You said yourself, he's changed.'

'But—but he can't have changed that much. Once he sees me...'

'You'll not see him alone, am I understood?'

'I've told you before, I don't take orders from you,' Madeleine snapped, confusion and weariness making her temper ragged.

'On the contrary. You will recall that that is exactly what you agreed to when I offered you my escort. You will do as I tell you.'

'Best that way,' McAngus intervened hurriedly. 'I don't want a pretty wee thing like you coming to any harm while you're under my roof.'

Madeleine's smile was wan. 'You are very kind to be so concerned, but it's not necessary.'

The timely arrival of a manservant put an end to

further dispute. He showed them up the steep stairs to their rooms. Calumn did not seem to notice she had not given her promise.

The bedrooms of the castle were icy cold. Madeleine shivered as she washed in the freezing water poured from a pretty china jug on the nightstand. McAngus had obviously fallen on hard times. Equally obvious to her, from the amount of cobwebs which hung from the rafters to the bed hangings, was that his lady wife was dead, and had not been replaced by any sort of housekeeper.

She leaned out of the leaded window of her room. On the second floor, it had a view out over the glassy water of Loch Catriona to the mountains beyond. That way, directly north through that valley she could see, then directly west from there, was the isle of Heronsay. And near there, another day's journey, were the lands of Errin Mhor. Calumn's lands.

Somewhere out there, too, perhaps watching the castle right now, was Guillaume. Since her host's revelations, it was harder than ever to conjure up the image of him in her mind. He sounded so changed, not at all like the gentle—in fact, she had to admit—rather submissive man she knew. But then war did terrible things to men. Look at the way it had affected Calumn.

Calumn. Every way she turned her mind, it always twisted back to him. He it had been who had upended all her beliefs, all her plans. Until she met him, she had never questioned the simple premise upon which she had built her life—that in making the people she loved happy, she would be happy herself. She knew now that this was not true. Knew, too, that she had never known real happiness, which came from being true to something in herself. Something which Calumn had awakened. Something she could never, ever regret having come to know, no matter what the consequences.

Love.

Love. She was in love with Calumn Munro, and this simple, wonderful, amazing, earth-shattering fact put everything else into the shade. She loved him. At his side, she had learned what happiness was. Through him, she had changed. Become stronger. A person willing to face up to truths, however awful. Or at least, that is what she aspired to.

She turned away from the window to pace nervously up and down the room. Willing to face up to them—yes—but not able to do so with anything less than extreme trepidation. Why did it have to be here, with their reunion imminent and no escaping it, that she finally faced the facts of the matter? Guillaume was a habit. Her love for him was a pale, poor thing compared to the overpowering, overwhelming, fiery creature which was her love for Calumn.

She took another turn around the room. The repercussions were like a quagmire. Guillaume, her father, home, her future—she seemed to have no solid foundations left, and with each question she asked herself, she sank more surely and more deeply into the boggy mess of her own stupid creation. For the one questions of utmost importance, the one which could change everything, was the one of which she was least sure at all. *What did Calumn feel for her?*

Disconsolately, she flung herself on to the bed. There were times when she hoped. Times when she dreamed. And times when she despaired. Though she felt she knew him at an elemental level, though after last night she felt she understood him, though their bodies had shared the most exquisite of intimacies, still she had no idea if what he felt for her was a passing whim or something more enduring.

That he could make her happy, as she could him, she did not doubt. That he would allow her to? That, she did indeed question. He seemed to think himself undeserving of happiness. There was one thing of which she was completely certain, though. Without him the future would be as dreary and grey as the lowering Highland sky she could glimpse through the dirty window panes.

Courage, Madeleine, she chid herself. First Guillaume. Then she must face Calumn. Proud and honourable, strong and desirable, such a man as he deserved a woman who could at least try to live up to him. She would face him. She would tell him. For it were better to have loved and lost. The old saying was true after all.

Footsteps halted outside in the corridor, and she heard Calumn call her name. Pasting a smile on to her face, she opened the door to find him waiting to take her down to dinner.

He had shaved; his hair was gleaming gold in the dark of the long hallway which was lit only by an oil lamp at the far end. He had discarded his *filleadh mòr,* but kept his jacket on, the tight fit of it showing off the breadth of his shoulders and chest, the neatness of his waist. Every time she saw him, he took her breath away. Every time she saw him, her heart seemed to expand to accommodate another little bit of love. And then another.

She took his arm, relishing the familiar ripple of sensation as her fingers felt the heat of him through his jacket sleeve. Calumn Munro, who had made Madeleine Lafayette into a new person. Calumn Munro, the man she loved. Would always love. She tripped along the stone flagstones at his side, down the two flights of stairs to where the laird awaited them in the great hall.

Chapter Seven

'*Feasgar math,*' Madeleine greeted her host in the carefully rehearsed phrase she had asked Calumn to teach her.

'*Bonsoir, mademoiselle,*' McAngus said in return, ushering her towards a chair on his right at a dining table which would seat an entire clan.

They were served soup, mutton broth thick with potatoes, barley and neeps, by the gloomy manservant who had earlier shown them to their rooms. Madeleine was beginning to suspect that he did the cooking too. There was more mutton to follow, a roast with fresh peas and an unexpectedly excellent claret. 'The lifeblood of the auld alliance,' their host told them with a chuckle. 'The wine of Bordeaux has been imported to Scotland for many years. Our new English masters would have us drink port, but ach, what do they know about drink!'

Madeleine's suspicions about the old man's family were confirmed. 'My wife Morag died five years ago now, and I've never had any daughters,' McAngus said in answer to her query. 'The place lacks a woman's touch these days, I know.' He dropped the mutton bone on which he had been gnawing to the flagstones, where one of the deerhounds immediately pounced on it. 'You'll find Lady Munro keeps a much better house than me when you get to Errin Mhor, eh, Calumn?' he continued. 'A right tartar is Calumn's mother, Christina. I mind her as a wee tearaway, when she was just Teenie, and after too, when she was married on to Finlay MacLeod. She wasn't more than sixteen, but she could make me tremble in my shoes with just one look. You're the spit of her, Calumn.'

'It means I look like her,' Calumn explained uncomfortably.

'A beauty, too, his mother. Still is,' McAngus continued oblivious. 'Oh, aye, as bonnie a lass as you've ever seen. I'd have asked for her hand myself if I'd thought she'd have me, but I had not the wealth of Finlay McLeod to tempt her, and by the time she was widowed, I'd wed my Morag, and Christina McLeod as was had set her sights even higher. Lord Munro is one of the wealthiest men in the Highlands, you know. That son of his here, he's quite a catch,' he said to Madeleine in a stage whisper, nodding in Calumn's direction.

She blushed at the blatant hint, but could think of nothing to say. Fortunately, no response seemed to be required of her. 'She'll be glad to see you, your mother,' McAngus said to Calumn, getting into his stride as he topped up his glass once more from the silver-mounted claret jug. Wine, it would appear, was one of the few things with which his castle was well stocked. 'I heard your father's been taken bad again, the pernicious old bugger. I mentioned your lands had been attacked, did I? Aye, Lady Munro's hired a factor now, but it's not the same, is it? You'll be wanting to take things in hand yourself, for if you don't mind my saying, your father's not long for this world. Though which world he's headed for, that's the question, eh?' McAngus wheezed alarmingly at his own joke. 'Are you calling on your brother first? If you do, you'll give him my best, won't you? I won't make the ceilidh, these old bones aren't fit for dancing.' He turned towards Madeleine again. ''Tis traditional to have a ceilidh for a bairn, once the mother's been churched. You'll have a rare old time, for it'll be a grand affair, celebrating the first born of the Laird of Heronsay, even if it is a wee lassie.'

'I don't think—that is, I…'

'And what about you, lass, what will you be doing with this fine fellow here, once you've done whate'er your business is with de Guise? You're only a wee thing, but you've a look that would keep a wilder man than Calumn Munro tied to your apron strings. He'll no wander far if he has you waiting at home for him,' the old man said with a leer which was comical in its blatancy.

McAngus's accent was becoming thicker, as the wine, which he was consuming at an alarming rate, took effect. Madeleine looked helplessly for an explanation to Calumn, but he merely shrugged, obviously enjoying her discomfort.

'A wedding on Errin Mhor, that'd set things to right, my boy. Think on't, but not too long mind, your faither's hanging by a fine thread,' McAngus advised owlishly. He raised his glass once more.

'We are not—Calumn and I are not—you are mistaken, Mr McAngus,' Madeleine said, finally realising the meaning the laird had put upon her relationship with Calumn. 'Calumn—Mister Munro is merely very kindly acting as my escort here.'

'Here's to you both,' McAngus said, ignoring her intervention completely. He drained the glass in one long swallow, smacked his lips together and got to his feet, refusing Calumn's offer to help him upstairs. 'I'll see myself up,' he said shakily, snapping his fingers at the deerhounds, which got reluctantly to their feet. They made a ragged procession up the stairs, the laird swaying precariously and humming softly to himself, the two shaggy dogs herding him upwards, nosing him gently into action when he paused, for all the world as if he were a sheep.

Madeleine chuckled. 'What an odd man. I think he must be lonely. I thought he was nice.'

'A likeable rogue. He certainly took a fancy to you.'

'Do you think he allows those great big smelly dogs into his bed?'

'Maybe they remind him of his wife,' Calumn said wickedly.

'That's a terrible thing to say. At least they'll keep him warm though. This castle is freezing.'

'I could keep you warm tonight.'

She struggled, her conscience warring with her desires. But she wanted to be able to look Guillaume in the eye. She had already been unfaithful in thought and in deed; it mattered to her that she had stopped short of the final act. 'Not tonight, Calumn.'

His lips thinned. 'If not tonight, then when? No, don't answer that question, for I have changed my mind. I have no desire to make love to a woman who gives herself to me knowing full well she is promised to another. Tomorrow or the next day, your outlaw betrothed will come to find you. I will not take another man's property and that is what you are.'

'No!'

'No, you don't like to hear the cold-blooded truth, do you, Madeleine? Any more than you like to admit you are wrong.'

'That is so unfair!' The whirlwind of emotions which had beset her over the last twenty-four hours took a sudden and violent toll on her temper. 'From the moment we met you have been unrelenting in your campaign to separate me from Guillaume. I use the word campaign deliberately, you understand, for it has been one planned attack after another. You think I don't know that our—our intimacies have been your weapons of choice? You forget, you warned me yourself that you would prove you could make me want you. That is all it was to you, though, a game. You had nothing to lose. But I—I have everything. Have you even thought about that, Calumn?'

'You will lose a husband you don't love. That sounds more like a profit to me.'

'It is much more than that. You and I, we have very different experiences of the world. For you, doing the right thing has eaten away at everything you believed in. Doing your duty by those you love and respect has forced you into conflict with those closest to you, including your own brother. It's not the same for me. In fact, until now, it's been the very opposite. It's not just that I'll be making Guillaume unhappy, he will be shamed. Everyone knows of our betrothal, the whole country. It is not just a bit of paper signed by our parents when we were children, it is a fact of our lives. My father will be devastated. All his hopes and dreams lost. Our home lost, when he dies, for it will go to a distant cousin if I do not have a son. Don't you see, all my life I've believed, really believed, that in doing my duty I would be fulfilled. If that is gone, it is like taking a part of me away.'

She stopped for breath, staring off into the distance in an effort to clear her thoughts enough, to make him see. To make him understand. 'You have always seen it in such black-and-white terms. I don't love Guillaume, therefore I should not do what I have promised publicly to do. It's not black and white. There are a multitude of shades of grey.'

'You don't love Guillaume! Finally, you admit it.'

'Yes,' she admitted, exhausted by her outburst. 'I admit it, I don't love him. You see, you were right all along.'

'You're not going to marry him?'

'No,' she said sadly, 'you were right about that, too. It would be very wrong of me. No matter how painful in the short term, I know that. But it does not mean that I look forward to telling him with anything less than dread.'

Calumn sat down abruptly on a seat at the head of the table. 'Why didn't you tell me before?'

'Because I've been running away from the truth. Because I've only just got it straight in my own head. Because I wanted to tell Guillaume first, with as clear a conscience as I can.'

'Which is why you will not share my bed.'

'Yes.' She smiled wanly. 'You have taught me many lessons, and one of them is honour. I'm not very good at it, but I'm trying my best.'

'I think you are doing remarkably well,' Calumn said, stretching out his hand to her, 'in the face of such temptation.'

She had to smile at that, allowing him to pull her into the lee of his body, and to hold her there, stroking her hair, rubbing the nape of her neck. 'I think I have mentioned before that you have a very high opinion of yourself.'

'I have a very high opinion of you, too. You're

right, I hadn't thought of it in such terms. You are being very brave.'

'I don't feel very brave. I just want it over.'

'And what then?'

She was tempted to throw the question back at him, but the time did not feel right. 'I'll think about that later. After.'

'After. Perhaps you're right.' Calumn got to his feet and fetched the best of the candles, burning in their pewter holders, from the table. 'Go to bed. Get some sleep.' He led her up the stairs. Kissed her cheek at the door to her room.

In his own damp and unwelcoming chamber, Calumn opened the window wide and gazed out. An owl hooted. He sniffed the soft sweet air. In Edinburgh, the seasons melded one into another so that the change was easy to miss, but it was not so up here, where summer burst on to the senses like a fanfare. He had forgotten.

No, he had not really forgotten. Boiling up mussels in a bucket on the beach at low tide. Endless fishing trips in his boat, the *An Sulaire*. Learning how to wield the claymore under the tutelage of his father's champion, Hamish Sinclair, a man with a beard so red it looked like he had set fire to it. The sound of the sea shushing on the shore from his bedroom window, lulling him to sleep every night. Calumn gazed sightlessly out at the black waters of the loch and remembered.

Though Lady Munro's letters had kept him

informed of the state of his father's health and the bad heart the land had fallen into, it had not seemed real until the old laird referred to them in such blunt terms, assuming—naturally enough—that Calumn was on his way to Errin Mhor to take up the reins. Only a few days ago, such an idea was unthinkable. But now?

Now hope, that long-absent visitor, peered through the door of his mind and took a step over the threshold. Errin Mhor sang her siren call to him, and Calumn knew the time had come.

And Madeleine? He had won his point with her, but it occurred to him only now that she had not said how. It mattered, he realised, it mattered that it was her need for him which had persuaded her, not some lack in de Guise.

He must have her. Could think of very little else but having her. He was not ready to let her go. Let her face de Guise first. And then—thinking about the delights in store, Calumn fell asleep.

Madeleine awoke the next morning depressed by the task which lay ahead of her, but determined to see it through. She wished she knew when Guillaume would arrive, for now she had steeled herself, she would much rather it were sooner than later.

Watery sunlight filtered in through the dusty panes of the window, showing a new-washed sky and mountain peaks cloaked with mist. Outside she could hear voices, men calling to each other in Gaelic. The hunt. She had forgotten. She washed and dressed, crept out along the corridor and down the first flight of stairs, pausing on the landing of the first floor to look down at the great hall.

It was a hive of activity. The long table was laden with tankards, bread and cheese, and a side of meat—no doubt the ubiquitous mutton. The men were all dressed in plaids of different colours: blood reds, bottle greens, dull gold and royal blue. Some wore trews instead of the *filleadh beg*. Most had beards. The few women present busied themselves with the food, pouring beer into pewter tankards, slicing bread, laughing together, their words lilting like a melody. They were dressed as Madeleine was herself, in skirts with *arisaidhs,* though all wore the kertch. McAngus's deerhounds had also found companions. There were eight or nine of the dogs lolloping through the great hall, tearing out on to the forecourt where she could see the horses tethered, then tearing back in again, barking wildly.

Calumn come through the front door, talking earnestly with another man about the same age as himself, dressed in a plaid of dull gold. The two men paused on the threshold, clasped each other's hands, and then the other man joined the throng at the fire. Calumn stood alone for a few moments, his height dwarfing all the others, his hair like a beacon in the hazy light.

He looked up and saw her watching him. He beckoned her down, but as he did so another man called his name. 'Calumn,' he said, waving him over. ''Tis

Calumn Munro,' he said to his companions, 'Rory McLeod's brother.'

'The Redcoat.'

The words rang out loud and clear in the hall, spoken in English by a dark-haired man dressed in the red and green which proclaimed him a Cameron. Silence fell. All eyes turned towards Calumn. His smile hardened, but his step did not falter. He walked firmly over to the Cameron, holding his gaze. 'That's right,' he said, 'Captain Calumn Munro, late of the fusiliers. At your service, sir.'

Madeleine watched with bated breath, cursing her lack of Gaelic, for the men had resorted to their native language. She became aware of a presence at her side and looking round saw it was Angus McAngus.

'Yon's Donald Cameron,' he whispered. 'The Camerons were staunch Jacobites. Wheesht now, and I'll tell ye what he's saying.'

Calumn was standing in front of Donald Cameron, his face grim as granite. 'Is there something you wish to say to me?' The challenge in his voice was obvious to Madeleine, even without McAngus's translation.

'I've nothing to say to the likes of you,' Donald Cameron replied. 'You're a traitor.'

A hiss escaped the onlookers, like the sound of damp wood thrown on a fire. Various men murmured unhappily. Calumn took a hasty step forwards. With enormous difficulty Madeleine suppressed her instinctive cry of disgust at the accusation. The word, the very word which Calumn used to lacerate himself, stuck like a knife into her heart. She felt McAngus's grip on her shoulder. Realising he was afraid she would interfere, she gave him a quick reassuring shake of the head.

'I was a Redcoat long before the Pretender set foot on Scottish soil,' Calumn said through gritted teeth. 'What would you have me do when they ordered me to fight, turn my back on them? Disobey orders? Well, I didn't.' There was a proud tilt to his head. 'I did my duty, though it cost me dear. One of your claymores damn near killed me at Culloden. I'll have the scar on my belly as a reminder for the rest of my life.' He shook his head sorrowfully. 'As if I need reminding. As if any of us need reminding.'

The rawness of his emotion was obvious to all. A good few of the other men growled agreement to his sentiments, and some moved towards him, ranging themselves by his side.

'Easy for you to say,' Donald Cameron said viciously. 'The Butcher hasn't laid waste to your lands.'

'And he wouldn't have been near yours either, if you had not risen in aid of the Stuarts,' Calumn said furiously. 'Where is your Bonnie Prince now, eh? Do you think he cares what's happened to any of us in his wake?' His fists were clenched tight, two flags of colour on his cheekbones signalling his rage.

'Steady now,' one of Calumn's supporters said, placing a hand on his shoulder. 'We've had enough feuding to last us a lifetime.'

Calumn shook himself free, but the words had an effect. 'You're right,' he said tightly, 'we've lost enough—' looking pointedly at Cameron '—all of us.'

There was an expectant hush as Cameron stared without moving at Calumn's extended hand. Madeleine barely noticed that McAngus had left her to join the men. Slowly, reluctantly, Cameron shook Calumn's hand. A sigh of relief went up. McAngus raised his tankard. 'Here's to forgiving and forgetting,' he said. *'Slange var.'*

'Slange var,' the subdued response echoed through the hall. Someone pressed a tankard into Calumn's hand. Very quickly he was surrounded. Madeleine heard the words, Rory Macleod, uttered several times. Obviously Calumn's brother was a well-respected man. She watched as his countenance resumed its normal colour. She saw from the way his shoulders relaxed how tense he had been. She continued to watch from her vantage point as the men talked animatedly, laughing and exchanging stories, though she had no idea what they were saying. She realised she had just witnessed an extraordinary event. Calumn had come home. Though it was what she knew was right for him, she felt as if she were watching him sail away while she was left alone on a distant shore. Though of course soon, very soon, it would be she who would be sailing away to a far-off land.

Eventually, she descended the stairs and made her own way to his side. 'I was watching, McAngus told me most of what was being said. I thought you did well not to hit that man. I was—I was proud of you. And you must be relieved.'

'It's a start, but it will be a long road.'

'And does it lead to Errin Mhor?'

He smiled enigmatically. 'In the end, all roads lead to Errin Mhor—surely you know that much by now. Right now, I've other things on my mind. Like our business with de Guise.'

So he was still determined to accompany her. She wasn't really surprised. It would be easier to move one of the Highland mountains than to change Calumn Munro's mind. 'It's not our business, it's my business, and it would be much better if I saw him alone,' she said tiredly.

'He's not the man he was, Madeleine. He's dangerous. I'm much more concerned about him hurting you, than the other way around. You'll mind what I said, you're on no account to see him alone, do you hear me?'

'I hear you,' she replied, crossing her fingers behind her back.

'Mind you pay attention, then,' he said astutely. 'Now come and be introduced to the rest of the party.' Taking her hand, he pulled her towards the crowd of men and women and horses milling in the courtyard of the castle.

'*Madainn mhath,*' Madeleine murmured shyly, pleased when her badly pronounced good morning was greeted with smiles and even a few friendly *bonjours*. 'They know I'm French,' she said won-

deringly to Calumn as he threw her on to her horse
and adjusted her bridle.

'They know all about you. Word travels fast up
here.'

A horn sounded to announce the beginning of the
hunt and they rode out from the castle to the edge
of the forest. The deerhounds stood alert at the head
of the group of hunters, their aristocratic noses sniff-
ing the air. Bits jangled. Horses snorted and pawed
the ground, anxious to be underway. One of the
hounds froze, his sensitive nose quivering, his tail
stiff, a forepaw lifted, so that his whole body seemed
to point in the direction of the forest at the other side
of the loch. McAngus called out something, a rally-
ing cry of some sort. And then they were off.

The dogs led them straight into the forest which
covered the gently sloping land on the western
edges of Loch Catriona, at the juncture with her
sister lochan, Johanna. Close up, it could be seen
that the two expanses of water were actually linked
by a small burn. The ground was soft underfoot, the
surface covered in needles dropped from the pine
trees which formed a dark canopy over their heads.
The air was heavy, all sound muffled. There was a
fretwork of little paths criss-crossing the forest, and
a huge number of little burns and ditches too, the
rocks beside them covered in dark green moss and
lichen. Clumps of fern, shorter and a brighter, fresh-
er green than that which grew in the open, provided
the only other ground cover. The gnarled branches
of ancient oak trees reached out like gouty fingers

to clutch at the riders as they passed. Silvery birch and mystical rowan, the witch's tree, grew along the edges of the larger burns.

Despite the density of the tree trunks and the many rabbit holes which made it madness to proceed at anything other than a slow trot on horseback, the majority of the hunting party forged ahead, anxious to keep up with the dogs. Madeleine lingered at the rear, enjoying the pleasant resiny smell of the pine and the quality of the light filtering down through the trees which reminded her of the forests at home. Stopping by a tiny waterfall, she spotted the tell-tale signs of a dam built by a beaver. So much here was familiar, she felt almost as if she were at home. Even as she drew the comparison, an enormous bird flapped out suddenly, making her horse start. Its green breast feathers seemed to shine like burnished metal, and it had a tail which spread out like a fan. She had never seen anything like it.

'A capercaillie, a male,' Calumn said. He had ridden back to find her. 'See how he flaunts his feathers to try to impress you. They've picked up the scent of the stag; if we don't hurry up we'll be left behind.'

He brought his horse close enough to hers so that his bare knee brushed against her skirts. He leaned over, holding his own reins in one hand, placing his other on her saddle to balance himself. Then he kissed her. A tiny, tender flutter of a kiss. Soft and warm, over before she had time to respond, but still enough to have her pulses leaping in response.

'Come on,' he said, slapping the rump of her horse, 'we don't want to miss the excitement.'

As they caught up with the rest of the party she saw the stag leaping balletically over the heather just a few yards ahead, with the dogs in hot pursuit. He was a magnificent creature with a fine set of antlers, like the one she had seen that morning a few days ago.

The antlers were a sign of his virility as well as his maturity, for he used them to fend off younger challengers to his herd, maintaining his supremacy and protecting his young. And his females. He rested for a moment, his slender legs having created some distance between himself and the dogs, looking frantically around him for a means of escape. Madeleine whispered a secret prayer for his safety. It seemed wrong to hunt such a beautiful creature, as much the proud laird of his own domain as she could see Calumn would be of Errin Mhor.

The dogs bayed. The stag leapt forwards on its muscular haunches, soaring elegantly, effortlessly, over an uprooted tree, as if he were flying. The hunters followed, shouting, blowing the horns, calling out instructions to the dogs. On they all rode in the wake of the deer, out of the forest into the lower slopes of the hills, through fern and bracken, leaping over ditches, along the sandy shallows of a river bed. Madeleine could smell the damp of wool from the Highlanders' plaids. The earthy smell of fresh-churned grass and fern. The sharp odour of sweat from the horses.

On and on they went, for what seemed like hours, with the stag finally slowing, his flanks heaving with effort, obviously blown. Dogs barked excitedly. The cries from the hunters took on a higher pitch as the stag was cornered in the shadow of a large rock. The poor creature was foaming at the mouth, his eyes blank with terror.

Though Madeleine had taken part in many boar hunts at home, for some reason this event seemed manifestly unfair. So many people, so many dogs and horses, all pitted against this one lone, regal creature. She could not bear to watch the end. It would be like viewing the execution of a king, seeing the brown eyes glaze, the mighty body topple. No, she could not bear it.

They were on the edges of Loch Fiona, on the far side from Castle Rhubodach. If she kept to the shore, she could get back without returning through the forest. Decision made, she turned her horse around and headed off.

About halfway to the castle she experienced the prickly feeling of being watched. Reining her horse to a halt, Madeleine peered around her, but could see no one. To her left was the gloom of the forest, seemingly impenetrable at this point due to a jumble of fallen trees. On her right was Loch Fiona, tapering into Loch Aileen. Behind her—no one. Yet the feeling persisted. Goosebumps raised on the back of her neck. Her hands on the reins were clammy.

She continued slowly, telling herself that she was

being foolish. It was an animal, without a doubt. Another deer, perhaps. Her sharp ears heard a rustle coming from the forest. She stopped her horse again and, carefully scanning the foliage, caught a glimpse of a pair of eyes. Not deer. Definitely human. She called out, *'Who is there?'*, in English. She was frightened, though she told herself she had no cause to be. Probably another member of the hunt who had lost their way. Her horse pawed at the ground. All her instincts told her to flee. She gathered the reins to do so. Too late.

A man appeared directly in front of her. He held a pistol in his hand and it was pointing straight at her. Another man emerged from the cover of the forest brandishing the lethal long thin knife she knew from Calumn was known as a dirk. He put the tip of it to her breast. 'Get down,' he growled in English.

She did not hesitate to obey. One look was sufficient to tell her that both men meant business, for they had an air of desperation about them. Clad in trews and leather waistcoats, their faces were tanned and fierce under their beards. She assumed they were after her horse. Snagging her foot in the stirrup as she dismounted, she was caught in a vicious clamp against the body of the man holding the dirk. She was shaking, and meeting her attacker's eyes flooded with another type of fear, for he had a lascivious look to him as his filthy hand clamped around her waist. She knew she should not show her fright, but it was there in her voice when she said, struggling, 'Get your hands off me.'

To her astonishment he did, laughing crudely. His companion grabbed the reins of her horse. She thought with relief that it was over, that they would be on their way, was already trying to calculate how long it would take her to walk back to the castle, when the man spoke again.

'You're the Frenchie.'

She was taken aback, then remembered what Calumn had said earlier, that there were no secrets in the Highlands, so she simply nodded.

'Come in search of Guillaume de Guise.'

She nodded again.

'We're to take you to him.'

Her jaw dropped in astonishment. What on earth was Guillaume doing associating with such men? '*You!* I don't believe you. Where is Guillaume? Why has he not come for me himself?'

The man looked at her contemptuously. 'Think he's daft, do ye? He's a price on his head—we were to make sure this wasn't a trap.'

'A price on his head! Do you mean he's an outlaw? *Non, non, non.* You must have the wrong man.'

'Do ye want to see him or not?'

She looked longingly back behind her, but the path along the lochside was empty. Calumn was too caught up in the hunt to have noticed her leaving. He had been adamant that she not meet Guillaume alone. She had thought him over-cautious, but looking at the two henchmen who had been sent for her, she thought now that he had been right to worry. But surely Guillaume would not harm her?

No matter how much he had changed, he could not have changed that much.

The man with the pistol gave an impatient exclamation and said something to his comrade in Gaelic. He nodded his agreement and picked up the reins of her horse, encouraging her with the blade of his dirk in the small of her back to walk into the forest. She had no choice but to obey. Gathering up the remnants of her courage, Madeleine did as she was bid.

Once under cover of the trees, the men bound her wrists and threw her back on to the saddle of her horse. They untied their own horses, which had been waiting sedately in a small clearing, and mounted, one in front leading Madeleine, the other following behind. They took a path which led steeply uphill into the depths of the forest where sunlight did not penetrate, making their way with the assurance of long familiarity.

The forest became less dense as they gained height. A small clearing appeared, with what looked like a large cave at the far side. A camp fire smoked at the mouth of the cave, with a large cauldron suspended over it on a complicated arrangement of sticks. Scattered possessions—saddle bags, some clothing, tin plates and cups stacked by the fire—betrayed the presence of other members of the group, who were obviously out foraging—or carrying out their evil business. For now, the camp seemed deserted.

Madeleine's escorts brought the little procession to a halt and dismounted, tethering the animals to a tree. She was pulled from the saddle and stood shakily on her feet. 'Untie me,' she said, looking around her warily. The men made no move to do so, one busying himself with the horses, the other heading towards a makeshift shelter formed from canvas and branches, whistling softly.

'Guillaume,' Madeleine called. 'Guillaume, *c'est moi, c'est* Madeleine.'

The man with the dirk sat down under the canvas and began whittling on a piece of wood. Trying to keep a lid on her rising panic, Madeleine took a step towards the cave. 'Guillaume?'

A tall figure emerged from the gloom. 'Well? What do you want?' he growled, speaking French with the guttural accent of the south-west.

'Who are you?' Madeleine countered. Though he was obviously French, tall and dark-haired, there the resemblance to Guillaume ended. Dressed in trews and a cambric shirt with a short woollen jacket, this man was older, perhaps thirty, his face etched with lines which told of a hard life. Under black brows which almost met over his nose, his eyes were cold.

'I am Guillaume de Guise,' he said.

'*Non.* You are not Guillaume. Where is he, what have you done with him?'

'I am Guillaume de Guise,' the man repeated threateningly. He smelled of sweat and whisky. 'Who are you, and what do you want?'

Madeleine cowered back, tugging on the leather which bound her wrists. 'I am Madeleine Lafayette, as you would know if you really were Guillaume,' she said, glaring at him. 'Where is he?'

'If you know what's good for you, you'll stop asking me that,' he hissed, putting a hand around her throat.

'Why did you bring me here, if you are not Guillaume?' She was trying desperately not to betray her fear.

The Frenchman's grip tightened around her throat. 'I was told you had news for me, something to my advantage. What is it?'

'News for Guillaume.' Madeleine struggled to free herself from his grip. 'For the real Guillaume.'

'What news?'

'It's none of your business. Where is Guillaume? I want to talk to Guillaume.' Her voice rose several octaves. The two henchmen abandoned all pretence of going about their own business and watched with interest as their leader struggled to control the Frenchwoman who had turned into something resembling a wildcat. Madeleine bit, kicked and squirmed like an eel to free herself. Though her hands were still bound, she managed to rake her nails down her captor's cheeks, making him drop his hold and yelp in pain. Blood dripped from the scratches. The henchmen grinned. Panting, Madeleine edged backwards, thinking only of escape. If she could outrun them, lose herself in the forest…

She glanced at the man who claimed to be Guillaume. He was busy wiping the blood from his face. The other two were watching her, but they were both seated, giving her a slight advantage. It had to be now. Taking a deep breath, she ran as fast as she could to the edge of the clearing, throwing herself into the forest, regardless of the branches whipping at her face and tearing her clothes, holding her bound hands out in front of her like a blind woman, concentrating on keeping her balance, on putting some distance between herself and her captors.

She got only a few yards before one of them grabbed her. They dragged her back to the camp and threw her on to the ground. Opening her eyes, the first thing she saw was the wicked glint of the long broadsword blade. It was resting on her stomach. 'Now, *mademoiselle,* perhaps you are ready to speak,' the Frenchman said. There was an equally wicked glint to his smile.

Angus McAngus insisted that the honour of bleeding the stag went to Calumn. Though it was not a task he relished, he knew it would be an insult to refuse, and executed it as mercifully as he could, taking his dirk swiftly and cleanly to the animal's throat. A rousing cheer went up from the rest of the hunters, and the men set about tying the carcase up to take back to the castle. There would be roast venison tonight, a welcome change from mutton.

Wiping the blood from his hands, Calumn noticed Madeleine's absence and guessed she had not wished to witness the stag's death. She must have taken the path back along the lochside but, scanning it anxiously from a vantage point on top of a crag, he could not see her. In an instant he was on full alert. De Guise.

Shouting an apology to his host, Calumn mounted his tired horse and headed off down the mountainside, his keen eyes on the lookout for signs of an ambush. Forcing himself to go slowly lest he miss anything, he retraced Madeleine's steps, picking up the prints of her horseshoes in the soft mud on the edges of the path. His caution was rewarded. Three horses, and a broken branch leading into the forest. They had not expected to be followed and had made no attempt to cover their tracks. Stealthily, all his faculties on full alert, he followed the trail until he saw the clearing in the distance.

Three men. And Madeleine, with a claymore pointing at her belly. The discipline of a trained soldier and the fighting instincts of a Highland warrior both took hold of him. Calumn tethered his horse well out of sight and sound of the camp. His dirk, still bloody from the stag, was in his belt. The wicked blade had been cut down from one of his father's own claymores, the hilt chased with ornate Celtic symbols copied by the Munro clan blacksmith from an ancient parchment kept at Errin Mhor Castle. He drew it from its leather sheath and felt for his *sgian dubh,* the secret dagger he kept strapped under his jacket. Thus armed, he crept soundlessly through the undergrowth. When he was within hearing distance he forced himself to pause, safe behind the shelter of a birch, surveying the scene before him.

Madeleine was lying on the ground, her hands bound, her hair and clothing in wild disarray. For a heart-stopping second he thought she had been ravished, but closer scrutiny reassured him. She had obviously put up a fight. Fierce pride heated his blood. He should have known she would not give in easily.

The man who must be de Guise stood over her, wielding the broadsword. He looked more mature than Calumn had expected. Battle-hardened. That would account for it. All soldiers grew up quickly in the heat of combat. He had the look of a man who had been living wild for some time, with his hair long and unkempt, though he was surprisingly clean shaven. A mean look about the mouth marked him out as a man to be taken seriously.

The other two Calumn dismissed as lightweights. Scrawny, shabbily dressed, they had a gaunt, hungry look about them, as of scavengers after an unsuccessful night's hunting. They were watching the tableau as if it were an entertainment, quite evidently unaware that their intervention would be necessary. All the better.

'Well, what's it to be,' de Guise was saying, 'what is this news that I'm told will be to my advantage?'

Calumn cursed, tightening his grip on his dirk as he saw the terror in Madeleine's eyes. Finding out that he was responsible for pillaging Errin

Mhor had given him a legitimate grudge against de Guise. Now, he despised him with all his heart. A cold rage enveloped him. Death was almost too good for this man.

Chapter Eight

Calumn leapt forwards from his hiding place with a blood-curdling cry, startling de Guise into raising his claymore, but Calumn was already upon him, a fearsome flurry of plaid and brawn and muscle, rushing at the Frenchman, breaking his sword arm with one brutal kick, causing the claymore to clatter to the earth seconds before its owner, with a howl of agony, followed it. On his knees, clutching his damaged limb, de Guise screamed at his men to come to his aid, but it was too late. Calumn stood behind him, his dirk at the man's throat, so close that a trickle of blood ran down the blade, and already Madeleine had scrabbled to her feet, kicking the claymore out of reach.

'Get over here,' Calumn called to her, manoeuvring himself so that the other two men were within his sight, with de Guise in front of him and Madeleine safe behind him. She held her wrists towards him so that he could cut her ties and, needing no encouragement, she picked up the heavy broadsword, using both her hands to hold it at waist level where it wavered, more threatening to the watching men in the hands of her amateur grip than if it were held by a champion.

'Good girl.' Calumn eyed the two henchmen, his eyes slits of dark, his mouth thinned into a cruel line. 'One move from either of you and he's dead, am I understood?'

The men nodded. 'Cowards,' de Guise snarled, but Calumn pressed the dirk tighter into his throat. The trickle of blood thickened.

'What's the game, de Guise?'

'Calumn, it's not Guillaume,' Madeleine said, taking a step forwards.

'Stay behind me,' he snapped, keeping his eyes on the henchmen, one of whom had a dirk. 'Keep the claymore up. If either of them move, you lift it as high as you can and slice it down on them.'

'Like this,' Madeleine said, demonstrating.

He could see from the reaction of the watching men that she had managed something effectively threatening, and chuckled bloodthirstily. 'Good. Now,' he said, returning his attention to the man he held pinioned, 'who the hell are you?'

'Guillaume de Guise,' the man replied, though all conviction was gone from his voice.

'That is not Guillaume,' Madeleine spat, 'he's an impostor.'

'One last chance,' Calumn said, 'who are you?'

'Droissard,' the man muttered.

'Speak up, laddie, your men will want to hear what you've got to say.'

'My name is Marc Droissard,' the man replied through gritted teeth.

'You see,' Madeleine cried triumphantly to the men who had brought her here, 'I told you it wasn't Guillaume.'

They looked astounded. 'What's going on? Who are ye? Why did you tell us your name was de Guise?'

'Well, are you going to answer that?' Though he was fairly certain that they were safe from attack, Calumn still retained his grip, for even with a broken limb, he knew that a rat in a trap was at its most dangerous. 'Speak up man, I'm losing patience.'

'I fought with de Guise. We were in the *Écossais Royeaux* together.'

'You were friends,' Madeleine asked in disbelief, 'comrades?'

Droissard laughed. 'Comrades, yes. Friends, hardly. He was out of my league. I was a humble tanner before I took up soldiering. I'm good enough to die for the likes of him and his precious Prince, but nothing more.'

'Yes, and I bet you've fought for a few different sides in your time, eh,' Calumn said. 'I recognise your type—you've got mercenary written all over you.'

'How can you be so sure?'

'I was a soldier myself. Let me guess, you joined the French army, but they threw you out for some crime or other—or perhaps you deserted. But you like killing and you like to get paid for it. And now you've got a price on your head and you can't go home. Am I right?'

Droissard struggled, cursing, but Calumn pulled his head back, gripping his hair by the roots so hard that he yelped. 'So, you've taken de Guise's name to avoid the guillotine, eh? Where is he?'

'Dead.'

'No!' The claymore dropped from Madeleine's grasp.

'When?' Calumn looked anxiously over his shoulder. She had turned ghostly white. Though he had suspected as much, from the very moment Madeleine told him this was not Guillaume, he would have spared her the pain of finding out in this brutal way.

Droissard had obviously decided to co-operate. 'Culloden. I saw him fall. A musket wound to the head. I knew he had no family, I thought no one would care. When I heard that she was looking for him, I couldn't resist. They told me she had something for me, something to my advantage. Money, I thought.'

'Aye, you thought to take it and then to kill her, didn't you?'

'No, no,' Droissard protested. 'I'd have released her.'

'Let her go to tell the whole country that the man

who called himself de Guise was an impostor! Don't lie to me. You had a claymore aimed at her belly. I know exactly what that does to a body.'

Droissard was shaking now, all pretence of bravado gone. 'What are you going to do with me? I've done you no harm. My men will be back soon, but if you let me go I'll make sure you and the girl get safe passage back to the castle. I'll—'

'You and your men are responsible for attacking my lands,' Calumn hissed. 'Munro lands.'

'So you're a turncoat then, I should have known it,' Droissard threw at him.

'I was loyal to my troops and to the army I was part of,' Calumn replied furiously. 'But you wouldn't know about that, would you? No, you fight for whoever pays you most. Do they know that, these men of yours? Do they know you're as much a Jacobite as Cumberland is? You're in this for the takings and naught more. Do you think they'll rush to your defence when I tell them that?' He wanted to slit the man's throat, to drive his dirk into the man's evil heart, to tear out the heart while it was still beating, to flay him, to...

'Dead?' Madeleine was standing by his side, her voice a mere thread. 'Calumn, ask him, is he certain?'

Pity and tenderness washed over him, draining away the bloodlust. 'Madeleine, de Guise took a bullet to the head, there can be no mistake.' No point in reminding her that even had de Guise survived the battle, he would have been slaughtered in the aftermath. 'Go and fetch your horse, and bring one other over. Go on, do as you're told. You two, make yourself scarce if you value your hide.' The two men needed no further persuasion and ran off into the forest.

'Are you're going to kill him?' Madeleine asked apprehensively.

'Killing's too good for him.'

'Then what?'

'He's coming with us. There are representatives from most of the clans at Castle Rhubodach. They can decide.'

She smiled bravely. 'Rough justice. More than he deserves.'

'Aye. It sticks in my craw, but I've enough blood on my hands.'

With Droissard bound by the wrists and nursing his broken arm, the journey back to Castle Rhubodach was made in sombre silence. In contrast, the great hall, when they entered, was alive with laughter. McAngus's claret was flowing freely. The appetising aroma of venison filled the air, the spit on which it was turning watched by a pack of drooling hounds. When the trio were spotted, they were greeted raucously, amusement which turned to concern and then anger as Calumn quickly explained what had passed. Calls for retribution mingled with fainter cries for leniency. An impromptu clan tribunal was assembled.

Prejudiced as he was against Droissard, Calumn

declined to take part, instead ushering Madeleine upstairs to her chamber, where he managed to coax the fire into life and even conjured up some hot water for her to wash in. She was shivering, her face ashen, seemingly beyond words. He should be furious with her for disobeying him, but her punishment already far exceeded her crime.

Madeleine's shivers had turned to shaking. She was fumbling with the lacing on her boots. He stooped to help her, then undid the belt and brooch which held her *arisaidh* in place and sat her gently down on the bed. Taking a washcloth, he cleaned the worst of the dirt from her face and hands, murmuring soothing nothings in his own language. Her hair was a tangled mess. He pulled the last of the pins from it, and, taking her brush, combed it rhythmically, gently, using long soothing strokes until it hung sleekly down her back. He unlaced the sleeves from her waistcoat, took off her stockings, rubbed her cold feet between his hands to warm them, massaging life into each of her little toes, doing the same to her hands. 'You should try to get some sleep. I'll get you a toddy, it'll help.'

'What's a toddy?'

'It's a hot drink. Whisky, cloves, honey and hot water. It'll soothe you.'

'No.' She gazed at him, as far from him as if she were on the other side of the ocean. 'No. I don't want anything. I just need to be alone.'

'I don't think that's such a good idea.' She hadn't cried. Not one tear. That couldn't be healthy.

'No!' She jumped up from the bed, clasping her hands together so tightly the skin strained at her knuckles. 'Please, Calumn, just—I need to be on my own. Please.'

As a soldier he was used to dealing with the shock of the bereaved, but he had not seen a reaction as extreme as this before. He had come to believe she did not really care for de Guise. Obviously he had been wrong. The realisation was unexpectedly painful. 'I'll come back later, see how you are.'

'Tomorrow.' She opened the door. 'Come and see me in the morning. Goodnight, Calumn.'

He waited in the hallway, ears straining for sounds of grief. But there was only silence.

Inside the room, Madeleine slumped to the floor in front of the flickering fire, hugging her arms tight around herself, for if she let go she would surely shatter. Guillaume was dead. Since last night, hearing McAngus's story of the renegades, she had half-expected this. The man McAngus described was not the Guillaume she knew. But to have it confirmed was a shock. A horrible shock, made worse by her being so certain that he was alive.

But worse, far worse, was the shock of discovering her own wickedness. For just a few moments, when the news of Guillaume's death was confirmed by Droissard, she had been relieved. Shamefully but unmistakably relieved.

'They've decided to let him go, I'm afraid, laddie,' Angus McAngus told Calumn. 'At the end of the day, he fought for Charlie and that swung the balance in his favour.'

'He was a mercenary.'

McAngus smiled wearily. 'So were half the Jacobite army, though I doubt they were actually paid. Don't take it to heart, Calumn. You did the right thing bringing him back here—that deed will stand you in good stead, I promise you. Your father would not have had the courage to show the man mercy.'

'Courage! I should have slit his throat when I had the chance.'

'Nay, you don't mean that. You did the right thing.'

'He would have killed Madeleine.'

'But he didn't, did he? You were there for her. As it should be. Don't let that one get away. In fact, what are you doing here? Should you not be up there comforting her? Take her up some of this venison and a cup of good French claret. I always find the world's a better-looking place myself, with a few cups of good French claret inside me.'

Calumn smiled, amused despite himself, but he shook his head. 'She wants to be left alone.'

'And here was me thinking you were an experienced ladies' man! Did you not know that when a woman says she wants to be left alone, she means the very opposite? Wait till I tell them this one.' With that, McAngus slapped Calumn on the back and went over to join the others at the head of the long table, where the haunch of venison was rapidly diminishing. A hearty burst of laughter followed Calumn up the stairs. McAngus had obviously shared the joke.

On the landing, he stood looking out over the grounds of the castle through a rather beautiful, if also rather dirty, stained-glass window. It was raining steadily now. The clansmen's decision left him strangely untouched. He wondered if Droissard had already been released. Hard to remember that only a few hours ago he had been intent on murdering the man.

You were there for her. True enough—this time. This time, he'd played the part of Madeleine's champion, a part he'd come to think of as his own, but it was not his for much longer. She would be going home soon. She had no reason to stay. Who would be her champion then? He didn't want to think about that.

Voices wafted up from the great hall. The sound of a fiddle being tuned. Soon they would be singing, and to the repertoire of the old songs would be added the new ones about their Bonnie Prince which would establish the undeserving Pretender as a legend. Calumn turned away from the rain-drenched window and headed up to the second floor. Nothing wrong with another legend, he supposed. Best way to heal a hurt. Right now, he had another hurt to deal with.

When there was no reply to his soft tap on her door, Calumn opened it carefully, assuming Madeleine was asleep. She was wide awake, hunched on the floor in front of the dying embers of the fire. She did not stir when he approached, looking at him through huge, unseeing eyes filled with something which tore at his heart.

'I came to see how you are,' he said, feeling helpless in the face of such dumb grief.

No answer. And still no trace of tears, either. He hunkered down beside her. She had her arms wrapped tight around her body, as if she were trying to stop herself from falling apart. Her bare feet were like ice. 'You're freezing. You should be in bed.' Still no response. 'Madeleine, you're going to catch your death.' He scooped her up into his arms. She was as light as a feather. Her hair was soft against his chin. She released the tight hold she had on herself only to clutch at him instead, her fingers on his jacket gripping like claws. A violent shiver racked her body. When he tried to release her onto the bed, she wouldn't let go.

'Stay with me.' Her voice was a thread.

'I'm not going anywhere.'

Quickly, he took off the rest of her outer clothing, careful not to alarm her, undressing her as tenderly as he would a child. Then he divested himself of all but his shirt, and, rolling back the covers of the bed, wrapped her tight against his chest, tucking the sheet up around her chin, warming her feet with his own, chafing her hands between his to make the blood flow, murmuring gentle nothings to soothe her.

Madeleine lay curled up against him shaking, then shivering, then finally still. She nuzzled her face into his chest, feeling the soft fuzz of his hair on her cheek in the opening of his shirt. Safe. Like an animal in its burrow. Safe and warm. And home.

A hot tear rolled down her cheek. Its path scorched her skin, for it was a bitter tear. The tear of the wicked. Another followed, then another. She pressed her lips tight together, she closed her throat, she held her breath, but there was no stopping them. Tears poured down her cold cheeks, dripped down her chin and on to Calumn's chest, soaking his shirt. Sobs racked her body. Her fingers clutched at his desperately, as if he could anchor her, as if she were being wrested from him by a storm, as if she would be washed up, broken and lifeless, as surely she deserved to be. And still the tears flowed, softer now, filled with sadness. Finally, tears of grief.

When she was empty, her grip slackened. She became aware of Calumn holding her, stroking her head, her hair, her shoulders. Of his voice in her ear telling her to hush, that she was safe, that he would keep her safe. Of the way her body was nestled against his, chest to chest, thigh to thigh, held tight but unthreateningly. She sniffed. Rubbed her damp cheeks on his shirt. It was wet through. 'Sorry,' she whispered, her throat raw, her voice husky.

She felt, rather than heard, him laugh, a deep rumble in his chest. 'A pleasure,' he said, making her smile weakly in the darkness.

More stroking of her hair. Her tense muscles began to relax. She was warm now. She did not deserve to be warm when Guillaume was cold. Cold and dead. She struggled to sit up.

Calumn pulled her effortlessly back against him. 'Where do you think you're going?'

'I don't deserve this.'

'I know it's difficult to accept, especially when you were so sure, but—'

'No, that's not what I meant. I don't deserve *this*. You. Me, lying here like this, feeling warm and—and safe.'

'Madeleine, what you're feeling is perfectly natural. It's normal to feel guilty to be alive when someone dear to you dies, I promise you. What you must remember is that Guillaume was a free man. He chose to fight, he chose to take the risk, as every soldier does who goes into battle. He died fighting for something he believed in. His choice. You've no need to be feeling guilty.'

She struggled to sit up. 'You don't understand, Calumn, I've every reason to feel guilty. I'm a wicked, wicked person.'

She was wringing her hands together, her breath coming short and fast, the rapid rise and fall of her breasts clear under the thin material of her sark. To his shame, Calumn felt himself stirring and quickly averted his eyes. 'It's been a shock, that's all. Of course you're upset, but you've no need to feel guilty. Nor to think yourself wicked, simply because you're alive and Guillaume is not.'

'You don't understand! That's not why I feel guilty. It's because—it's because—when I found out that Guillaume was dead I was relieved.' She waited for the disgust to show on his face, but he simply returned her gaze. 'It meant I didn't have to face him. Now do you see what I mean? I wished him dead.'

Instead of pushing her away, Calumn pulled her back against him. 'There's a world of difference between being relieved that you don't have to face something, and actually wishing it. You didn't wish him dead, but he is dead, and now you don't have to face something you were dreading. That doesn't make you wicked. It makes you human.'

Madeleine shifted in the bed, turning to meet his gaze in the flickering light of the lamp, the fire having died out long ago. 'You don't hate me?'

'I could never hate you. Come, it's been a hell of a day. Do you think you could sleep?'

She nodded wearily. 'Will you stay with me, just for a little while? Just to hold me? Please.'

'You're asking a lot. It would be a first, you know.'

'I'm sorry I—'

'It was a joke, Madeleine—the first bit, anyway. The second bit was true.' He pulled her against him so that her head rested on his shoulder and tucked the blankets up around her.

'Calumn?' Her voice was the faintest whisper.

'What, lass?'

'You saved my life today, I'll never forget that. Thank you. And thank you for being here now.'

'Hush.' He cradled her in his arms until the

rhythmical sound of her breathing told him she was asleep. Exhausted, he, too, soon fell fast asleep.

Madeleine awoke with her heart pounding, completely disorientated. It was still dark. Outside the rain had stopped, leaving a clear sky dotted with stars. The moon was almost full, shining high in the sky. She was hot. She tried to push the blankets down and found they were anchored to her by a muscular arm. Calumn. Then she remembered.

The guilt which had rocked her off balance seemed to have dissipated. Calumn had a way of putting the world in perspective for her. He sighed in his sleep and Madeleine wriggled closer, spooning her body into the nook of his. The movement revealed his state of undress. He had only his shirt on—how could she not have noticed that last night? She wriggled closer, relishing the feel of her contours against his.

Over the past few days, the building blocks of her life had tumbled into disarray and must now be rebuilt in a different shape. Nothing felt real any more. Nothing, except the man lying beside her. This warm, alive, solid man, who had rescued her, taken her under his wing, and now saved her life. The jolting reality hit her like a blow to the stomach. If Calumn had not arrived when he did this afternoon, she would almost certainly be as dead as Guillaume. He had been quite fearless. Only now, thinking back on the event, did she realise how incredibly brave he had been. Three to one. Exactly as it had been the first night they met, only much more dangerous.

Wanting surged through her like a tearing hunger. She felt cavernously empty, cravingly needy. As if she were a husk which needed to be filled. Made into flesh and blood. Made to feel. Made alive again. She was thirsty for life. And here beside her was the perfect person, the only person, capable of slaking that thirst. Something primal bubbled through her veins. She needed him. She needed him now, especially now that there were no more barriers.

She eased herself carefully from Calumn's loose embrace, lifting her sark over her head. Naked, she turned around to face him. The rough hairs of his bare legs against hers. Skin. And heat.

Was he awake? His eyelids were closed. His lips slightly parted. She smoothed his hair back from his forehead. Kissed the tiny scar on his brow. Now the cleft on his chin, feeling the rasp of his bristles on her tongue. Still he did not stir.

She pressed closer, putting an arm around him, feeling, under the shirt, the indentation of his waist, the rise of his buttock, to the scar on his belly. She traced the curve of it down to its ending, her fingers brushing the rougher hair there, her breath coming quicker as the feel of him sent arousing messages back, through her fingertips, into her blood, heating her all over. *Wake up, Calumn.*

She felt the weight of his erection on her thigh. She allowed her fingertips to flutter near, nearer, caressing the tip of him, adjusting her body so that she could feel more of him. Wriggling again. Nearer. Breathing quickening. Closer.

'Madeleine, what are you doing?'

'You need to ask?'

'This is not a good idea.'

'Yes, it is. *I* think it is.'

'Well, I don't.'

'Part of you does.'

Her fingers fluttered over that part of him again. A sharp intake of breath. His hand clenched on her thigh. 'You're naked.'

'Yes.'

'This is definitely not a good idea,' he said, struggling to sound convincing.

'Calumn, it's what I want. There's no reason, now, for us not to.' She pressed a feverish kiss to his chest. She kissed his throat, where a pulse beat fast against her lips.

His hands smoothed their way over her skin, her arms, the line from her shoulder down to her waist, on to her thigh. She lifted her head to look at him, saw indecision and desire writ equally large in his heavy-lidded eyes.

'It wouldn't be right,' he said raggedly, meeting her gaze.

'You're wrong. It's the one thing that feels exactly right.'

Calumn groaned. The temptation was unbearable. He prayed for the strength to match his resolve. 'It's just your grief talking. You've had a traumatic day, your emotions are all over the place.'

'It doesn't feel like grief,' Madeleine said, a little desperately. Despite the ample evidence of his arousal, she could see he had made up his mind, and she knew that once he had, it would be as easy to change it as it was to breach the walls of Edinburgh Castle. 'I'm not confused. I want you, Calumn, I can see you want me.'

His expression set. 'No,' he said, and now the word held a world of conviction. He wrenched himself free of her. 'No.'

He retrieved her sark, pulled it over her, keeping his hands strictly, strictly to the business of fastening it at the neck, refusing to allow his mind to dwell on the vision of her gloriously naked. Parts of him persisted in clinging to that image. He forced himself to ignore the urges of those parts too, though it cost him dear. 'You're in no frame of mind to know what you want, Madeleine. I'm not going to let you do anything that you'll regret in the morning.'

'I wouldn't regret it.'

'You won't have to.' He pushed back the bedcovers and got to his feet. 'When we make love, it will be because you want me, and for that reason alone. I'm going now. Try to get some rest.' Hastily pulling on his plaid and gathering up the rest of his clothing before he changed his mind, Calumn fled.

Madeleine shivered violently, all traces of desire gone so completely that she wondered where they had come from in the first place. She curled up under the sheet into a tight ball. Hot tears leaked from her eyes. Calumn's abrupt departure left her feeling lonelier than she had ever felt in her life.

When we make love, it will be because you want me, and for that reason alone. He had said when, not if. One word, but it brought immense comfort. She clung to it. Held it close like a talisman. She dreamt of being shipwrecked. Of drowning, only to be tossed up in a strange land. Like Viola, she thought, waking the next morning with a start. If only, like Viola, her own journey could end in lovers meeting.

She found Calumn sitting alone in the great hall, the other houseguests clearly still busy sleeping off the effects of the previous night's carousing. He looked preoccupied, jumping to his feet when she greeted him, obviously unaware until that moment of her approach. 'Madeleine. I hope you managed some sleep.'

'A little. What about you?' she asked politely, unable to quite meet his eyes.

'The same. I'm afraid I can only offer you cold meats and leftovers for breakfast. Everyone is still abed, including the servants—what few there are of them.'

'I'm not really hungry.'

He gestured for her to sit opposite him. 'You need to eat something, you had no dinner. Here, I've made up a plate for you.'

She took her place reluctantly. 'Thank you.' She picked up a knife, looked at the food in front of her, felt a wave of nausea, and replaced the knife on the table. 'Calumn, about last night... I don't know what came over me, I think maybe I'm losing my mind. I should never have...'

He reached across the table to take her hands in his. 'You have no need to apologise. For what it's worth I think you're doing a remarkable job of preserving your sanity, given the circumstances. Any other woman would have succumbed to strong hysterics at the very least, by now.'

Her smile was tentative. 'At least I've not subjected you to that.'

Calumn pressed her hand reassuringly. 'You've been through enough trauma in the last few days to last you a lifetime. You've made your way on your own to a foreign country. You've travelled for days through an alien wilderness, been abducted and near enough killed, and, to top it all, you've just found out that the man you were to marry is dead. What you felt last night was a desperate need for solace. There's no shame in that, it's a perfectly natural and very human reaction.'

'Thank you.' Unwilling to allow him to see how much his words had touched her, she strove for a lighter tone. 'You're being so very nice about it, you must think me a poor soul indeed.'

'I think you're a very brave soul, and I am simply telling you the truth.' He eyed her with concern. There were dark circles under her eyes. She looked wan, her skin had lost its translucence. 'It's a bonny day outside,' he said bracingly, 'we should head off as soon as possible, make the most of it.'

Her heart plummeted. Nausea churned in her stomach. The smell of food was making her ill. She pushed her plate to the side. 'Head off? Yes, yes, of course, I suppose I should be thinking about my journey home.' Home. The image the word evoked was like a painting, rather than a real place.

'You're not going home, not yet. I am, and you're coming with me—as far as Heronsay anyway.'

'What? What did you say?'

Calumn grinned. 'We're going to Heronsay, to visit Rory. It's high time I cleared the air with my brother.'

She looked at him speechlessly, then a smile spread across her face like the sun rising, and she clapped her hands together with delight. 'That's wonderful news. I'm so happy for you. And I know that it's what will make you happy.'

Her unaffected response touched his heart. Not one word of "I told you so." She was happy because he was happy, despite all her own cares. A rare creature. It felt good to have her on his side.

'And Errin Mhor?'

Calumn laughed. 'You're quite a taskmaster. Yes, all roads lead to Errin Mhor, I told you that. But I don't think you heard me right. I'm taking you with me, to Heronsay.'

'Taking me with you,' she repeated stupidly.

'To Heronsay.' He reached over to take her hand. 'We have unfinished business, you and I.'

Now her heart began to pound. *When* we make love, not *if.* She remembered her dream and wondered if it was a portent. She wanted to go with him. No matter what the future held, no matter what the consequences, she wanted to go with him. For not to do so would be to regret for ever what might have been.

'Madeleine?'

She smiled, a slow curling smile she had learned from him, had learned he liked. 'Yes. I'd like that very much.'

'If—when you are ready to return to France, it will be a much simpler matter from there. Rory will be able to arrange a passage for you on one of the boats which ply their trade down the west coast to the channel ports.'

Her smile faltered. He made her no promises, but she had already decided to take her chances. She would not fail for want of trying. 'Yes, that makes sense. Thank you.' Despite the looming unknown of her future, and the knowledge of poor Guillaume's death, she felt a lightness of spirit which was a prelude to a new kind of happiness. She was in love and was taking her fate into her own hands. How far she had come from the woman who had landed at the port of Leith, content to entrust her future happiness to others.

She took a deep breath. 'Calumn, last night—it wasn't just about solace.'

She had taken him by surprise, but she could tell from the way he smiled that it was a pleasant one.

His eyes smouldered with promise. 'Next time, it won't be about solace at all. Next time, it will be about you and I and nothing else.'

She blushed furiously, a heat which spread rapidly through her body, making her breathless.

Satisfied, for now, Calumn laughed huskily. 'Eat. I want to be away from here. I have not Castle Rhubodach in mind as an appropriate setting, you can be sure of that.'

Madeleine picked up her fork and took a little of the mutton, unable to face the venison. 'Will I like Rory?' she asked in an effort to direct her thoughts to a less distracting channel.

'He's very like me.'

'Ah, then I'll be bound to like him.'

'And if he has an ounce of judgement, he will like you! Now, eat your breakfast, the sooner we set off the better.' Calumn picked up his own knife and addressed himself to his plate with a renewed appetite.

'I'll be sorry to see you both go, we haven't had this much excitement for months,' Angus McAngus said with a whimsical smile when Calumn sought him out to announce their departure. McAngus was looking distinctly the worse for wear, his hair and beard so dishevelled he resembled a walking gorse bush. 'You seem uncommon happy this morning, young Munro, if you don't mind me saying. The prospect of going home, I expect.'

'Why else?'

McAngus fixed him with a gimlet eye and winked extravagantly. 'Why else, indeed? God speed to you, Calumn Munro, and to your lovely companion. Remember what they say, a misty morning may become a clear day. Now, you'll forgive my rudeness, but I won't see you out. I must go in search of a hair of the dog that bit me.'

'Quite a large hair, I suppose,' Calumn suggested with a smile.

The old laird shrugged and tilted his head to the side. 'Indeed. But then it was, after all, an uncommonly big dog.'

The approach to Heronsay was marked by a series of little villages, no more than clusters of cottages—crofts, Calumn called them—surrounded by a patchwork of fields planted mostly with potatoes, oats and barley. There were plenty of sheep roaming free on the hillsides, looking like puffs of cotton stitched on to the heather, but very few cattle. Though the villages were pretty, whitewashed and thatch-roofed, Madeleine thought the people seemed rather dour. A few smiled at Calumn, but none met Madeleine's eyes, nor returned her smiles.

'They're wary of strangers, especially after what's happened,' Calumn explained.

'I thought McAngus said that you'd protected Rory's lands. I can't see any signs of damage.'

'My influence didn't extend to those of his neighbours. You have to remember, we're a very close-knit community. Everyone here will have kin who've lost something—or someone. What happened in the aftermath of Culloden up here—I can't describe it, Madeleine, it was beyond words.'

'But you saved all of this—' she made a sweeping gesture '—you kept all these people safe.'

'A small enough reparation.'

'I'll wager your brother doesn't think that.'

Calumn shrugged. 'We'll find out soon enough. Heronsay is not far now. I hope it lives up to your expectations.'

And I hope it lives up to yours, Madeleine thought with some trepidation.

It was late afternoon. Clouds scudded across the paling sky. They had been travelling due west towards the sun for some miles now, following the level track as it wended its way from village to village. The scent of the sea grew stronger with every step their tired mounts took. Madeleine was excited, nervous, and anxious that Calumn's new-found confidence might be deflated in the face of a tepid welcome.

They rounded a bend and suddenly there it was. Heronsay. Of one accord they brought their horses to a halt. A cluster of fishermen's cottages, surprisingly like those her mother's family had occupied, perched so close to the sea that they looked as if they would float away at high tide. A gently shelving beach covered in white-and-grey pebbles. A small fleet of fishing boats bobbing a few yards offshore, sleeker in line than the galleon-shaped Breton ones.

'That's Heronsay there, the island across the

sound—though all the land hereabouts is Rory's, too,' Calumn said, pointing across the narrow stretch of water which separated his brother's home from the mainland. 'You can just see his standard flying above the turret of the castle.'

'Will he be expecting you, then?'

'It wouldn't surprise me—and expecting us, not just me. I told you, news travels like wildfire.'

The island was almost flat and very green, a verdant contrast to the mainland. Heronsay Castle was built along the same lines as Castle Rhubodach, though it had two towers, and even from here Madeleine could tell it was well maintained. All around, in fact, the land, the villages, the boats and the island, spoke of care, attention, and wealth. 'How does it feel, being back here?'

'The last time, Rory had just escaped from the Campbell dungeons. I told you how he brought Jessica with him. They were married as soon as he could get the banns read, but I didn't stay.'

'He'll be pleased to see you now, then?'

Calumn's grin was only a little rigid. 'Only one way to find out.'

They made their way to the inn at the far end of the village, where the landlord greeted Calumn like an old friend and stabled the horses. As Calumn had predicted, they were expected. A boat, flying Rory's standard, was crossing the sound. The man at the helm, with his mane of gold hair, was unmistakably the laird himself.

Madeleine felt sick with nerves. She clutched

compulsively at Calumn's hand, glancing first to him, then to the boat, then up at Calumn again.

'Stop that, you're making me nervous,' he said, without taking his eyes off the figure in the boat, which had reached the shallows now.

Rory Macleod leapt lithely into the water, pulling the sturdy wooden craft on to the beach with effortless ease. He stood on the pebbles, scanning the village, the expression on his face impossible to read, obscured by the dazzle of light from the sun setting directly behind him. He looked to be about the same height and build as Calumn. Together, they would make a fine-looking pair.

Rory was dressed in trews, a shirt and waistcoat. Clean shaven. Now he had seen them and was waving. A grin split his tanned face. Madeleine tugged her hand free of Calumn's. 'Go on, I'll wait here.' He seemed rooted to the spot. She gave him a little push. 'Go on.'

Calumn walked down to the beach. Rory gave a whoop of welcome which reverberated across the water. He enveloped his brother in a bear hug. Madeleine's knees gave way in relief. She slumped in an undignified heap on to the ground, her eyes wet with tears.

Chapter Nine

'So this is your French companion, then.'

Madeleine looked up to find two exemplary spec-
imens of Highland manhood standing over her, two
pairs of eyes, one set brown, the other blue, staring at her from two extremely handsome faces.
Rory Macleod was as good looking as she had
expected, but not nearly as attractive, in her eyes, as his
brother. The aforementioned brother reached for her
hand and pulled her easily to her feet. 'Madeleine,
this is Rory.'

'*Enchanté, mademoiselle,*' Rory said, bowing
gracefully over her hand in just exactly the same
way as Calumn had the first night they had met.

Madeleine curtsied daintily. 'The pleasure is all
mine, *monsieur.* I've heard so much about you.'

Rory laughed, clapping Calumn's shoulders. 'All
bad, if you've heard it from this one.'

'*Au contraire,* all good, I promise.'

Rory grinned, but looked unconvinced. 'I can't believe you're here,' he said, turning back to his brother, 'I've so much to tell you. Do you know I'm a father? A wee girl. Christina.'

Calumn raised an eyebrow. 'Named for our mother? You kept to the tradition then.'

'Aye. But we call her Kirsty.'

'It must have been a worry to you, her arriving so early.'

'Early?' Rory frowned. 'Not at all, she was a full nine months. Whatever gave you that idea?'

'The fact you'd only been married seven,' Calumn said, laughing delightedly at his brother's sheepish look. 'Congratulations. Is Jessica well?'

'Blooming,' Rory said tenderly. 'I'm a lucky man. I look at her sometimes, and I can't quite believe she's still here. She's a lowlander,' he explained to Madeleine, 'had never been north of Glasgow when I met her.'

'Kidnapped her, you mean,' Calumn interjected. 'She was on her way to visit her cousin in Inverary and Rory here took her captive.'

'You're joking?'

Rory laughed. 'Not a whit of it. I tied her up and galloped off with her. She started off my hostage and ended up my wife. I married her out of hand too, for her parents disowned her. You'd think she was living on the moon, rather than a few days' ride from Glasgow.'

'How romantic,' Madeleine said, her eyes shining.

Rory laughed again. 'Don't be saying that in his hearing, you'll give him ideas,' he said, nodding at his brother, 'and that one doesn't need any encouragement.'

'Oh, I don't know,' Madeleine said mischievously, fairly entranced by the idea of Calumn carrying her off as his captive.

She was rewarded with one of his slow smiles, was basking in it, so she did not notice the startled expression on Rory's face as he looked first from his brother to the pretty little maid at his side.

'Come on then, into the boat with both of you.' Rory ushered them down to the shore. He couldn't wait to see what Jessica would make of this!

Calumn helped Madeleine on board, and the brothers pulled the little craft out into deeper water, working together with the instinctive harmony of two people who have carried out the same task in just this way most of their lives. 'The last time I sat in a boat with a woman was that very day you brought Jessica here,' he mused as he unravelled the sail, leaving Rory to take the tiller.

'We've missed you.' Rory's voice was gruff. 'You've been away long enough.'

'Aye, well, we'll see,' Calumn said, his own voice equally gruff.

'No, I mean it. We've missed you. I'm glad— really glad—you're home.'

Calumn sat down on the narrow bench beside

Madeleine and put his arm around her. Though the day had been warm, there was a cooling wind blowing across the sound. Perhaps it was this which made his eyes water? She snuggled close to him, nestling her head on to his shoulder. Or perhaps not.

They landed as the sun set behind Heronsay, a spectacular sight, streaking gold and crimson across the horizon. Jessica Macleod was waiting to greet them at the jetty. Her husband enveloped her in a hug, sweeping her off her feet and kissing her hungrily, as if they had been parted for weeks. She was a slight thing, more curvaceous since her pregnancy, with ebony black hair dressed high on her head and a classically beautiful face. The plain green gown she wore was well cut, and she had overall an air of elegance which made her look as exotic here on this Scottish island as a hothouse flower.

'Put me down, Rory, we have guests,' she said, laughing up into her husband's face. But it was obvious she was as in thrall to him as he was to her. The intimate look they exchanged was a secret promise.

After the introductions had been made, Calumn and Madeleine followed the Macleods up the path from the beach to Heronsay Castle. Madeleine watched the couple in front feeling both dowdy and envious.

She jumped, as Calumn slipped his arm around her shoulder. 'Married life obviously suits Rory,' he said. 'You wouldn't believe it, but before he met Jessica, he was a worse man than me for the ladies.'

'You're right, I don't believe it,' Madeleine replied. 'They certainly do look very happy, though. They're obviously made for each other, and they obviously know it. And now they have a baby, too. How lucky they are.'

'You like bairns?'

Madeleine smiled wistfully, imagining a whole brood of children, each with Calumn's blue eyes and golden hair. 'Lots—it comes of being an only child.' Her smile faded. 'What about you? Isn't it funny, I've never asked you.'

He imagined them, a little row of miniature Madeleines. It was a painfully pretty picture. 'I've never thought about it,' he said dismissively. He closed his mind to the bewitching image of his daughters, wondering why doing so hurt, as if he had killed them.

Conversation over dinner was wide ranging, mainly concerned with the changes in the Highlands which had taken place since the end of the Rebellion, with Rory lamenting the ban on the plaid, due to be implemented in a few weeks' time, and extolling the worth of the new black-faced sheep which were being introduced by some of the more modern landlords. Jessica left the table early to nurse her child, bidding Calumn and Madeleine a graceful goodnight before directing a meaningful look at her husband.

Toying with her wine glass, Madeleine stifled a yawn. The food had been excellent, beef served with a red wine sauce and not a turnip in sight. The castle, too, was beautifully appointed, unexpectedly homely compared to Castle Rhubodach, and warm, for the glazing was all in good order. On top of everything else, Jessica was obviously an excellent housekeeper.

From the expression on Rory's face every time his gaze fell on his lovely wife, it was clear that her talents were not confined to domestic duties. Lucky Jessica.

Madeleine drained her glass and pushed her seat back from the table. 'If you'll excuse me, I think I'll go to bed. It's been a long day, and you must have lots of things to talk about.' When Calumn and Rory made to rise, she shook her head. 'Please, there's no need to get up on my account.' She dropped a curtsy and swept out of the room without giving either of them a chance to object.

There was a large copper jug of warm water waiting for her in her bedchamber. Fresh flowers sat on the escritoire at the window. There was a warming pan between sheets smelling of heather and sunshine. The pillows were soft, the mattress firm. Even as she snuggled gratefully down, wearing the clean nightdress Jessica had thoughtfully draped at the end of the bed, trying to stay awake just in case Calumn decided to pay her a visit, the home comforts of Heronsay Castle conspired against her. Madeleine fell into a deep and dreamless sleep.

Downstairs, Rory poured a measure of whisky into two heavy crystal glasses. 'Pure malt, fifteen years old, you'll not taste a finer dram.'

Calumn rolled the smoky spirit on his tongue 'You're right. It's grand.'

Silence reigned. Rory sipped his malt and waited patiently. His relief at seeing Calumn looking almost his old self again was palpable. Throughout Calumn's long months of self-imposed exile in Edinburgh, the temptation to hunt him out and drag him home had been overwhelming. It had been Jessica who had convinced him to wait. 'He needs time for his wounds to heal,' she had told him.

Rory smiled to himself as he remembered his reply. 'It's been six months since he was near disembowelled, he's fine.'

'Not those wounds,' his wise wee wife had said, laughing.   And it looked as though she had been right. It went against the grain, but he had left Calumn to it, and now here he was, looking—healed.

He decided it was time to break the silence, for it looked as if Calumn never would, and much as he wanted to talk things over, Rory had a wife who had informed him earlier that day with a promising smile that she had fully recovered from the birth of their daughter. 'You seem well,' he said to his brother. 'You had a peaky look about you the last time I saw you.'

'Hardly surprising. A claymore's a vicious weapon.'

So much for tact. Rory decided not to waste any more time. 'Aye, but it was more than that, wasn't it? We didn't get a chance to talk properly. I told you at the time that all I cared about was seeing you alive and well, but you didn't believe me, did you?'

Calum shrugged awkwardly. Though he knew this discussion was the reason he had come to Heronsay, he and his brother had always been men of few words. He detected his sister-in-law's influence on Rory. He thought of Madeleine's influence on himself. He could almost hear her now, urging him to speak up.

Calum sat back in his chair, the better to see his brother's face by the light of the large candelabra on the table. 'Aye, you're in the right of it, I didn't believe you. I know you meant it when you said it, but I thought when you'd had time to reflect—well, at the very least that you'd hate me for choosing the wrong side.'

'But you didn't choose, did you? If you'd had a choice, you might not have followed the Prince, but I know fine and well you wouldn't have fought against him—against me—of your own accord.' Rory ran his hand through his heavy fall of hair, a gesture which Madeleine would have recognised instantly. 'Do you not think I've been in a frenzy of worry about you, lad? You might be twenty-six years old and every bit as big and brawny as I am myself, but you're my wee brother, and you always will be. There were times when Jessica had to hold me back with her bare hands, I was so set on heading off to Edinburgh to find you.'

Calum grinned. 'Bare hands? All Jessica has to do is look at you sideways and you fall at her feet.'

'You know what I mean. Why has it taken you so long to come home?'

Go on! Once again, he could hear Madeleine's voice in his head. Calumn started talking. Slowly and hesitantly at first. Then the words began to flow in a torrent, rushing and tumbling as the dam broke and he finally unburdened himself.

The candles were guttering when he finished talking, though the level on the whisky decanter had not dropped at all. As he talked and Rory listened, explained, contradicted and reassured, his brother's words echoed Madeleine's so precisely that Calumn wondered fleetingly if she had somehow managed to counsel him before dinner. Foolish thought. More like his brother had been counselled by his wife. But though the words might be in part Jessica's, there was no doubting the sincerity of them. Calumn felt the black weight of the past finally lift itself free from his shoulders.

'And what of Errin Mhor?' Rory asked, never one to shirk the difficult questions. 'Our mother has been on at me for months now to *fetch you back,* as she puts it. Her urging me to do so was one of the things that kept me here. I knew it was probably best to do the opposite of anything she demanded.'

'You're not wrong there. So she's been here, then? Has she seen her grandchild?'

Rory's face darkened. 'No. I've had a surfeit of letters from her, though. No point in expecting her to change now. And your father is in a bad way, I hear. Not just from our mother, I've had it from Ailsa, too.'

'Ailsa! I haven't seen her in six years. Things must have changed a bit if she's allowed to visit you.'

'All Ailsa's doing. She's as stubborn as a mule, puts you in the shade. She's grown into quite a lass, she has all the lads at her feet and takes great pleasure in trampling on them. You'll see her tomorrow, she's coming for Kirsty's ceilidh. You haven't answered my question. Are you going to Errin Mhor?'

'Yes. Yes, I am,' Calumn said decisively. Not just because it was the right thing, he realised, but because he wanted to.

'Good. I can't tell you how glad I am to hear you say that. Your father's dying, but if you're thinking he's as feeble in mind as he is in body, you're wrong. He's perfectly capable of holding his own. You'll have to be ready to take the reins off him in the teeth of that. I tell you now, if you do, your tenants will greet you with open arms. That factor our mother has employed is not up to the job, and to be honest, Calumn, your land's in very bad heart. Your tenants are starting to leave—for America, some of them. It wouldn't surprise me if the old man was neglecting them deliberately.'

'To ruin my inheritance, you mean? Or to force me to do his bidding and come home?'

'Aye, I know it sounds fanciful, but it's the sort of thing the thrawn old bastard would do. He won't ever admit it, but he needs you. Enough of Lord Munro— tell me more about this Madeleine of yours. She's a bonny wee thing.'

'Bonny! She's a sight more than that.'

'Aye, well, I prefer dark-haired women myself.'

'Just one dark-haired woman, I hope,' Calumn said with a grin.

'Oh, there's no need to worry on that score,' Rory replied with a wider grin. 'As I said earlier, marriage suits me. You should try it.'

'Me!'

'Don't tell me you haven't thought of it,' Rory said in surprise. 'You're head over heels in love with that wee lassie. I know a man in love when I see one—from looking in the mirror, you understand. You're a changed man, Calumn, you look—dare I say it—happy.'

'Relieved, more like. I've been a long time in coming back here.'

Rory shook his head. 'It's not just that. I reckon it's got more to do with the presence of that wee green-eyed lass. And just in case you haven't noticed, she's every bit as besotted with you as you are with her.' Rory got to his feet, snuffing the last of the candles before lighting two lamps with a taper lit from the embers of the fire. 'I'm off to bed, where my lovely wife will be waiting for me. Hopefully, she'll not have fallen asleep.'

Calumn pushed back his chair. 'You should have said.'

Rory handed him one of the lamps. 'I was under strict instructions not to come upstairs until you and I had cleared the air. And one of the many wonderful things about marriage is that there's no hurry. We have the rest of our lives together.'

'I used to think that was the worst thing about marriage.'

Rory clapped his hand to Calumn's shoulder. 'Used to?' He left the room, laughing softly to himself.

All hands were required for the preparations for the ceilidh, which began early the next day, leaving no room for privacy. Madeleine was eager to help and Jessica was only too happy to accept. 'Bless you, would you come and give me a hand with the flowers? We don't have a lot to work with, I'm afraid,' she said, leading the way down a flight of steep stone steps to the stillroom.

Once they had agreed on the containers for the arrangements and the overall colour scheme, the two women set about their work in comfortable accord. 'Rory's taken Calumn over to the mainland to look at sheep, would you believe?' Jessica said, frowning over the centre piece for the dinner table. 'He's obsessed with this new breed, something about the quality of the wool, but I have to confess when he talks to me about it I stop listening. I'm hoping he'll take the trading side of it up with my father, though. He's a merchant, based in Glasgow. It might help mend a few bridges if they can do business together.'

'I take it your parents still aren't reconciled to your marriage, then,' Madeleine asked. 'Don't you mind?'

Jessica shrugged. 'Not as much as Rory does. I

mind it more for Kirsty, missing out on both her grandmothers, since Lady Munro will have nothing to do with her either. It's their loss, is how I think of it.' She was silent for a few minutes, weaving heather into a long garland for the great hall. 'No, that's not quite true. Of course I mind. I miss my sisters, and I don't like being at odds with my parents, but—well, in a way it's simple. I can get by without my family, but I couldn't live without Rory. My parents will come round in the end, I'm sure. They seem to think I'm living in some sort of Highland hovel, they've no idea what a wealthy man my husband is—and I haven't told them. I want them to approve of us for our own sakes—maybe for their granddaughter's sake.'

'Kirsty's adorable. I've never held such a new baby before.'

'Wait 'til you have one of your own to hold. It's the most—I can't describe it, it really is like a miracle. You should have seen Rory, the first time he held her.' Jessica blinked back a tear. 'You wait.'

'Oh, I don't think…'

Jessica smiled. 'I've seen the way you look at Calumn. I look at his brother in the exact same way.' She placed a last rose in the ornate silver epergne she had been filling. 'There, we're done here. And if I'm not mistaken, that's the men back, too. Just in time.'

As the hour of the ceilidh approached, Calumn had ample opportunity to observe the changes in his brother which marriage had brought about. Marriage did not just suit Rory, it had improved him beyond measure. Gone were his flashes of temper, his impatience, even his indifference to matters domestic. Here he was offering his wife advice on the placement of an arrangement of roses. Calumn watched with amusement as Rory moved the cut-glass vase from the oak chest and placed it instead on a small teak cabinet in an alcove. Jessica clapped her hands in admiration. Rory selected a bloom from the vase and presented it to her with a flourish. Jessica reached up to kiss him. Not a peck on the check. A proper kiss. Completely unnoticed, Calumn slipped from the room.

Madeleine was standing on the landing, directing the set up of tables in the great hall. She saw him watching and smiled fleetingly before returning to her task, frowning down at the paper she held in her hand—Jessica's plan, presumably—and then waving and pointing at her helpers below. Her lack of Gaelic was confusing matters. When she got into a flap, as she had now, she lapsed into French, which confused matters more.

One of the wonderful things about marriage is that there's no hurry. Calumn was climbing the stairs to go to her assistance, but his brother's words made him stop in his tracks. Rory was right. He had always seen marriage as a sort of life sentence before, but Rory's marriage was obviously a very positive thing. Rory was certainly transformed by it, and blissfully happy too, a happiness that went deep to the bone.

Madeleine was leaning precariously over the banister flapping her arms about and shouting, *à gauche, à gauche, à gauche.* She looked like a baby grouse trying to fly, and even more endearing. Calumn wrested Jessica's plan from her and repeated the instructions in Gaelic.

Madeleine made him laugh. She told him uncomfortable truths. She never let him get away with anything, yet he never doubted that she was on his side. He liked the way she looked at him. She knew him, in a way that no one else did, and he liked her knowing, for he trusted her with the knowledge. He liked the way her body fitted so perfectly into his, too, as if it were a space made specially for her to fit. And as for the way he desired her—the way she desired him—he had never felt anything like it.

Did she make him happy? He looked at her, the frown of concentration on her face, the slight pursing of her infinitely kissable lips, the entrancing line of her spine, curving out to the roundness of her bottom. Yes. She did. And it felt right. Was it really as simple as that? How ironic that he, who had spent most of their acquaintance preaching to Madeleine about the nature of love, should have omitted to ask himself the very question he had forced upon her numerous times.

'Calumn, what is it?'

He jumped. 'What?'

'You were staring at me.'

'Just thinking.' Mechanically, he continued to help her with the directing of operations, but he felt dazed and dazzled, aware that she was casting covert glances at him, unable to stop himself from looking at her, as if he was seeing her for the first time.

Forcing himself to imagine life without her, the future, which had begun to seem so appealing, took on a bleaker hue. Without her, he knew for certain that he would be unhappy. Not even Errin Mhor would compensate for her absence. Maybe it really was that simple.

'Is that the last one?'

Calumn hastily consulted the plan. 'The last one. Yes, I think so.' He knew he was staring again, but he could not help it. *Why had she agreed so readily to come here to Heronsay with him? Had she, too, discovered happiness?*

A distant baby's wail came from upstairs, followed by another, louder and more determined one. The door to the dining room burst open and Jessica appeared. 'Kirsty's due a feed,' she explained, rushing past them, seemingly oblivious of the fact that the fastenings of her robe were undone at the neck. A single pink rose petal clung to the white skin of her breast.

'What can she have been doing?' Madeleine asked.

'I think her husband was showing her some flower-arranging techniques,' Calumn replied with a grin.

Madeleine's mouth formed a round *oh* of surprise. A delightful blush pinked her cheeks, the same colour as the rose petal. He could not resist her. He kissed her full on her infinitely kissable mouth. A fleeting kiss, in full view of the servants, and of Rory, too, who had emerged from the dining room looking even more dishevelled than his wife. The merest touch of his lips to hers, but it had the strangest effect, for as he kissed her, Calumn could have sworn he heard his heart speak to him. It was the merest whisper, but the words were clear, none the less.

When Madeleine came downstairs that evening, having soaked luxuriously in a large bath brought up to her room before dressing in a clean shift and her Breton blue dress, Heronsay Castle had been transformed. Garlands of heather were draped around the banister leading down to the great hall, which was blooming with flowers, and where Jessica was holding court with baby Kirsty in her arms. Mother and daughter were both in white, the child's robe of satin and lace intricately embroidered, Jessica's dress a simpler but no less effective creation with only a long length of Macleod plaid worn as a sash to provide contrast. Madeleine felt dowdy in comparison. She had never been one to give much thought to her appearance or her clothes, but she wished she had a dress more suited to the occasion.

Gifts for Kirsty were laid out on a large table— spoons carved from wood and bone, silver rattles and pewter quaichs, the traditional Scottish drinking cup. Skirting the edge of the crowd, Madeleine made her way out into the gardens, feeling unaccountably shy and out of place in what was, after all, a family celebration. She chided herself for being so feeble—they were just people, after all—but her usual confidence seemed to have deserted her.

On the lawn in front of the castle long rows of trestle tables covered in snowy white cloths were laid out, decorated with wild flowers and heather. A steady stream of people were making their way up the path from the jetty, where Madeleine could see at least four boats ploughing back and forth across the sound. Men pushing carts laden with food and drink. A rowdy group with fiddles and bagpipes. Rory's tenants in their Sunday best, children bubbling with excitement, women bobbing nervous curtsies and apologising for the excited screaming of their bairns. Dour men looking uncomfortable, sweating in their heavy formal jackets under the warm evening sun. Well-dressed neighbours and their wives in a colourful assortment of beautifully woven plaids.

Rory was standing in the doorway, greeting his guests. Madeleine noticed he knew the name not just of every one of his tenants, but of their wives and children, too. He had a way of putting people at their ease, of knowing just the right thing to say to make the dour men laugh, the nervous ladies blush. As she watched, admiring his finesse, Calumn joined him. The two men were in traditional dress, though their plaids were different colours. Calumn's belt and buckle had been polished. The pin he wore to hold his *filleadh mòr* in place gleamed. His mane of hair had been washed and brushed into submission, and he was clean shaven. The light tan he had acquired over the last few days seemed to make the lines of his face more defined. The more subtle changes that had taken place in him since coming here were evident in his stance, in the pride he so obviously took in wearing his clan plaid, in the confidence with which he joined Rory in greeting each guest.

'It's almost unfair, how handsome they are together, isn't it? I feel like I can't compete.'

Madeleine jumped, for she had not heard Jessica approach. 'You have nothing to worry about, you look stunning. You make me feel so plain.'

'Plain, with that hair and those eyes of yours—don't be ridiculous. Oh, look, there's Ailsa.'

'Where—oh!'

'I know, there's no mistaking who her brothers are. Though apparently she's the image of her mother.'

The tall young woman with a mass of golden hair and eyes the same blue as Calumn's had spotted her brothers. With a very unlady-like screech, she threw herself at Calumn, wrapping her arms around his neck. 'Is it really you? I can't believe it.'

Calumn was looking at his sister in astonishment. 'Ailsa? My God, you've turned out bonny. The last time I saw you, you were just a wee lassie.'

'Well, that's not my fault.' Catching a warning look from Rory, she smiled apologetically. 'You're here now, that's the main thing. I have a thousand things to tell you and a whole load of messages from our mother. What's this I hear about you having a mysterious French beauty in tow? Where's Jessica?' she asked, turning to Rory. 'More importantly, where's my niece?'

Rory looked over his shoulder. 'Kirsty's in there. Poor wee soul, she's being passed about like a parcel but she's being as good as gold and not making a sound. Jessica was with her, but—'

'There. With Madeleine,' Calumn said, waving at the two women, who came forward arm in arm. 'Madeleine, come and meet my sister Ailsa.'

'*Mon dieu,* you are exactly like the portrait of your mother,' Madeleine blurted out.

'So everyone says. What portrait?'

'The one on the wall in the house in Edinburgh.'

'You've been there,' Ailsa exclaimed. 'How—?'

'Ailsa, come with me and see Kirsty,' Jessica intervened hastily. 'She's needing changing. You can catch up with your brothers later, when they're finished greeting everyone.'

'There's no need to pull at me.' Laughing, Ailsa followed Jessica. 'I'm more than happy to keep you company. You can tell me what's going on between my brother and Mademoiselle Lafayette. She looks exactly like the picture of a fairy in a book I had when I was wee.'

Jessica giggled. 'Everyone looks like a fairy to you, you're so tall. But I know what you mean, she has a fey look about her. She doesn't seem to have any idea how pretty she is, though.'

'My brother does, he can hardly take his eyes off her.'

'I know, it's so romantic, only Rory says that—oh, wait and I'll get Kirsty, then I'll tell you the whole story.'

When the two women came downstairs again, it was time to eat. A chosen few were seated in the formal dining room, but most sat at the trestle tables in the great hall and on the front lawn. Toasts were made to Kirsty, who was brought back down from the nursery for the occasion, and Rory spoke proudly on behalf of his daughter. Beside him, Jessica dabbed at her eyes with a wisp of lace.

Once the tables had been cleared, the scraping of fiddles being tuned signalled the start of the dancing. Rory led Jessica forwards to the head of the first set, amid much applause and cheering. He nodded to the fiddlers and the first notes of the opening dance were struck. Soon the floor was thronged with graceful couples executing the complicated steps to the lilting, haunting music.

Madeleine watched the dancers enviously. She had been placed on the opposite side of the table from Calumn at dinner, and was exhausted with trying to maintain her part in a rather stilted conversation with two Highland lairds who, though they spoke both English and French, were interested only in the subject of a new breed of sheep Rory had brought to Heronsay as an experiment. The fascinating topic of wool yield, fleece oil content and texture signally failed to enthral her. Eventually she gave up the attempt to feign interest, sat back in her seat and allowed the men to continue their discussion without her assistance.

She saw Calumn deep in conversation with a group of men over in the corner of the great hall. She was thrilled at the warmth of the welcome he had been extended. Not a single snub had she seen, and though some were reserved, most men had greeted him like a long-lost friend. It had been immensely satisfying to watch.

A piper had joined the fiddlers. The bagpipes he played looked uncommonly like the Breton version—though the sound was quite different. A reel was called, with sets of six couples birling wildly around in circles, then breaking apart and progressing round the room. People were beginning to relax. Jackets had been discarded, neckcloths loosened. The next dance was even more raucous than the last. Standing in the front doorway, Madeleine watched as the men and women threw themselves into it with gusto, jigging and clapping, one minute executing the most intricate of steps, the next jumping high into the air, or whirling their partner around so fast their faces were a blur. She noticed several pairs had taken a tumble. She noticed, too, that some did not rejoin the dance, but disappeared off into the night giggling, wrapped in each other's arms. Obviously a blind eye was being turned for the occasion. Madeleine wondered if there would be a little crop of babies in nine months' time and how many would be named Christina in tribute to Kirsty.

'Would you care to dance, *mademoiselle?*'

Calumn stood before her, looking magnificent. She smiled up at him. Even in this well-dressed throng of handsome Highlanders, he was, for her, the only man in the room. As if by magic, the fiddlers struck up a slower tune. 'I don't know the steps,' she said hesitantly, looking at the sets which were already forming.

'We'll make up our own.'

He did not lead her on to the floor though, but out, over the lawn and round the corner of the turret, where Jessica had made a start on setting out more formal gardens. The strains of the music and the noise of the ceilidh were fainter here. Roses perfumed the air. Stars hung low, glowing softly in the ink-black night sky. Calumn pulled her into his arms, making no attempt at all to dance, simply holding her, nuzzling his face into her hair and swaying gently in time to the music. 'I've hardly seen you.'

'You've been busy. Everyone wants to talk to you. It's nice.'

'Not as nice as this. I've been thinking about this for hours.'

'Dancing?'

'No. Just being on my own with you.'

His tone was unexpectedly serious. He pulled her closer to him. 'You feel so lovely,' he said, smoothing his hand down the line of her spine, nestling her head on his chest. 'Perfect.'

He smelled so delightful. Of sun and fresh linen and soap and Calumn. He sounded strange, though. Not flirting. As if he meant it. He had been looking at her oddly all day. As if he didn't know who she was.

The music had come to an end, but he showed no signs of releasing her. If anything, he held her closer. She tightened her own hold on him, slipping her hands under his jacket, feeling the warmth of his back through the silk of his waistcoat.

'Have you missed me?'

How was she to take that? 'Well, I've been busy with Jessica and everything,' she prevaricated. Looking up, she saw that her light-hearted reply had hurt him. 'Of course I've missed you,' she said simply.

'Madeleine…'

A couple came arm in arm around the corner, bumping into Madeleine in their haste to find their own dark haven. Calumn turned on them with a growl, the young man bent almost double apologising while his more brazen companion eyed Calumn with blatant interest.

'Let's get out of here,' Calumn said, grabbing Madeleine's hand.

'Where? We can't leave the ceilidh, it's rude.'

'I've done my bit being polite, I want to be on my own with you.'

She found nothing to argue with in this sentiment,

since it exactly matched her own, so she tripped
after him, clinging to his arm as he loped through
the gardens, out the back of the castle, and unerringly through a gate, down a little path which wended
its way down to a secluded cove at the bottom of a
steep set of steps.

The sand curved white and perfect down to the
sea. The beach was sheltered by the high dune on
which the steps had been set. Stars gleamed so bright
in the summer sky that they looked as if they were
hung closer to earth than anywhere Madeleine
had ever seen before. The moon was full. The sea
shushed, waves rippling gently on to the hard sand
and ebbing, rippling and ebbing.

'It's magical,' Madeleine said, her voice hushed.

'Magical,' Calumn echoed. He was nervous. It
mattered so much. Nothing had ever mattered so
much. 'You're so beautiful,' he said, turning her
towards him, running his hands down her arms, just
brushing the sides of her breasts, wanting to mould
her to him and never to let her further from his side
than this. 'I love you so much.'

Chapter Ten

She was imagining it. She must be imagining it.
'What did you say? Calumn, what did you say?'

'I love you, Madeleine.' He gazed at her, frowning, as if he could not quite believe what he had said. Then his frown cleared. His mouth softened. A tender smile suffused his face. 'It really is that simple. I love you.'

She felt as if his heart was speaking to her through his eyes. He had never looked at her like that before. She never wanted him to look at her in any other way. She gazed at him in wonderment. 'You love me.'

'Yes, I do. And if you don't say that you love me back very soon, I think I'm going to expire. I feel as if I'm waiting for the executioner's axe.'

She threw her arms around his neck. 'I love you, I love you, I love you. I love you, Calumn Munro,

I love you so much.' Happiness made her feel as if she were taking flight, like a flock of seagulls from a windswept Breton beach. Swooping, soaring, gliding happiness such as she had never known. 'Say it again. I want to hear it again.'

Laughing, Calumn swept her into his arms, pressing her tight against him. 'I love you.' His kisses were hungry. He was greedy for her, needy for her, his hands feverish. 'I love you,' he said again, whispering it huskily as he pressed his face into her neck, breathing in the scent of her, filling his lungs with her sweetness, for it was the essence he needed to live. 'I love you.'

Madeleine shivered under his touch. Felt her skin blossoming and blooming. Different. He sounded different. It felt different. She reached her hands under his jacket, running her hands up his back. 'I love you,' she whispered, dizzy with the delight of saying the words. 'And I'm in love with you, too, and I see now that you were right, it is quite a different thing.'

'A very different thing. I'm going to show you how different. Let me make love to you now. Make love, real love, not just give you pleasure—though there will be that too, I hope,' he added with a wicked smile.

She pulled his face towards hers, feeling the clean line of his jaw, the silky soft of his hair. 'Please,' she said simply.

His lips were gentle, as if he was afraid she would bruise. The sweet taste of him. The breath of him.

The smell of him. She wanted it all, all of him. His kisses supped and licked, his hands stroked and caressed, trailing heat and lighting sparks. He was murmuring to her now, kissing her eyelids, her brow, her cheek, her ear, soft words she could not understand, though they poured over her like honey.

Calumn laid her down on the sand, covering her body with his, cupping his hands on either side of her face as if she were clay to be formed into whatever shape he desired. Warmth flooded her like sunlight, its rays emanating out and up, melting her into pliancy.

He disrobed her slowly, almost reverently, his lips pressing little patterns of kisses on her flesh as he bared it. When he removed her stockings he kissed the tender flesh in the crease behind her knees, the delicate bone of her ankle, her instep. Unlacing her bodice, he traced the line of her shoulder to where it joined her arm, licking into that tender crease too, then the nook of her elbow, the pulse on her wrists, each one of her fingers. Removing her petticoats allowed him to run his palms along the outline of her body through her shift, from the curve of her breasts down to the indentation of her waist, the swoop of her hips.

She was being unwrapped, layer by sensitised layer. She was quivering with desire. He was watching her in that way he had, which made her feel as if she was bared to the bones for him. Her body was his vessel.

Calumn relished everything about her. The way

her lids grew heavy when he touched her here. Like this. Or here, like this. The way her pulses jolted into life with each stroke, each kiss. The way her flesh cleaved to him. He watched each flicker of response with the gravest attention, learning her, as if she were the first woman he had ever studied. For that is how it felt. The first. And the only.

He lifted her shift over her head and she was naked, her skin gleaming like moonlight. 'So beautiful,' he sighed, kneeling before her, watching, looking, drinking her in. 'So very, very lovely.' His voice trembled with emotion. His hands were not quite steady. He was her first. He felt as if she were his. He undressed himself hastily, wrenching his clothes from him as if they were burning.

Calumn tugged his shirt over his head. Madeleine watched the flexing and rolling of his muscles, feeling the flexing and clenching of her own in response. Naked, he rendered her breathless. So broad, so lean, so deeply, perfectly, wonderfully male. Never had she felt so intrinsically feminine.

She reached up to touch the curve of his scar, running a fingertip along the ridged outline, placing her palm flat on his belly, feeling the heat of his skin beneath her. Her palm. His scar. Intimate. Sensual.

Calumn took her hand in his and kissed the palm where it had touched his flesh. When she looked at him like that he thought he would die for wanting her. The need to plunge into the sweetness of her was painful. He wanted to worship her, but he wanted to possess her too. He was shaking. Aching. Sweat glistened on his brow. On the small of his back. *'Gràdh, mo chrìdh,'* he whispered into the soft flesh of her belly. *'Gràdh, mo chrìdh,'* he whispered again, into the white skin at the top of her thigh. He could feel her hands on his hair, clutching at him. He could wait no longer to taste her. Parting her thighs, he kissed her and lost himself in the delight of it.

The shocking, unbelievable, unimaginably sensual touch of his mouth on her most intimate self almost sent her immediately over the edge. She clung desperately, but it was a tenuous, delightfully tenuous, grip. Licking and kissing so different, so similar, so wildly exciting. His tongue circling and then plunging into her, then out, then back up to circle and lick. She was jolted to another plane of emotion, tugged high with him to another galaxy of passion. Too-stretched. A strumming, thrumming vibration emanating out from where he touched, reaching out to every part of her body, so that she was pulsing with it, and every pulse like a wave that she must catch. Riding it, but knowing, that soon, soon, she would let go and it would break over her and she would crash.

A surge of something hot and wet shot through her. His grip on her thighs held her firmly, tilting her so that there, there, there, exactly there, his tongue touched and lingered and held, and a wave rolled over her so high she thought she was drowning and she heard moaning and perhaps it was her, and she clutched at him. At his hair, his shoulders, thrusting her body unashamedly at him as her climax shook and eased and shook and ebbed and she was left floundering and spent, like a starfish on the beach.

She heard someone calling his name, over and over, the sound hoarse and guttural, and it must be her voice, but it sounded so strange and so far away. He held her until the waves ebbed, kissing her thighs, kissing her stomach, kissing her breasts, covering her with kisses, heating her again, unbelievably stirring her, so that just when she thought it was receding it started again like the turning of the tide. A new feeling. Or the next stage of the old one. She did not care.

Need, primal need, urgent and irresistible, made her cling and clutch and drag at him, pulling him up towards her. Her mouth hot on his, his hot on hers, and even while they kissed she could hear that moaning of his name, begging and pleading, because though she had thought herself spent, now she knew she was not. Not an ending, but the beginning of the end. She wrapped her legs around him. She heard *him* moan. Heard *him* say *her* name.

He was fanning the flames of her fire. He kissed her greedily and heat leapt high inside her. His tongue thrust and his lips sucked and pulled as if he would devour her. He rolled her nipples between his fingers, making her arch in ecstasy, so exquisite were the shards of sensation. Like glass melting. Hungrier kisses. Her own hands roaming over him, his shoulders, his back, his buttocks, his thighs, her palms and fingers caressing and sculpting.

His expression was clenched with passion. A

dark flush slashed across his cheekbones. His hands held her by the waist. She felt the tip of him nudge between her thighs. She felt him enter her slowly, saw the stress of the slow movement on his face, saw the pains he was taking not to hurt her.

She breathed. Tried to breathe. He eased into her slowly, gently, pushing just a little harder when he met the resistance that was the end of her maidenhood, waiting, breathing, then pushing on until she sheathed him and he held her still, tilted her so that she could feel all of him inside her, deep inside her. She saw from the heaving of his chest, the opening out of his ribcage, the glaze of his eyes, what the control cost him, and his being so caring made her open out to accommodate him more.

He was breathing hard, as if he had been running for days. Sweat dripped from his brow. Sheathed tight inside her, he wanted to stay there for ever. He did not want to move. He needed to move. She was watching him, eyes dark and slumberous, hands clinging.

'Madeleine, are you all right?' he asked, and she gave a strange little laugh, for she felt as if she could never be more all right. The tiniest tilt of her hips, and he felt himself swell inside her. He leaned down to kiss her, his tongue thrusting slowly into her mouth in such a delicious echo of how he had pushed into her that she moaned and felt it again, that swelling. Of her. Of him.

Calumn moved, withdrawing slowly, pushing back into her, relishing the feel of her unfolding and holding against his shaft. Again, struggling to control himself as her heat urged him onwards to plunge harder and faster, as her hips arched up when he thrust, as she moaned with pleasure when he moved inside her. She was like a new world, one he had been created to explore, one made for him, so perfectly did they fit together, so hot and wet and unbearably, wonderfully taut was she around him. He pushed harder with each plunge, tugged her body closer. The soft clutch of her calves and ankles around his waist. The drum of her heels on his buttocks as he pushed again, withdrew and plunged. Plunging again, he felt the ripples of her climax reviving around him. The delight, the too-painful delight. A new urgency.

It happened, all at once. His thrust, his hoarse cry, his hands around her like a vice, the pouring into her, the hotness and pulsing of it, her echoing pulse, her own clutching, clinging, surging, clamouring. He poured into her, and she fell too, with a soft moan of submission, clamped so tight to him it was as if they were melded, and she knew that this was the final shape she was to take. Not sated, but fulfilled. One body formed from two. One skin. No edges. No borders. Just one.

He felt raw. Stripped, his old skin sloughed away. Reborn. Tenderness overwhelmed him. He had never held anyone so precious. It was terrifying and earth-shattering and wonderful and just—just so right. Calumn gathered Madeleine to him, cradling her against his chest, as if he could lock her there, safe against his heart, for ever. This was how it was supposed to be. Nothing could ever be so important. His world shifted on its axis and realigned itself.

Madeleine opened her eyes, looking up at him dreamily, still caught in the floating, sparkling aftermath of their love-making. He looked so different. She kissed him softly, a kiss stripped clean of everything save love. 'I didn't know. I never thought it would be like this.'

Calumn's smile twined its way around her heart. 'Neither did I.'

The next morning, the family gathered for breakfast, which was served in a small room at the back of the castle with a view out to sea. Helping himself to a substantial platter of food from the sideboard, Calumn looked up to find Madeleine's eyes upon him. A warm glow suffused him as he remembered last night, a glow which amazingly quickly manifested itself in the beginnings of arousal. He smiled over at her. A blush tinged her cheeks with colour. Obviously their minds were in exactly the same place. As he took his seat beside her, he pressed a swift kiss to the nape of her neck, his lips so attuned to her that he felt the tiny shiver of her response.

He would take Madeleine for a sail. He had not yet proposed. They would land on one of the little islets out west. He would do it there. Then later, much later, they would share their news with his family. Under the pretext of shaking out his napkin, he stroked Madeleine's thigh under the table. He looked up to find his sister-in-law watching him rather too knowingly.

Jessica arched a delicate brow, nodding at his breakfast. 'Goodness, Calumn, you must be hungry.' She was nibbling on a thin slice of bread and butter. Despite several attempts, she had failed signally to make good on her promise to Rory to learn to like porridge for her breakfast.

All eyes were now on Calumn's plate, which was piled high with kippers, eggs, bannocks and bacon. 'Must be the Highland air, gives a man a healthy appetite,' he mumbled.

'Or maybe it was all the dancing you got up to last night,' Rory suggested with a twinkle.

'Dancing! I did not see Calumn dancing,' Ailsa said. 'In fact, I hardly saw him at all.'

Jessica cast her husband a reproving look. 'You were that busy encouraging that poor Cameron laddy to make sheep's eyes at you for most of the night, I'm surprised you noticed anything at all,' Rory said hastily.

'He knows it was just a bit of fun,' Ailsa said, with a careless shrug, exactly like Calumn's. She turned her attention to Madeleine, furiously concentrating on her breakfast. Ailsa watched, fascinated, as she removed each of the feathery little bones from her fish, laying them out carefully on the side of her plate before taking a first tentative bite. 'It's just smoked herring,' she told her encouragingly. 'Most people eat the bones. Surely you must have herring in—where is it you come from, exactly?'

'Brittany.'

'Oh, yes, that's in the north of France, isn't it? I don't know if you realise it, but there are quite a few of your countrymen still in the Highlands. They were all pardoned after the Rebellion, and some settled here. We've one from Normandy who married a local girl, the daughter of one of your tenants, Calumn, and my friend Isla was telling me of another at Inverlochan. I'm sure he is from Brittany.'

'Oh, yes,' Madeleine said vaguely. 'I like this fish—what is it you call it?'

'It's a kipper,' Jessica told her, pouring herself another cup of tea.

'Anyway, he's apparently lost his memory, all he remembers is his first name,' Ailsa said.

'Who?'

'Keep up, Rory, the young Frenchman I was telling Madeleine about. He was wounded in the head. Lucky to be alive by all accounts; for a long time they thought he wouldn't make it.'

'Where was he injured?' Rory asked.

'Culloden.'

'Likely he was part of the Royal Scots, then,' Rory said. 'They were on our—'

'Culloden,' Madeleine interrupted, dropping her fork.

Calumn looked up. 'Madeleine, you can't think…'

'But she said he was wounded in the head,' Madeleine said to him, 'you did say that, didn't you, Ailsa?'

Ailsa looked confused by the sudden interest. 'Yes. He was shot, Isla said.'

'Who's Isla?'

'Isla Morrison. Calumm, you must remember her, she's Iain Morrison's daughter, who owns the lands at Inverlochan. I keep forgetting how long you've been away. Well, 'twas her brother Hamish who brought this Frenchman back after he was wounded and no one claimed him. He has one of the Morrison's crofts now.'

'Who cares about the Morrisons! What does this Frenchman look like? How old is he? What colour is his hair?' Madeleine threw the questions at Ailsa in a flurry.

'Goodness, give me a minute. Isla said he's young, maybe twenty-four or five. Dark and handsome, she says, though what she means by handsome I'm not sure. Much as I love her, Isla's the type you'd call homely, rather than bonny.'

'His name, you said he remembered his name,' Madeleine reminded her impatiently.

'Give me a minute, it'll come to me.'

'For God's sake, Ailsa, think. It's important,' Calumm snapped. Beside him, Madeleine's face was drained of colour. She was lacing and unlacing her fingers in her lap, something she always did when she was nervous. Her eyes were fixed upon Ailsa, wide and blank, like an animal caught in a trap. He reached for her hand. Icy cold. 'Droissard seemed very sure that de Guise was dead,' he reminded her gently. 'Men like that don't make mistakes.' He did not want de Guise to be alive. Did not want him to rise from the grave like a Lazarus. 'It's likely a coincidence,' he said to Madeleine. 'You must not pin your hopes on it.'

Pin her hopes on it! Did he think she wanted Guillaume to be alive? God help her, she did not. Though she could not wish him dead either. She should be happy for him. Yet all she felt was a sick dread. Selfish, sick dread! 'Calumn, I—'

'Guillaume,' Ailsa announced suddenly. 'Guillaume, that was it!' She beamed triumphantly. 'I knew I'd remember. Is it him? How amazing.'

Madeleine nodded. Her mouth was dry. She was incapable of speech. Guillaume was alive. Just when her world had settled so beautifully into its new orbit, the ghost of her past had risen up to confront her with her sins. She looked around the table, becoming vaguely aware that all eyes were upon her: Jessica's looking kind and concerned, Ailsa's eager expression fading into one of bafflement, Rory frowning heavily.

And Calumn, looking at her with his face set, his eyes dark and distant. Her fingers clutched at his. Her rock. She did not want to slip anchor, but she felt the tug, the pull of the past like a rip tide, strong enough to make her wonder whether she should. Whether after all, she had the right to sacrifice others upon the altar of her own happiness.

Her head whirled. The urge to flee was irresistible. She got to her feet so hastily her chair fell back on to the wooden floor with a clatter. She was at the door when he caught her, strong fingers on her arm, his solid bulk looming over her. He pulled her out of the room, shut the door fast behind them. 'Where are you going?'

'I don't know. Away. I don't know. I can't think.' Tears started in her eyes. She was trembling.

'Running away, Madeleine?'

'Yes,' she said frantically, struggling to release herself from his grip, 'yes, I am.'

'No.' He did not raise his voice, but it felt as if he had. 'No,' he said again, quieter, but even more implacable, 'you're not running away. I won't let you. We've both done enough of that.'

'What do you mean?' A churning in her stomach. Legs so wobbly it felt as if the bones had been removed.

'Truths must be faced, no matter how unpalatable, you know that. Devils must be confronted. There can be no room for doubts. I love you. I know you love me, but we both need to know that it's enough. It's been a long road we've travelled together, we're different people from the ones who started out. I don't want us to be haunted by the past, yours or mine. I don't want to win you by default. I don't want second-best.'

'You could never be second-best,' Madeleine said brokenly, overwhelmed by his resolution in the face of the calamity which was threatening to dash their hard-won future to pieces. Awed and humbled by the strength of his love for her. 'I love you.'

'Then prove it,' he said gently. 'I'll take you to him. Go and fetch your *arisaidh*.'

He watched her make her way slowly towards the stairs. Then, heart sore but set on his course, he returned to the breakfast room to inform his relatives of their imminent departure for Inverlochan.

Madeleine sat in silence as Calumn steered the little boat out into the sound. When the wind caught the sails, he pulled in the oars and took his seat at the tiller. The breeze caught his hair, whipping it over his face. He stared out over the strait at the shoreline, effortlessly holding their path, his expression as distant as the mountains on the horizon. Solid. Unshakeable. Sure.

Would that she had his certainty. She loved him. Every time she looked at him, her love rushed over her like a wave. She could not imagine life without him. Her love did not waver for a second, but she was terrified that her resolution would. Faced with telling Guillaume that she could not marry him, knowing that by doing so she was cutting the ground from beneath his feet, would she hold strong? She could only pray that it would be the case. Calumn had handed her his heart. She did not want to let him down. Would die, rather than let him down. But still, was terrified that let him down is what she would do.

The pebbled shore of the mainland drew near. Calumn pulled in the sail and beached the boat, heaving the craft high on to the shale before reaching to help her out. She waited in the morning sunshine, watching a woman mending a lobster creel, as Calumn went to the inn to have their horses readied. He threw her into the saddle. She managed a tentative smile. The one he returned did not reach his eyes. Her heart beat slow and sluggish in her breast. Like the drum which preceded a tumbrel on its way to the gallows.

They rode to Inverlochan village in silence. Calumn had no difficulty in finding the croft that one of the villagers directed them to. It sat on its own at the northern crossroads, a well-kept thatched building, with smoke rising from a hole in the middle of the roof. A few hens scratched contentedly on a freshly dug strip of land which had been prepared for planting kale. A peat stack piled up against the side of the croft gave off a loamy smell.

Beside him, Madeleine's face was as white as her sark. Desperate thoughts of killing de Guise, of pushing ahead of her into the cottage and throttling the life out of him, rushed through his fevered brain. But his own words gave him strength. He would not be second-best, no matter how much pain it caused him. He could not choose for her. De Guise was one dragon his lovely maid must slay for herself. Or not.

Lifting her down from the saddle, he held her close, pressing her tight against him, as if to imprint for ever the shape of her against him. 'Whatever you choose, I will stand by you.' Even as he said the words, he doubted his ability to keep such a pledge.

She was his. Pray God it would not become necessary to prove it.

Madeleine clutched at him, her hands tugging at his shirt, his plaid, pulling him close and closer. Gently, he detached himself. 'Ready?'

She nodded. Calumn knocked on the door, but there was no answer, so he pushed it open. The room was dark, the tiny unglazed window letting in little light. A pot was suspended over the fire, from which arose the smell of barley broth. A rough-slatted partition separated the living quarters from those of the animals. The place was empty of both man and beast. Back outside, the sunlight blinded him. 'We'll try the fields round the back. The fire's lit, so he can't have gone far.'

They rounded the corner of the croft, where more narrow strips of crops grew in orderly lines. A hen house. A cow in an open barn. A burn feeding a tiny pond. And beside the pond, a man, bending over with a bucket. He straightened when he saw his visitors, shading his eyes, putting the full bucket carefully down on the ground before walking slowly over to greet them.

He was a tall man, with the gaunt frame of a long-term invalid. Pale blue eyes, rather deep set under dark brows. Dark brown hair, growing raggedly round a livid scar which ran from the top of his skull to his ear, giving him a distinctive appearance. For all that, Calumn could see that he was good-looking, with an amiable countenance and a shy smile. Young, no more than three- or four-and-twenty, the fretwork of tiny lines around his eyes and mouth evidence of trauma rather than passing years. He was dressed simply in the trews, shirt and jacket of a crofter. The boots on his rather large feet were held together with leather thongs. His toe could be seen peeping through the left one. But his hands, though roughened, were those of a nobleman, long-fingered, shapely and surprisingly well cared for.

Madeleine's fierce grip on his hand was becoming painful. He had no need to ask if this was de Guise. 'Guillaume,' she said, her voice coming out in a croak.

'Yes?' Guillaume de Guise looked from Madeleine to Calumn with a puzzled expression. 'Can I help you?' He spoke Gaelic with a French accent.

'Guillaume, *c'est moi. C'est Madeleine. Tu me connais?*' Madeleine looked up anxiously into his face. 'Don't you remember me? It's Maddie,' she said, continuing to speak to him in French.

'Maddie?' Guillaume stared at her. He shook his head, closing his eyes as if in pain. He stared at her again. 'Maddie?'

He clutched his head and swayed on his feet. Instinctively, Madeleine reached out to support him, staggering as he slumped against her, his eyes clouding. His knees buckled, and Calumn caught him just before he slumped to the ground. 'Take his other arm,' he ordered Madeleine. 'Help me get him inside.'

Half-carrying, half-dragging him, they made it to the croft with Guillaume between them, white as a sheet, barely able to hold himself upright, collapsing weakly into a chair. Madeleine poured some water from a jug into a wooden cup and handed it to him.

Guillaume sipped, and after a few moments, seemed to recover. He pulled himself upright, his pale blue eyes focusing on Madeleine, hovering anxiously at his side. '*C'est toi, vraiment?* I can't believe it. How did you come to be here?' He reached out a hand towards her.

She took it. It felt strange. His clasp was weak. His hand did not envelop hers the way that Calumn's did. She sat down in a hard wooden chair beside him. 'I came to Scotland to find you. I ran away.' He was much thinner than she remembered, and older too. No longer a boy, the traumas of the last eighteen months were etched upon his face, giving him a gravitas he had not possessed before. Despite the horrible scar, he was an attractive man, she could see that. But she was not at all attracted.

'Ran away? You mean you are here alone? Then who is this?' he asked, looking at Calumn.

'It is a long story. Are you sure you are well enough to hear it? You look very pale.'

'My head, but I am used to that. Tell me, it will help me, I think.' He took another sip of water. 'It's so strange. All these months, it's been like a black curtain in my mind that I couldn't see behind. Yet just the sound of your voice and it has lifted, as if it were never there.' He tightened his grip on her. 'I can't believe you are here. It's so good to see you, Maddie.'

His words stung her conscience, his unaffected pleasure in seeing her eating into her resolve. Her smile wobbled as she snatched a glance at Calumn, propped up against the door with his arms crossed across his chest, his expression unreadable, his mouth a thin, hard line. Once more the urge to run held her in its powerful grip, surging up inside her like a tidal wave. With an immense effort of will, she suppressed it. *She would not let Calumn down. She would not.*

She turned back to her betrothed. 'And you, Guillaume. It is good to see you.' The relief of realising that this was true gave her courage. She did not wish him dead. She had not stooped so low.

In a low voice, faltering but never halting, she told him the salient facts, from his cousin's claim on La Roche, which had been the trigger to her journey, to the discovery of his whereabouts at breakfast on Heronsay this morning. Her eyes never left his face. In his eyes, she saw surprise, shock, disgust, when he heard of Droissard, who had taken his name. Admiration for her, too, and—there could be no denying it—love.

'You never gave up hope,' he said, when she had finished. 'I can't believe what you've put yourself through for me. I'll make it up to you, I promise. I've always taken you for granted. I won't ever do so again. So brave. My own Maddie.'

Tears started in her eyes, but she would not let them fall. She breathed deep. Forced herself to take it out of the box to which she had confined it, her affection for him, and to take a long hard look at it. To take her time, because it was now or never. She had to be sure. Completely sure. No matter what.

And there it was. A real thing but paler, and quite a different shape from her love for Calumn. Not dead, but fixed in size. It would not grow, nor would it ever be transformed into something else. And in time, untended, it would fade. Beside it, her love for Calumn glowed, vibrant and potent. In the end, it was not a choice. There was no question.

If only the doing of it were not so very painful! Her heart was tolling like the harbinger of death again. The way Guillaume was looking at her, so tenderly—he had never looked at her like that before. Would never look at her like that again. For surely he would hate her after what she had to tell him next. 'Guillaume, the thing is—'

'It's like a dream,' Guillaume interrupted, smiling happily. 'Or as if I've just woken up,' he added with a chuckle, 'I can't decide which.'

'Guillaume! Listen, there is something else I need to tell you.'

'What is it?'

'I can't. I'm so sorry, but I can't.'

'Can't what? Maddie, you're scaring me—what's wrong?'

She got to her feet, took an anxious turn around the room, sat back down, her fingers laced so tight together that her knuckles showed white. 'I can't marry you. I don't love you, not in that way, and I know now I never will. I'm so sorry.'

'But—I don't understand, what has changed?'

'I've changed.' She took his hand again, her eyes pleading for understanding. 'I've changed so much that there is no question of my ever going back.'

'You've met someone else.' He wrenched his hand out of her clasp.

She closed her eyes, unable to face the pain she saw in his face, but forced herself to open them again. 'Yes, I have. But even if I had not— Guillaume, it is not just that I love someone else, it is that I—I'm sorry, but I've never loved you, not in that way. Not as you deserve to be loved. I still love you as a friend, but I know I will never, ever love you as a lover. I'm sorry.'

'Why did you come here then, knowing this? Why didn't you just stay in France, give me up for dead?'

'She didn't give you up for dead because she believed, despite what everyone else was telling her, that you were alive.'

Calumn could restrain himself no longer. Pushing himself away from the door he took two hasty strides to stand protectively over the woman he loved. His woman. For he had heard enough, more than enough, to know that Madeleine was his, irrevocably, wonderfully, certainly his.

Relief, joy, pride, and that thing he had begun to recognise as happiness swelled inside him so that he could hardly restrain himself form picking Madeleine up and making off with her there and then. 'She came because your cousin was laying claim to your property,' he said through gritted teeth. 'Had she not come, there is every chance you would have lived out your life here with no name, no fortune and no past.'

Guillaume flinched in the face of the unexpected menace now lowering at him over Madeleine's shoulder. 'Who *are* you?'

'Calumn Munro.'

'Yes, I know your name, but who—oh! It is you.' Guillaume turned to Madeleine in astonishment. 'When you said you had met someone else, I thought you meant another Frenchman. Does this mean you came here—that when you arrived in Scotland there was still—that you still considered yourself my betrothed?'

'Well, yes, but that does not mean—'

'But if your acquaintance with this man is of such short duration, then surely—Maddie, you can't possibly know enough about him to make any sort of commitment.'

'She already has,' Calumn said threateningly. 'Were you not listening?'

'I know everything there is to know about him, Guillaume,' Madeleine hastened to intervene. 'All the important things. I just know. I love him.' She dashed a tear away from her eye, and looked up fleetingly Calumn, still lowering with his fists clenched. 'The only thing that time has to do with it is to make me love him more. I'm sorry. I am truly sorry, Guillaume, but you have to accept that. I can't go back. I'm not the Maddie you knew before. I'm sorry it has to be like this, I'm sorry to have to hurt you, but the one thing I can't ever be sorry about is finding Calumn.'

Guillaume was silent for a long moment, then he got to his feet, rather shakily. 'It is my own fault. I didn't know what I had until I left you. I missed you, you know. More than I thought possible. I should have told you in my letters.' He kissed Madeleine's cheek. Then he held his hand out to Calumn. 'You had better deserve her. You will have me to answer for, if you do not.'

Calumn shook his hand. He even managed to smile, though its effect was to make Guillaume flinch. 'It shall be my life's mission, you can have no worries on that score.'

Guillaume slumped back down in his seat. He was still very pale. Madeleine suspected that he had not yet felt the full impact of the series of shocks he had been dealt. 'What will you do now?' she asked him tentatively.

'I have absolutely no idea.'

'Give the man time to gather his thoughts, for heaven's sake, Madeleine,' Calumn said, 'he's only just getting his memory back. What he needs is rest. Time to think. Take stock.'

'Yes,' Guillaume agreed gratefully, looking paler than ever. 'Time to think. To grow—accustomed— to what you have told me.'

'But we can't just leave you here,' Madeleine protested. 'You don't look at all well.'

'She's quite right. I'll tell you what, my brother Rory is Laird of Heronsay. We are staying with him, and shall take you back with us for the time being. Then we can decide what's best to do next.'

'You're very kind, but I can't impose,' Guillaume replied, finding the prospect of another such as Calumn to contend with rather terrifying.

'You won't be imposing,' Calumn said, his tone softening slightly.

Madeleine beamed her support. 'Say yes, Guillaume. Please. You can't stay here.'

He looked bemused. 'Well…'

'Excellent. We'll be back for you in—say, a couple of hours,' Calumn said, shaking Guillaume's hand, magnanimous now that he had achieved his purpose.

'Where are we going?' Madeleine asked.

Calumn did not reply. He nodded at Guillaume, took her arm and led her firmly out of the croft.

'But I have not…' Guillaume called, but he was addressing thin air. Looking out through the window, he saw the intimidating Highlander throw Madeleine into the saddle. She did not protest. In fact, she looked as if she were accustomed to it. He remembered it was one of the things she always prided herself on, the ability to mount Perdita without help. Come to think about it, had he tried to manhandle her out of the room the way Calumn Munro had done, he would have been rewarded with one of her set downs. Yet off she went with Calumn Munro, quiet as a little lamb.

Guillaume turned away from the window and reached into the cupboard for the decanter of whisky he kept for the occasions when the pain from his wound became too much to bear. His wound was not bothering him. But still, the pain felt almost as if it was too much to bear.

Calumn led the way out of Inverlochan, taking a path which headed directly west towards the sea. Realising he had no intentions of explaining himself, Madeleine had ceased to question him. Though the encounter with Guillaume had been painful beyond words, it had also been an incredible relief. She had not let Calumn down. And she knew, without any room for doubt, that she had made the right choice.

They reached a shallow border of pine trees, where the narrow path led down to a sheltered cove. Calumn tethered the horses, then sat down in the white sand, pulling Madeleine with him. 'Look over there.' He pointed directly ahead, where a spit of land in the distance reached far out into the turquoise sea. 'That's the Heads of Errin. At high tide it's cut off completely, but at low tide it's the perfect place for gathering mussels and clams. All the land you can see to the north from there is Munro land.'

'Munro land. You mean I'm looking at Errin Mhor?'

'It is your home, where your heart is,' Calumn quoted. 'That's what you wrote in your letter to me. Your words, they were a turning point, but they weren't the whole truth. My heart is with you. Home is wherever you are.'

'Oh, Calumn, I love you so much.'

'I know,' he said. 'But it's no more than I love you.' His kiss was long and languorous. The kiss of a man who had been drowning, but was saved. The kiss of a lover. The kiss of a man in love.

Madeleine's heart strained at its tethers, slipped anchor and sailed free. She kissed him back without restraint. Love bubbled in her blood, filling her with light and a happiness so pure she thought she would expire from it. They kissed as if they would never stop. As if there could be no end. And indeed there was not, for it was the beginning of a lifetime of love. A love which they sealed making long, slow magic together, pledging their hearts by uniting their bodies.

Later, they lay entwined in one another's arms. 'I feel as if I'm floating,' Madeleine whispered, her fingers idly tracing the shape of the scar on Calumn's abdomen. It seemed fainter now. The angry redness had faded.

'Well, I hate to bring you back down to earth, but there's something I want to ask you.'

She knew by the tone of his voice that he was smiling his curling smile, but she pushed herself up just to check. Sure enough, there it was, and sure enough, it worked its magic on her. 'What is it?'

'I want you to marry me, of course.'

She had not thought any question in the world could be more delightful. Though it required the simplest of answers, it rendered her speechless. Even as she tried to form the word which would make her happiness overflow, Calumn set her gently from him and knelt before her in the sand. 'I'm only ever going to do this once in my life, so I'm going to do it properly.'

Deeply serious now, he took her hand. 'My darling, loveliest Madeleine, marry me. Be my wife. Be my first and my last lover. Be my heart and my conscience. For I love you, and I can think of no greater honour, nor no greater happiness, than to be able to call you mine. For always.'

Madeleine's eyes filled with tears, which seemed to come direct from her heart. 'Oh, Calumn,' she managed, and flung herself into his arms, sending the two of them back down into the sand.

'Is that a yes, then?' he asked her, his own voice hovering between tears and laughter.

'Darling, lovely, Calumn, that is the biggest, most perfectly wonderful, completely irrevocable "yes" that it is possible to give.'

Epilogue

One week later

Madeleine and Guillaume sat together on the edge
of the jetty at Heronsay, looking out towards the
mainland. The fishing boat which would take Guillaume to Oban, from where he would board a larger
vessel heading south, was making its way towards
them across the sound. It was a dull day, the sun
hidden behind a thin layer of sullen grey cloud, the
type which Madeleine had learned portended that
mizzling rain so typical of a Highland summer.

'You have Calumn's letter,' Madeleine asked anxiously.

Guillaume grinned. 'For the tenth time, yes. And
yours.'

'He will be so angry with me. I still think perhaps
I should come with you.'

'We've been over all this, Maddie. Remember, your papa is to be so pleased to see me that he will forgive you.'

'That is what you say, but…'

'Trust me. Just this once, trust that I know best.'

She chuckled at that. 'Papa will be astonished at how much you have changed. I can't believe it myself.'

Guillaume looked grim. 'Battle tends to do that to a man.'

She laid a gentle hand upon his arm, her expression tender. 'I know. Do you regret it?'

He looked thoughtful. 'I don't know. When I signed up to the Stuart cause, to be honest it was more because I was looking for—well, a bit of excitement, a challenge. I suppose what I was really doing was proving something to myself. I didn't think about what I was leaving behind. I didn't think what it might cost me. And it did cost me. Not just you, but maybe my health. Definitely my stupid pride. But I don't regret it. If nothing else, it's taught me to appreciate what I have. I've grown up.'

Madeleine blinked back a tear. 'Are you looking forward to seeing La Roche?'

'Oh, yes,' Guillaume replied. 'It's lovely here, but it's not home. What about you, won't you miss Brittany?'

She shook her head decisively. 'No. Never. Isn't it funny, I haven't even been to Errin Mhor yet, but already I'm thinking of it as home.'

'Provided your Calumn can sort out his differences with his father.'

'Oh, I don't doubt that,' Madeleine said sunnily, 'Calumn can do anything.'

Guillaume laughed heartily. 'You really have changed.'

'Yes. For the better, I hope,' she said anxiously.

'Definitely. So much for the better, that I fear you are right. We would not suit.'

'Guillaume, do you mean that? You're not just saying that to make me feel better?'

'Only a little,' he said with an awkward shrug. 'You will be happy, won't you, Maddie? You are sure of that? I couldn't bear the thought of you being otherwise.'

'I am sure, I promise.'

'Good, because although I did tell that hulking Highlander of yours that he would have me to answer to if you were not, I have to say it's not a prospect I'd face with anything other than terror.'

Madeleine chuckled again. 'You won't have to. Here he comes now, with the rest of them, to say goodbye.'

They got to their feet. Calumn was ahead of the rest, his usual loping stride making his hair fly out behind him, the pleats of his plaid swinging with the motion, showing her a tantalising glimpse of finely muscled leg. Madeleine's heart did its special little Calumn flip, and she ran to greet him, throwing herself into his arms, finding herself whirled off her feet, and her mouth firmly kissed. 'I missed you,' she said.

'God, you're insatiable, lass,' he murmured wickedly into her ear, 'it's only been a couple of hours.'

She giggled. 'That's not what I meant.'

He let her slip back down to the ground, sliding his hands up her body, and pressing her close against him as he did so, leaving her in no doubt about the effect she was having on him. Again. A delightful shiver of anticipation set her own pulses racing. 'You're not the only one who's insatiable,' he whispered wickedly. Then, putting his arm around her shoulder, he turned her back towards Guillaume. At the jetty, the fishing boat was being tied up. 'Did you say your goodbyes?'

'Yes. It's fine, don't worry.'

Calumn nodded, then released her, holding out his hand to Guillaume. 'Safe journey to you. You know you are always welcome here.'

'Thank you. I have your letter safe. I'll do everything I can to persuade Monsieur Lafayette to do as you suggest. I know how much her father being at her wedding means to Maddie.'

'Aye. But she does not need his permission. She will be my wife, whether her father comes or not.'

Guillaume laughed. 'I am aware. I shall tell him that, too.'

Rory, Jessica and Ailsa arrived on the jetty now. Jessica handed Guillaume a large wicker basket. 'For the journey,' she said.

'She thinks she's feeding the five thousand,' Rory said. 'There's some of my best malt in there, too.'

'More than you think,' Calumn said, pulling two more bottles of his brother's precious supply from his jacket pocket and handing them to Guillaume. 'These are for Madeleine's father.'

'You must go, or you will miss the tide,' Ailsa said to Guillaume. *'Bonne chance.'* She kissed him on the cheek, as did Jessica. Then Rory and Calumn slapped his back and shook his hand.

Finally Madeleine hugged him tight. 'Take care of yourself.'

'And you, Maddie. Be happy.'

Madeleine gave him a watery smile. Guillaume jumped into the boat. Ailsa handed him the loaded basket. Rory unlooped the rope from the jetty. Calumn pushed the boat off, and the fisherman unfurled the sail. Guillaume waved once, then turned away from Heronsay to look forwards, out to the open sea.

Madeleine wiped her eyes, and snuggled gratefully into the shelter of Calumn's body.

'You'll owe me for that whisky,' Rory said to his brother as they all began to make their way back towards the house.

'Oh, I'll pay you back, don't worry, and from my own cellar. Everyone knows that Errin Mhor malt is the best,' Calumn told him.

'I'll hold you to that,' Rory said.

'Calumn, are you sure about us coming to the

wedding?' Jessica asked anxiously. 'Lord Munro has made his feelings about Rory very clear and Lady Munro has never shown any signs of wishing to meet me or Kirsty. We will not be welcome.'

'You are coming to Errin Mhor for my wedding and that's an end to it. I can assure you that you will be extended the warmest welcome it is possible to give. You, and Rory, and Kirsty, all. Whether my father wants to accept it or not, you are my family. Our family,' he said, his hold on Madeleine tightening. 'Is that not right, Ailsa?'

Ailsa beamed. 'Completely. Don't worry about my mother, Jessica, she's a tartar, but she'll dote on wee Kirsty when she sees her, I just know she will. And she'll be that glad to have Calumn home, he'll be able to wrap her round his wee finger.'

Calumn and Rory exchanged a look. The idea of their austere parent either doting on a bairn or allowing herself to be wrapped around anyone's finger was not an image either could conjure. They burst out laughing. Ailsa could not help joining in. 'Well, in time, maybe,' she conceded.

They had reached the front steps of the castle now. Looking at the two brothers and their striking sister, Madeleine could not imagine a more attractive set of siblings. Surely even Lady Munro, the dragon lady as she had secretly named her, would be won round by such a combination?

'I must go and see to my packing now,' Ailsa said,

looking up at the sky, where the sun was making a valiant attempt to appear. 'When do we leave,' she asked Calumn.

'A couple of hours.'

'Then I'll go and see about getting you something to eat before you go,' Jessica said. 'What about you, Madeleine, do you need help with anything?'

'Madeleine and I are going for a walk,' Calumn announced. 'She wants to see the beach again before we go.'

'Do I?'

'Yes,' Calumn said with a look which sent her pulses quivering.

The walked along the path hand in hand, down to the little crescent of sand where they had first made love. Kneeling down opposite each other, they began the pleasurable ritual of taking off their clothes.

'Madeleine,' Calumn said huskily, as he unlaced her sark, his fingers trailing heat over her skin, 'you'd agree, wouldn't you, that there should be no secrets between a husband and wife?'

'Yes.'

'Only, I have a confession to make.'

She stilled, her hands on the buckle of his belt. 'What is it?'

'I can't swim,' Calumn said ruefully.

Madeleine tried to suppress her smile, but her dimples peeped. 'I've got a confession to make too,'

she said, her eyes brimming with laughter and love.
'I guessed.'

Then she kissed him, and he kissed her back.
Slowly. For there was no rush. They had the rest of
their lives together.

* * * * *

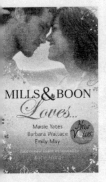